TO ENTER
JERUSALEM

TO ENTER JERUSALEM

Craig Eisendrath

THE PERMANENT PRESS
Sag Harbor, NY 11963

For information, address:
  The Permanent Press
  4170 Noyac Road
  Sag Harbor, NY 11963
  www.thepermanentpress.com

Library of Congress Cataloging-in-Publication Data

Eisendrath, Craig R.
    To enter Jerusalem / Craig Eisendrath.
        p. cm.
    ISBN-13: 978-1-57962-161-2 (alk. paper)
    ISBN-10: 1-57962-161-9 (alk. paper)
        1. Male sexual abuse victims—Fiction. 2. Incest victims—
    Fiction. 3. Fathers and sons—Fiction. 4. Family—Psychological
    aspects—Fiction. 5. United States—Politics and government—
    Fiction. 6. World politics—Fiction. 7. International relations—
    Fiction. 8. United Nations. Secretary-General—Fiction. 9. Magic
    realism (Literature) I. Title.

PS3605.I84T62 2008
813'.6—dc22   2008002522

Printed in the United States of America.

For Roberta,
the love of my life

INTIMATIONS FROM THE FATHER

Dwight stands in front of Father, who gropes around his back; with the other hand, he opens Dwight's bathrobe, and draws him in still closer. Now sweaty hands are moving down his stomach. The space around him has no density, makes no obstruction, as the hands move through it like satellites; beyond them, inaccessible, are planets, stars.

Father turns him around, then penetrates—their bodies, now connected, swing into orbit. Father is panting as he speaks: "I missed you all day, Dwight. I thought of you as I was sitting in the NSC. I wonder why then. . . . You have the most beautiful face—not from me, God knows—it's your mother's, lucky for you." His own face stares back at Dwight as if in a mirror, its blue eyes, red lips, pale skin—the face Father sees.

The phone jangles, their two bodies crack apart, and begin to drift away, as if hit by a missile. "Of course, Henry, I went over the whole matter at the NSC. . . . No, if the Paks want to commit national suicide in Kashmir, and take the Indians with them, there may be little we can do. . . . Really, you'd commit American forces? For what? . . . A UN peace force? Don't be absurd! . . . There are almost a billion of them, so ten or fifteen million more or less. . . . Scrooge?—I was trying to be funny, Henry."

Father sits naked, sprawled in a chair, pot belly, a huge balding head, loose jowls, rimless glasses, an irascible look in his eyes, his nose a pitted appendage of meat hanging over his mustache. "What interest have we got in the area that would be worth it?" The trail runs into white noise, then silence. Father smirks, puts down the phone, still holding Dwight.

"If he objected, he should have objected at the NSC!"

". . . Who was that?"

"Henry Morgenstern—some puffed-up Jew who's written a mammoth study of the region, and now he's caged the number two job at State. I've nothing to worry about on this issue, unless he talks directly to the President, but the President and I just talked. You see, Dwight, you have to keep all these lines in your head so none gets around you, out of your control."

Father's hands begin to pass over his body, but again the phone rings. "Just a minute." He covers the receiver. "Mix me a martini, will you, light on the vodka? I *do* have to work tonight." Dwight runs out of the room. When he returns with the drink—he'd remembered the pitted olive—Father is still on the phone. "Yes, I know Singh will be at the British embassy tonight, which is why, Leonard—it should be obvious enough—I'm making an appearance. . . . Yes, we will talk, and Singh will be vague and discursive for perhaps ten minutes, alluding to his years at Cambridge, and, of course, his genuine admiration for the West. But as his time runs out, or, by his calculation, my patience, he will finally get down to the business at hand, which is to tell me that war can break out at any time. . . . Yes, yes, I am prepped, you'll receive an A-plus on your efficiency report for 'Care and Repair of the Secretary.' Good night, Leonard!"

Father puts down the receiver, takes one more look at Dwight, sighs, lights up one of his stinking cigarettes, and stands up. "I suppose I'd better get ready." He lurches toward the bathroom as Dwight glances about the empty bedroom, suddenly alone, like a piece of junk or garbage abandoned in space; he is crying, even as he makes no sound, emits no tears, but only stares inside the room as if it were the black sky.

In another few minutes, his mother, Alicia, descends the stairs in a red silk gown, long earrings, diamond necklace, her hair swept up in a stylish bouffant. Her full-length portrait hangs in their living room, the one painted in Spain before Father married her fifteen years ago. She poses in a ballroom, her dark eyes delicately underlined with mascara, bitter, vacuous, like a Goya painting of a princess Dwight had seen at the National Gallery of Art. Father had told him the story of how he had met her in a swirl of social engagements when he headed his company's subsidiary in Spain.

She is perfect in her red gown, earrings, necklace, adding grace to Father's ugly nose, his irascible temper; but then the image detaches from some deep shadow, as if her face were simply colors, lines, in some arbitrary combination. She stares three-quarters into space, as the lamplight moves down from her hair, and then over her body, like a river rushing over smooth stones, plants waving in the current. . . .

Father emerges in his tuxedo, and as he adjusts a cuff link, emits a false sigh, "Oh, the *ardures* of political life." The word didn't exist—Dwight had looked it up. Was Father perhaps making a connection to what he had just done to him? Or was it simply that he really didn't know the right word, or was he just being pretentious? Yes, he looks splendid, as if his clothes, his position, have transformed him into a magnificent caricature—those drawings of famous people in the *New Yorker*, more real than life, whose lines come together like this, or in outer space, when Father's hands move over his body.

Father and Mother leave the house, with the limousine waiting at the curb. Why couldn't he tell her what Father did to him, and if he told her, would it matter—would she do anything to protect him? She must know—is that why when they are together she stares into space? He stands looking out at the dark street. From the doorways of the homes down the block, with their quaint brick walls and iron gratings, he hears the mix of gossip, the shuffle of waiters, the intimacies and innuendoes—he is inside one of those houses now, holding his drink, in a future time when he, like Father, will call himself a public servant. Someday, after four more years at Georgetown Elect, after Harvard, after perhaps an advanced degree—of course, it will be in Economics—could he possibly study Literature? No, Father would not permit it—he will enter this life, and stand where Father stands now, his name, Dwight Lockwood, to be inscribed on the stones of schools and institutes. . . . Is it true she cares nothing for him?

The limousine pulls up in front of their door, and Mother, with a quick gesture of irritation, darts back into the house—she has forgotten her wrap! It's hardly necessary on such a warm, sensuous late spring night, and yet it would serve to subtly complement her gown, add a flourish to her perfect decor. . . . Even as a small boy, he had wondered what it would be like to be held by her, enveloped by her warm body—"And so live ever—or else swoon to death." Would it be like in the poem he had just read in school—"Pillow'd upon my fair Love's ripening breast/ To feel for ever its soft fall and swell/ Awake for ever in a sweet unrest"? Or would the lines of her body converge on his, like the dive of a hawk or an eagle on a small animal, after a swirl of wings and shrieking cries?

The years stretch back without a moment in which to find himself. . . . Nannies in starched uniforms, tutors caught gazing abstractedly into space, little outings with selected, carefully dressed friends, trips to museums, country resorts, instruction in foreign languages, while grown-ups speak meaningfully in the background— that was real life, and his, only a preparation.

His grandfather, Eduardo, sits him on his knees, while the nurse, specially engaged for his brief stay in Spain, chants, "*uno, dos, tres; quatro, cinco, seis*," and then his grandpa's knees open, and Dwight falls into the space between, only to be rescued and set upright, to be repeated again and again. He had walked through the huge mansion, with the portraits of ancestors on the walls, the swords and suits of armor, and yes, the gilded framed portrait of Mother, which must have been an anniversary present, which now hangs in their living room. . . . Trips to unremembered countries while his father, the mad king, had conferred with someone called the Shah—yes, that would be the Shah of Iran, or attended a meeting in Paris, with someone—he'd actually thought it was a person—called NATO.

Yes, Father, after becoming the CEO of his corporation, had then been appointed Secretary of Defense, surrounded by his generals, his name in the *Washington Post* and the *New York Times*, his irascible face lit up in a smile—or is it a leer or a scowl?—on the television screen. He is sarcastic, yet somehow the reporters, and the public, actually like him. His quips, emitted through puffs of smoke from his eternal, disgusting cigarette, are taken up by the opposition, but then dropped as the public sounds them again and again like a bouncing ball, chuckles, laughs, remembers Father for his good humor, for his common touch, for the sheer pleasure of his sharply defined presence—Father!

He tells Dwight of his sessions with the "Gipper," of working with "a man who hardly knows what he is talking about, but can, in his public appearances, in a way which, Dwight, is simply astounding, combine simplicity with seeming wisdom. No one, no one *I've* ever worked with, has such magic. None of us, even if there were a science of imagining a perfect politician, of conceiving him, creating him, and empowering him, could have done it so well. We all know, God bless him, he speaks for us, for our interests, which are, they really are, Dwight, you must believe me, the interests of the country." Father smiles and shakes his head—what does Father really mean? Is the "Gipper" just an image, but then what's behind it? The lines of the Gipper's face with its cobwebs for eyes, its indentations of flesh, continue to weave back and forth until someday he will lie in the dark ground and the lines will slowly decompose.

No, Mother says, as she stares into space, when people die they go to heaven, and there they live for eternity with God—does he understand that? Would dying, then, be like going to the theater, with its aura of expectation, its swirl of music, its bright lights, with the director somehow hovering in the background, managing the play? She crosses herself—"Though I go to the Episcopal Cathedral, because your father demands it, my Dwight, I am still a Catholic, I will always be in the true church." . . . What really happens to people when they die? Do their lines unravel and stray until their images disappear, or do the lines continue to shuttle back and forth, until they reweave a new pattern?

They sit together in the pew at St. Paul's Cathedral in the swell of the organ, as God the Father speaks: "Thou shalt have no other gods before me." "Thou shalt not make unto thee any graven image, or any likeness of any thing that is in heaven above, or in the earth beneath." A matter of law rather than faith, from this august figure who rules the world. Then where is Jesus? His face looks out over the waters which his Father has created, or at the sky to see the stars which He has fixed, only to find himself in a simple village with an earthly father and mother, and numerous brothers and sisters, and yes, sheep and cows. He is poor, "below the head-lights," Father would say, yet precocious, his eyes staring out, the memory of his father like a dream.

The Bach fugue ends, and then the chorus begins with the voices of the *St. Matthew Passion*, and now Jesus appears in front of him, washing the feet of the disciples, or sitting at the common table at Emmaus with that preternatural look—"Dwight, do what is in your heart"—or he has decided to enter Jerusalem, knowing full well that he will die, yet completing his mission, and for a moment, Dwight enters his body, and extends his hands with the stigmata of the Cross.

Mother sits next to him in their own pew prominently forward and covered with purple felt, but she has only left her image there. The voice of the priest falls like rain on the earth. Her eyes widen, her breath quickens. How can she be just what he sees, the beau-tiful, vacuous face, the list of social duties, the separate bedroom?

On Saturdays, Dwight "shops" with her at Bonwit's, or Helena Rubinstein, or Bergdorf Goodman, or at her personal dressmaker, sitting while she changes only to emerge again and again in dresses or wraps or hats which seem to be mere subtle variations of each other, forcing him to define the most delicate criteria. "Which one would you choose?" she asks him, always in Spanish. The designer makes a minute adjustment, suggests she drape the shawl over her left shoulder—"Madam, will the gown be worn at a reception, at an opening, or at the theater?" Why for years had she brought him, waiting for Saturday, so he might attend her?

She had always taken his decisions as final, and purchased just that gown, that wrap, just as she had let him do whatever he wished around the house. "He will put away his toys, Brad," she had told Father, and, of course, he would do it—to protect her. Now, each week, he buys her a bouquet of flowers from his allowance, which always brings a quick smile, followed by a tightening of her lips and her staring eyes.

It had begun to rain at first almost soundlessly, then stridently like bad news or an international crisis that Father must handle.

The rain catches the light of the street lamps in electric glints, currents of fire run in the street, a truck flashes into incandescence, and then explodes.

The novel he's reading keeps its own pace, as the rain beats down on the cobblestones. The young man is clearly some version of Henry James himself, ambitious, diffident, gay, yes, clearly gay—has anyone ever doubted it? Is that why the hero cannot talk to the heroine, but just mechanically makes love to her, as once his father must have made love to Mother? And at the end, to speak of her eyes, how revealing, how self-deceptively sentimental, when the young man had not cared at all for her, and had only attempted, however futilely, to serve himself.

Dwight follows the young man through his encounters in London, and then in the country houses of England, as the novel maintains a surface of expectation, only to reveal its final deceptions. He stares out the window in the room where Father and Mother hold their entertainments, where, had he been Henry James, he might have made the observations which later would become his novels.

It is still a few hours until his parents return, and almost twelve hours before he must dress for school. The crisis with India and Pakistan will end, Father has told him privately, not with a war but with continued petty killings. "There is no end to human hatred," Father says. "Like human wants, human hatred is unlimited, and creates a continuous market for my services. It is the same everywhere in the world—Europe, Africa, and, of course, the Middle East." Father tells him the story of the Arab and the Jew who have died and gone to heaven, and had their first audience with God. "'When, O Lord,'" they ask"—Father gives their voices the appropriate agonizing tone—"'will there be peace in the Middle East?' The Lord answers, 'Not in My lifetime.'"

Dwight finishes the novel, mounts the stairs to his room, and types out his review as if he were merely transcribing it—then who has written it?—and slips into bed. His hand is clutching the novel, but then is releasing it into outer space. He stands looking up at the book, as it slowly begins to circle the earth.

He is climbing a mountain in Switzerland—Father had con-
signed him to an assistant, while he meets with the United Nations
in Geneva. With boots, knapsack, and even a little pickax, they
ascend the mountain, as he pushes himself higher and higher, past
moments when he is dizzy and breathless, until they reach the tree
line with only snow and ice above them, and circling hawks and
eagles, and then nothing but the limitless sky, a flash of light before
the darkness of outer space, and the whirling planets.

The house boy, García, wakes him up—"Is there anything I can
do to prepare you for school, Mr. Lockwood?" he asks with a little
snigger, and just a trace of suggestion that he could do to him what
Father had done, if his position would not be threatened. As he
descends the stairs, García is whistling *Dònna Immòbile.*

At the breakfast table, Dwight sits across from Father who, after
two smelly cigarettes, a second cup of coffee, and his perusal of the
Times, demands he tell him what happened yesterday in the soccer
game with Capitol Friends High. "I want a full report, Dwight."

"Well . . ."

" 'Well' is no way to begin a report."

"We won."

"That is how you *end* your report."

"Mansfield Vane scored the winning goal."

"What was the score, Dwight? If you think you can play some
kind of goddamn game with me, you're mistaken!"

"In the first half neither side scored. In the second, I scored the
first goal. Capitol Hill Friends tied the score with five minutes to
go, and Mansfield Vane scored the second and winning goal—would
you like to hear the whole game, kick by kick?"

"No, that will do, thank you!" Father resumes his reading of the
Times. Mother sits tight-lipped, says nothing.

The limousine, the same one which had escorted his parents last
night to the British Embassy, and has just returned from driving
Father to the Pentagon, now stands waiting to take him to school.
Peter, the Lithuanian chauffeur, sits impassively in his uniform.

Then the limousine is passing through the Georgetown streets until it reaches the main gate of Georgetown Elect, and halts behind a long line of limousines and foreign cars, as if it were an embassy, before depositing him in front of pillared Bennington Hall. He carries his books in a pack, but, unlike most of the other students, he disdains the deception of baggy blue jeans with holes in the knees and pock-marked sneakers.

"Hey Manse," "Foster," "Hi Parks." His "friends" seem utterly absorbed in their walkmen, their portable tape recorders, their concerts, films, TV programs, the group gossip, noting how the girls— Gwen, Polly, Dunsey—resemble their heroines of the media, a world made up of bits and swirls of electronic light.

He jokes with Parks—Dwight is already one of the stars of the soccer team, so Parks can't just ignore him. "Cool day," Dwight says, "if you can believe in a blue sky." Parks shakes his head.

Dwight says, "You gotta believe in the sky, man."

Parks blinks. "Yeah, like it's blue, huh?" They keep it up another minute or two, before they shuffle into class, as Dwight's skin slowly spreads over his body like a rash.

"Silly stuff," Father says, when every minute matters in the relations of India and Pakistan, or in the latest crisis in the Middle East, or in the formulation of a new policy, to be shortly announced, on the use of nuclear weapons in space, which, Father smirks, will "scotch the treaty." He's only in ninth grade—he's first in his class, he's already one of the stars of the soccer team—what *else* does Father want? Dwight glances down at the novel of Henry James, and his paper which describes its hero's self-deception that he is in love. . . . Now there is a buzz in the room as Gwen Bloomfield makes her appearance in the classroom. Her face is white like a mask, her eyes are accentuated by dark eye-liner, she wears all black clothes, her expression a studied apathy, setting a new "Gothic" style for the school. Between classes she attracts a knot of girlfriends, while the boys approach and recede like diffident filings in a magnetic field.

His favorite teacher, Dr. Reginald Herrington, enters, raps for attention, and begins speaking of Henry James as a mirror, and a lens, but also as a man whom he deliciously describes as "a floating cognitive function." Isn't that who he is himself? Dr. Herrington is speaking to Dwight, to the future writer of still another generation of novels, of another record of civilized life, but then he adds, "if it needs one, if it has not already moved beyond literature to television and, in the future, to computers, and all that vapid nonsense, to ultimately—can there be any doubt?—to consume itself in destructive wars."

Has Dwight been born to write, or is he simply the son of his father, who today is meeting with a Dr. Teller to design a system of nuclear weapons which will orbit in outer space and send beams of energy hundreds of miles to destroy the swarms of rockets sent by the "Soviets." Father had shown him the summary plan—"top secret, my boy, top secret," but if that were true, why had Father shown it to him, sworn him to secrecy, and then quizzed him on its contents? Did he trust him that much, or was it some subtle way to control him?—if Dwight knew, would he then be in league with him; would he already have been compromised, and so have to accept his demands? Walking down the street, a beam of energy will burn him alive, or he will be asleep, and his head will suddenly explode like a bomb. . . . "And so," Dr. Herrington continues, "Henry James reconfigured the world inside his mind into the words and worlds of his novels, a continuous process that lasted his lifetime from his earliest stories in the *Atlantic* until his final publications." . . . What if the Soviets really launched an attack, and the missiles were arching in the sky, then falling, like the golden grains of the Holy Ghost? The energy beams would be emitted and somewhere in the deep vacuum of space they would strike the missiles . . . "A man who looked like a banker or a politician, who then periodically slipped away from the social world in order not just to record it, but to recreate it." . . . Father, who is now meeting with Dr. Teller, will create with his words the future defense of the world . . . "a series of novels, *The Portrait of a Lady, The Wings of the Dove, The Ambassadors, The Golden Bowl . . .*"

Foster Nottingham slips his arm under his in some proprietary manner—did he suspect, did he know? Foster stares at him with his bulging eyes, upturned nose, imposing shoulders. Would he steer Dwight off the grounds of Georgy Elect and take him into the woods? "Foster, just what are you doing?" Dwight removes his arm; Foster shrugs, and saunters away.

Dwight sees Gwen out of the corner of his eye, and then she is actually talking to *him*, she is talking about Dr. Herrington, who "just happens to be the most boring man in the world," that she "tunes out" in his class—"who could possibly understand him?"—and doodles little stick figures who troop around the margins of her paper, while he "barfs" on endlessly. "Oh, Dwight, please rescue me from all this. Take me to some faraway island, Tahiti, or Pago Pago—is there a place in the world named Pago Pago?—where his voice will be so far away no one will even *imagine* he is speaking—oh, please, please!" She puts her arm around him, and steers him down the brick path which leads away from Bennington Hall.

Will he ask her to the school dance, will he buy her a gardenia, and then will he have to kiss her good night? . . . Father's hands move over his body, his fingers like the energy beams of the new weapons circling the world, contracting, clutching it hard. Then Father is exploding inside him, so that the world will be blown apart, and again he will be circling the earth amidst the stars, and then be staring into the emptiness of outer space. . . . She laughs. "Can we skip class and go for a walk?"

"It's Math."

"So, why not?"

"If in the class," he says, "we are going from *a* to *b* to *c* to . . . well, if tomorrow, when we will be at *d*, how will we ever know how we got there?"

They laugh, and skip the class, and buy ice cream cones, and walk along Wisconsin Avenue, and then into the woods.

Gwen will run her fingers over his face, her fingers dipping into the crevices and pockets around his eyes, his cheekbones and nose, her fingers moving down his chest, his waist, as a fragrant cloud passes by, drowning his senses—or will they be like the legs of a voracious spider? . . . Gwen says, "It must be strange being the son of so famous a father. How do you do it?"

"I don't."

"You're so beautiful," she says.

"That's what, I guess, we're supposed to say to you, and it's true, I look at your face, and . . ."

"Yes, yes, please go on."

"And then I close my eyes, and, well, then everything just disappears except the last image of you in my mind which," he lies, "is, I guess, your face, and . . ."

"Go on."

She has placed her hand on the back of his head, and drawn him toward her, and then she kisses him, there in the woods which are just off Wisconsin Avenue, not far from Georgy Elect, on a spring day. They walk back. He has just been kissed for the first time—he rubs the spot on his face, as if he would wipe it away.

* * * * *

"We all have our intimations," Father says. "We all want to dip into our private feelings, and entertain ourselves with our own sensibilities, but it's a luxury, Dwight, people in our position simply cannot afford." No, he would not major in Literature at Harvard; he would, of course, take Economics—"If you can prevent yourself from dying of boredom, it's really quite useful. You see, old Karl was right—everything or almost everything is ultimately reducible to economics, so why not go to the source? Is it odd my citing Karl Marx? It's nothing I would do in public, God knows, not in *this* Administration"—he laughs to himself—"but the old boy spoke the truth—the rest *is* mainly superstructure."

At the dinner table, Father has him analyze editorials in the paper, chart economic trends, report on turns in foreign policy. He dutifully submits his "reports" to Father, sometimes in writing, sometimes as if at a meeting or a conference. With all that "investment," of course, what could he do but what Father demands—major in Economics, and relegate Literature, at best, to a pastime? "Do you think I've been investing my time all these years so you could just waste your life?"

"And, of course, you'll room in Manning Hall, my old stomping ground." But over three years ago Father had stopped abusing him, or whatever the phrase is—it had been that night, after Gwen had kissed him—why had he waited so long?

Father had called him into his room, and had started to undress him, and Dwight had taken his hand and held it very hard, and then had moved it away, and stared into Father's eyes. Father had smiled, nodded, then sighed. "I've always loved you, Dwight," as if with that one phrase he could sift back over the years, and erase all that time. A week later, Dwight had stopped in the middle of the street—"I've always loved you, Dwight." Was it true—had Father just hinted then at asking his forgiveness for an emotion he had really felt?

Dwight looks out over the Harvard campus. Little paths seem to connect all the buildings in the Yard. Centuries ago, a student guide tells his freshman group, young men in dark robes had moved along these same paths clutching their scriptures, eventually to take their places as stern divines in the righteous churches of New England. In the winter, students and professors still follow the same paths, though buried in snow, as if they were the lines of a collective memory.

No, Gwen will not be here. In their senior year, she had been arrested for possession, which, even while it titillated, had carried the message that she had forgotten her obligation to her social class, and so slipped off the register—of course, she had been selling, as well. She had been expelled, and then treated as if she had never existed—the school purported to have no idea where she had gone. Would someday, along a street, in a strange city, he see her face?

They had been rehearsing *My Fair Lady* with Gwen playing Eliza Doolittle and Dwight, Professor Henry Higgins. They, and all the class, had continually laughed as they tripped over the exacting English, as "the rain in Spain fall gently on the plain." It was a release from care, a projection into the thinnest air of expectation, an invitation to play among the stars! How stunning Gwen looked; she had become the confirmed beauty of the senior class! What "superb fun" they were having, as scene by scene they played it out until the final scene, after the ballroom, when he had stood before the audience holding her hand as the applause filled the auditorium. . . . When he had arrived in Cambridge, and thereafter for a few years in each new city, he would search for her name in the phonebook.

His roommate at Manning Hall is named Richmond Kerry, or Rich for short. His father, Morgan Kerry, Father had told him, is CEO of Pathways Inc., a cable complex which "through aggressive takeovers, Dwight, has already snapped up most of the East Coast." Are his classmates like junior boards of directors? Are they the future rulers of the world, now only seeds or sprouts, waiting to be planted in the boardrooms of their fathers' corporations? Rich sits up at night in his bed, then slouches into the bathroom to mas-turbate, while Dwight finishes his romance with Henry James, and begins what promises to be a long affair with Marcel Proust.

Within a week, he finds a Spanish coffee shop, the Pamplona, where he spends hours drinking cup after cup of *espresso*. The wait-resses are from Guatemala, Colombia, Chile—he jokes with them about the muddy coffee, and "whatever goes on in the back room, where the dark brew is made," and hears their startled or amused answers, and, if he is not speaking Spanish, their awkward attempts to answer him in English. He sits writing his papers, as he begins the long string of courses which four years from now will produce his Harvard B.S., and reads in *The Remembrance of Things Past* of still another reception offered by Madame Guermantes, with its echoes from his Georgetown home of a game which has been played for hundreds of years.

In his introductory class, the cases of Russian begin to reveal their logic and this language its special genius. Father had fur-nished the tutors for him to supplement his courses in school, first in French, then in German, and, of course, he had always spoken

Spanish with Mother. . . . Sometimes, as he and Mother would be speaking together about the most mundane things, she would smile to herself like someone admiring a neighbor's cat.

As he sits in Political Science, Father says, "This isn't just about how the system works, but about how some people, Dwight, take responsibility for the world they live in." "No, Father," Dwight says under his breath, "this is also about how some people serve themselves at others' expense." In course after course, he learns how these selfish needs are met, while the needs of the peoples of the world remain unfulfilled—isn't that clear?—and yet Father had kept up the charade year after year.

Yes, he learns now how Father feeds on conflicts, with all their tension and stress. They frighten the Congress into greater appropriations, and the public into fearful acquiescence. They enhance his power, as, with his stinking cigarettes, he sits day after day watching it grow—his is the mind to dominate the world, like his body: huge, bloated, yet always unsatisfied.

Father looks to the rulers of the world, but what of its peoples? They matter to Father only because they can be manipulated, like his body that Father had touched, and dominated; but what if they said no, what if they pushed his hand away—what would happen then?

The courses pile up one on top of another, Nineteenth Century European History, Intermediate Russian, International Economics, Corporate Finance. . . . He sits in the Pamplona reading *Crime and Punishment*, while he consumes still another *espresso*, and jokes with a new waitress, Sabrina Montenegro.

She is light skinned, with dark hair and intense, dark eyes, and flower-like lips. She is small yet statuesque, a vertical line moving directly parallel to the earth, like the sweep of the eye, or a wave, or a gazelle. Sometimes when they speak together, they switch unconsciously into a deliciously rich Spanish.

"Ah, Dwight, did you, perhaps, forget to bring your money, and think that I will serve you this coffee out of love?"

"After all these years we have been together, how can you even speak to me of money?"

"Yes, it is true, my darling, we will always have Paris. . . . I will ask our manager, *Señor* Mendoza, if he believes in you as fervently as I do, and perhaps then he will even forgive you the bill."

She tells him her family is from Nicaragua, and owns a huge estate, some of which had been confiscated by the revolutionary Sandinistas, who now form the government. She had grown up with her personal maid, and had attended the best schools—"I was a little princess, Dwight, with dancing classes, a French tutor, and Pepe, my own horse, until the war." Her father, of course, had backed the dictator, Anastasio Somoza. "My father was not really political, just corrupt, or," she shrugs, "unconscious. Then the war started, and Father took out his hunting gun, and shot at some guerrillas—for him it was like shooting rabbits on his estate, but they returned the shots, and they killed him. . . . Now I think, I think, he was an ugly man, although he was my father, and, and I loved him." She shakes her head and begins wiping a table. After a few minutes, she says brightly, "Another coffee, *Señor*?"

Dwight does not tell her about Father—wouldn't she, doesn't everyone, already know he is the son of Bradford Lockwood? For weeks, they talk and exchange glances in some subtle language he had spoken only once, with Gwen, and then, without thinking, he asks her, "Would you like to see a movie, with me—it's *Last Year at Marienbad*?"

Five hours later, they are shadows in the lights of the theater, as the crowd slowly drifts into the street, and then they are walking under the lamplights to her Radcliffe dorm. They continue the French of the film—she speaks the language perhaps as well as he does—as she tells him, with her delicious laugh, how beautiful he is: "I do not know, *Monsieur*, if it is your blue eyes, or your delicious red mouth, or the whiteness of your skin, which so attracts me."

"'How do I love you?'" Dwight translates, "'Let me count the ways.'"

"Have we enough time for such a description? When does your first class begin? Hmm, or how long does the semester last?" She puts her arm around him, again as if this were a joke, and he whistles "*Dònna Immòbile*," while her dorm draws still closer. He says, "The film was like memory; it could have gone on forever, repeating itself endlessly, except then we never would have been able to leave." She says in English, "Always I wanted to go to France, but, with the war, of course, I never went," as they walk down the street, and then inevitably stand in front of her dorm.

"Come, we go in the back"—she takes his hand, which now has begun to sweat, while he walks with her, as if they were shadows, and the building itself could turn on them like a huge menacing dog, while the trees drip darkness, and he sees the glitter in her eyes, before her hand reaches behind his head, as they see again the fountains at Marienbad, and hear the same conversations they had heard last year, and the year before that, as she draws him to her, without laughing, and a dog barks, and she kisses him. . . . In the darkness, he finds his way back to Manning Hall, and Richmond, who is already asleep, and all that night he reads, as Raskolnikov emerges in little clumps from the English-Russian dictionary.

Will he ever go out with Sabrina again, or will he just go on living as the embarrassment keeps possession of his stomach? Weeks pass, as each day he stiffens his body to go to the Pamploma and order his coffee, and again make small talk with Sabrina, whose gaze drifts over his face. He says, "Still another coffee and then it's back to Mother Russia," or "Learning Russian is like being lost in the snow." Once he jokes, "Why is a beautiful princess like you working in a place like this?" "Because"—her face now is without a trace of humor—"so I will not be dependent on my mother—can you understand this?"

He tells her who his father is, as if it were a confession. "Yes, Bradford Lockwood," Sabrina says. "Of course, I know Bradford Lockwood. Everyone knows Bradford Lockwood. I read the newspapers, I look at the television, and there he is, Bradford Lockwood."

He gives an embarrassed little laugh, and sips his coffee.

In the dream, he is asleep, a small, helpless mass, as Father's form passes into him—in the next room, Mother, impeccably dressed, sits staring into the night beyond her window.

Dwight tells Sabrina, "I always thought of him as if he effaced the sky."

He says, "When he is in the room, he is the only one present!"

"And then constantly to see his picture in the papers, or see him on television, or hear his name!"

"Dwight, Dwight, this is not the drama of your life—can I tell you?" She looks into his eyes, and for just that moment, she disappears. "It is *you* who are the drama—I know someday we will talk about him." Could he ever tell her? Could he even begin? She smiles, "Ah, the drama of Bradford Lockwood, except that drama is being played in Washington, D.C., and we, Dwight, our drama is here in a little provincial city, called Cambridge, Massachusetts." No, he could never tell her.

He is running, as the players configure and reconfigure their patterns on the field. His first year, he had made the varsity team—unlike Father, he is lean and fast and hard. . . . There is a moment as he approaches the ball when he can stop and then kick, or he can run through the ball to the other side of a magic circle he and his opponent have drawn. Now, in this game with Haverford College, he runs through the circle and kicks the ball perfectly to the center, Allenby, who heads the ball for the goal.

He moves into the circle of the opponents' fullback, and impacts; a bomb explodes in his head, stars light up in the sky. Father looms over him, and then he has abducted his body into outer space, and is beginning again to draw him in with his hands. . . . Father is advancing still another scheme, this time another vision of Dr. Teller of thousands of little satellites, called "brilliant pebbles," which will circle the world, and, like a storm of angry bees, attack the incoming missiles. . . . Dwight opens his eyes—before him is the soccer field, his teammates gathered around him. He rises unsteadily, and stays in the game—the teammates say, "Way to go!"—the audience cheers.

Back in Washington, Father draws him aside to tell him that his "brilliant pebbles" have now become "kinetic kill vehicles" and have grown larger and larger, needing more and more complicated guidance systems until, he laughs, they're "apt to become brilliant boulders." He shows Dwight the diagrams—"Do you see the problem—if we add all the radar and the sensing equipment how their size will become simply impracticable?" On the same visit, he sees Dr. Teller, with his bushy eyebrows and grave, end-of-the-world voice, sitting in their living room still lobbying Father for his scheme, while Father's eyes widen and he slightly tilts his head in the gesture Dwight knows is disbelief, as the lights begin to dim, as now—Dwight had learned just an hour ago—Father is suffering from prostate cancer.

Two weeks later, Mother calls him in Cambridge. "Your father's cancer has already metastasized"—had Father known, and not told the press to preserve his position?—"and is rapidly spreading into his bones and organs."

Father lies in a hospital bed, his arms and legs hanging from their sockets, his pot belly protruding from his bony hips—he laughs, "This is where it ends, Dwight." By his bed are copies of the *Post* and *Times*, and a small pile of letters from well-wishers, who must think that perhaps, if he recovers, he will remember them. Yes, the large lens of his life has suddenly narrowed. If it were an infection, the doctors could send antibiotics into his blood, which, like the brilliant pebbles, could swoop down on the incoming bacteria, but, of course, his very system is corrupt. "There is no help for it now," Father says. "I try to read the papers, but then, what difference will it make? Years from now, after I'm gone, and then, until there is no life at all on this planet, each day will have its *Post* and *Times*, with still another set of dire events and names—of course, to be eventually forgotten. Does it matter, Dwight, I honestly ask myself now, does it matter that once I was part of all this, that once I had a name, an influence, that I was a figure to be reckoned with, whatever the phrase, that I belonged to that small group of people who sit up late at night and rule the world?"

Dwight says nothing. Mother sits by the bed, or silently confers with the doctors. "They give him another three months at most. I come every day. He rarely talks to me." She turns her head, "I will come every day until he dies, as this is what I have been sent to do!"

Father continues reading the papers and watching the news channels—"What else is there to do," he says, "except indulge in lugubrious conversations? What is there to say to a dying man? Can you tell him that 'Brilliant Pebbles' was a silly idea, can you fault him for his policy in the Middle East, or the *Contra* War in Central America—or praise him for his handling of the Soviets, as if any of this matters now? Or can you wish him luck in the next world, and then, perhaps, issue an *amicus* brief to his Maker?"

When Dwight comes home again, Father will be too weak to talk, or perhaps will already have died; but no, he is still talking to him: "What are you waiting for, Dwight? Some confession, an abject apology from the dying man? No, I close my eyes and see your face and your delicious body when you were a boy or a young adolescent. Your lips were so red, your eyes so blue, your skin so fair—dazzling, dazzling, as they still are, and I open your robe, and I do it again, and again, and again! Take that! Take that!" Father's voice has steadily risen until he is shouting, or emitting as much of a shout as now he can muster, and then he turns away, and coughs, and wipes the saliva from his lips, and goes about his business, which is to read the *Post* or *Times*, and then to die.

Dwight returns to Harvard—there are only three weeks left of the semester, and then he will be in Washington for a summer internship, which Father had arranged months before, at the CIA. He calls Sabrina to see *The Tempest* at the University Theatre. They sit together as the old man accepts with good grace the guile and accidents of the world, and then benignly takes control, guiding his daughter into a marriage of love, and, at the end, is taken up into the pure light of grace. As he and Sabrina leave the theater, they both are crying. Is she crying for her father? Who is he crying for? No, no, not for Father, but for Prospero, for the beauty of this old man—"I'll deliver all; and promise you calm seas, auspicious gales, and sail so expeditious that shall catch your royal fleet far off"—yes, for him!

As they are walking under the street lamps, Sabrina says, "Dwight, I know you are disturbed because of your father." He says nothing; they continue walking in the dark near her dormitory. Above, the brilliant pebbles circle the earth, as Father, surrounded by his generals, gives the command, and the pebbles scream down on their target. Dwight takes her hand. "I'm not very sure of myself. I don't even know what I want. If I think of myself, I'm paralyzed." She doesn't go away; she continues walking with him. He says, "If I kissed you, it would be not because I have desire, but because I owe you this."

"What do you mean?"

"I . . ."

"No, no, you should not think about it. Not now, not now, Dwight, if you truly want to kiss me, as I know you do," and she smiles.

"If you were me, you would have to think about it."

Is their seeing each other enough? Is she like the heroine of James' novel, whom he only pretends to love? Could he ever love her? . . . He walks back to Manning Hall, and his roommate Richmond, and yet another Russian novel.

Two nights later she cannot go with him—she has a meeting of her "group."

"Is there some secret in your life you haven't confessed?" Dwight asks in their joking manner, as his stomach begins to fill with a black liquid.

"Ah, it is something only we *Centroamericanos,* and a few *Norteamericanos,* would understand. It is about my Nicaragua and the *Contra* war—it is not for you, I think."

Is she making it up? . . . Two days later, he notices a placard in a corner of her room—"USA OUT OF NICARAGUA!" At the bottom, "Christian Solidarity for Peace." Of course, she must know Father's role, and that he will be working that summer for the CIA—is that the reason she hadn't told him? Was she just protecting him? Yes, she says now, there had been other meetings that year, and she had simply not told him.

She packs up for her return to Nicaragua—he will write her, of course; they will talk on the phone. A week later, he enters CIA headquarters dressed in a suit, with shined shoes and a briefcase, and registers at the security desk. Ramsay ("The Rod") Hensley, an old friend of Father, and Deputy Director of the CIA, has left a note inviting him to his office. As he sits listening to Ambassador Hensley recalling his "times" with Father, as the stories proliferate—an incident in Egypt, a confrontation with the Soviets in Geneva, an amusing interchange with the "Gipper"—Dwight keeps on saying, "Yes, sir, yes, sir," as if he had nothing better in his head.

With his new proficiency in Russian—does he really know as much as the CIA must think he does? What had Father told them?—he is assigned to the Russian country desk to analyze documents which have been slipped to an embassy official in Vienna by a double agent. His immediate supervisor explains, "The Agency wants to know, Dwight, if these documents can be relied upon, or are they still just another screen for KGB deception?"

"Well, sir, I'll do my best." He is the only person in the room with a striped tie.

As he sits in his little office in the CIA, Dwight writes out a translation, begins taking notes. Father is quizzing him: "So Dwight, what is Alsop getting at?" "What's Safire saying?" "Is Buckley making any sense—what's his real agenda here? I don't want your goddamn conjecture, I want to know what's in the language. Now go over this again, and report back to me in an hour!"

Dwight pours over the documents, as he takes in the tonality of the Agency, its eastern college pretensions, its relish of classification, its disdain for other branches of government. Slowly he descends into its world of deception, where words have no dependable reference, where motives are equally unclear, and lives are spent in a purgatory of suspicion or disbelief. He is breathing through his teeth as if his office were filled with Father's cigarette smoke.

He sits having lunch in the CIA cafeteria with some junior agents, though still years older than he is. "Are you about to become one of us, one of the despicable breed of spooks? Take care."

"I'm just here for the summer."

"A season in hell?"

Dwight blinks his eyes. "No, not at all. I'm finding it quite interesting, actually. Who knows what I will do next—I guess, I'll probably go to graduate school." It sounds so lame.

"Ah, the refuge of the lost."

"And you," Dwight smiles, "you came to the Agency directly from the playground?"

An agent tells him that on Thursday nights all his associates are taking a Great Books course—for the next session they are reading Plato's *Republic*. "You won't believe this, Dwight, we are actually discussing civic virtue. It's delicious—I can only compare it to theater."

Dwight listens to the professor, replete with beard and pince-nez, as he intones the text, and the agents offer their comments. Plato stands like a stone statue on a pedestal, as the agents approach him, laying at its base their reports, staff studies, National Intelligence Estimates. "What did Plato really mean?" the professor asks, but then doesn't wait for an answer: "His message is that beneath the phenomenal world is a force which is the true reality, which can dispel all appearances. He believes that this force, the mind of God, is the basis of civic virtue as it is the basis of the mathematical laws, and of beauty and truth, and that we have it implanted in our souls."

One of the agents lights up a cigarette, and smirks.

Dwight makes up a list of questions and takes the documents from the double agent to an older analyst, then another, then a third. He quizzes the analysts on their Eastern European contacts, evoking from them a detailed construction of the KGB, its ideology, its organization, its recruitment. He digs out old reports from Biographic Intelligence, collates dates and references—Father stands over him, impatiently tapping his pen on his desk.

As Dwight works into the early morning hours, the documents reveal their targeting of people now fallen from favor, certain contradictions, expressions which break stylistic continuity, and behind them, the continuing deceptive hand of the KGB—the documents are fake. With less than a week to go, he submits his report.

Two days later, he receives a call from Ambassador Hensley. "The analysis is quite brilliant—you are to be commended, which will be so recorded in your, I suspect, still rather short record of government service, but one that, I am sure, will grow. Congratulations, Mr. Lockwood"—he shakes Dwight's hand, and smiles to himself. Dwight says, "Thank you, sir," and "Yes, sir," several more times, then packs up and shreds his notes.

He is talking with Dostoyevski over a table in a coffee shop that looks like Emmaus, except Dostoyevski is constantly glancing around as if he were being overheard. "I need to tell you this, Dwight, I need to tell you this." Dostoyevski is sadly shaking his head, as Mother wakes him up. "I've just heard from the hospital. Your father died twenty minutes ago." She is already dressed, pacing, pale, her face stiff. "Your father *would* die on the one night I was not there!"

In a few hours, the phone is ringing with reporters, as the mechanism of an official death begins to whir like a virtual machine. Working with Mother and the family staff, he edits an official press release, allocates times for radio and television statements, takes endless phone calls offering condolences, some from people he has never heard of; and, with officials from the Department of Defense, he arranges the details of the funeral and public burial. Mother silently watches him, as if now he had replaced Father as head of the house. . . . A snake crawls out of its hole, its tongue flashing, then menacingly coils.

At the funeral, St. Paul's Cathedral is packed with well-wishers; he and Mother sit alone in their prominent family pew. As the organ sounds, and the hymns rise from the choir loft, the priest proclaims, "Bradford Lockwood was a man who shaped our times. If we survive as a species, it will be at least partly due to him, to his shrewd sagacity in the service of his moral purpose. His was a life given not in silence but in dedication . . ." Yes, his salvation is assured, as if his attorneys had already negotiated the judgment—Father is approaching the heavenly gates in a chauffeur-driven limousine, smugly smoking one of his cigarettes.

Dwight stands with Mother in Arlington National Cemetery, as a troop of soldiers fire their impotent rifles into the air; the drums sound, as the casket, draped in the American flag, is lowered into the ground. "No," Dwight says to himself, "he is not even the rich man who seeks to enter the kingdom of heaven. He would not even have thought it necessary to ask." As Dwight stands amidst the mourners, Jesus looks upon Father, and opens his hands. "Don't you know," he asks him, "what goods you should have given away?"

The next morning, there is Mother; the maid, María; the house servant, García, his thighs swishing under his pants. Mother has already dressed, sat for her coffee and croissant, and taken her morning walk. "It is over now," she tells him. "No, he did not empty the planet of human life!" Dwight stops in the middle of the street—yes, she had said this.

A week later, Sabrina returns to Cambridge from Nicaragua. "Why didn't you tell me your father had died. Why didn't you write or call me?"

"I think, I . . ."

"I am not only for the school year, Dwight!"

He turns his head, and stalks off down Boyleston Street—how can she care so little for him that she can scold him at a time like this? He passes the shops, the churches, block after block of colonial homes, until, after more than an hour, he sees a phone booth, and calls Sabrina at her dorm—"I'm sorry, I shouldn't have walked away. I . . ."

"If I am part of your life . . ."

"No, it isn't that."

"Yes, that!"

It sits like metal in his stomach—"Yes, yes, we will talk," he had told Sabrina, as he walks to her demonstration. Cars honk, unruly demonstrators shout, "STOP THE WAR, USA, CIA OUT OF NICARAGUA!" It's all so crude, so disorganized.

Father is decomposing in the ground, and yet he is speaking to him: "Why are you getting into this left-wing nonsense? Have I just been wasting my time all these years?"—no, not dead yet. Should he even be here? Yes, isn't all this "subversive"? Isn't Father right—if the government finds out, won't he lose his security clearance? The traffic piles up, the honking grows even louder. One blocked car careens out of the traffic onto the curb and almost runs down two or three demonstrators.

There, there is Sabrina—she is in the middle of the crowd handing out flyers! As she turns to wave to him, a policeman grabs her. He starts to run over to protect her, but she shakes herself loose, and then she disappears into the crowd. A police truck arrives. The police pour out and begin to arrest the demonstrators—on what basis? Has any law been disobeyed? The demonstrators go limp. There is Sabrina lying in the street, as if she were about to be violated—then the police are dragging her body over the rough cobblestones.

At the police station, he waits with a small group of demonstrators as toughs, prostitutes, policemen, and lawyers mill about in the smoke-filled halls. Hours later, as the demonstrators are released one-by-one, the group cheers. Then, with a policewoman by her side, he sees Sabrina smiling, holding up her small fist.

As they sit having coffee at the Pamplona, Dwight says, "Do you know that story of William James . . . when he experienced the famous San Francisco earthquake?"

Sabrina shakes her head.

"Of course, when his friends read about it in the papers, they were all worried about him, and wrote him letters expressing their concern, but William James answered that he was perfectly fine, and then he wrote, that all his life he had heard the word 'earthquake,' but now, by this visit, he had 'verified it concretely.'"

"I think, Dwight . . . I think, maybe we go to Nicaragua, and then you see it for yourself." . . . With Sabrina and a few other students, he is playing softball—it is a pickup game in the street. Sabrina is at the plate, small but enthusiastic, holding a broken bat. The ball arches toward her; she swings, and scampers to first base with a hit. She stands on the base raising her small fist. He is up next—his heart is pounding—he is holding the same broken bat.

TRAVELS WITH MARY MAGDALEN

Sabrina waits for him, as members of Christian Solidarity for Peace go around the circle. "Yes," Dwight announces, "I will do civil disobedience, and 'risk arrest,' in the current phrase." The CSP people nod their approval. In the training session, he goes limp on the ground, as one of the members, impersonating the police, pretends to drag away his body. . . . The policeman stands over him, leering at his helpless form.

"I must say, I'm a bit dubious about all this nonviolent business," he says as he walks back to Sabrina's dorm. "Frankly, letting someone abuse you without resistance will just make him feel he can get away with anything."

"Nonviolence is not just passive, it is very active, my Dwight . . . and you will see"—Sabrina laughs—"it is ennobling."

On the highway across from the Marine air base a dozen demonstrators hold a forty-foot banner, "HONK IF YOU WANT THE USA OUT OF NICARAGUA!" Each honk from the passing cars brings cheers from the demonstrators.

Dwight turns to Sabrina. "Is this their idea of having an impact?"

"Why are you being so critical of us?"

Behind a fifteen-foot cyclone fence, a squad of crew-cut Marines with M-16s are squinting like confused cattle. Then he sees Art Fenton from the CSP group climbing the gate. As he reaches the top, Art is winking—at *him*. . . . The group takes up a rhythmic clapping: "One, two, three, four, we don't want your stupid war!"

Dottie Berriman, an elderly lady from the group, approaches a Marine guard. "Young man, would you mind opening the gate so I might be arrested?"

"Ma'am?"

Then—what is he doing?—he is scaling the fence! As he rises over the crowd, he sees Sabrina smiling up to him. He easily reaches the top, clears the barbwire and spikes without getting cut, and drops to the other side. Immediately, two Marines put their hands on him, holding his arms and chest. They turn him over to the police, who put cuffs on his wrists, and then push him into a police truck.

He finds himself sitting in a corner of a cell which is filled with smelly drunks and criminals, who give him knowing looks. As he wakes up in the middle of the night, he had been dreaming that one of them was grabbing him, pulling him down on one of the cots. As night turns to dawn in the prison cell, he sees in a high inaccessible window a white knot of the purest light!

As the police take him to sign papers, he hears Father snap, "What the hell were you doing? Do you want this on your permanent record, for Christ sake?" He is led into the main hall to be released. There, with a small group of CSP demonstrators, is Sabrina—she must have been waiting for him the whole night. He holds up his fist; the group gives him a rousing cheer.

"It is so important," Sabrina tells him. "It is your body, Dwight, which makes the commitment, it is your body, my darling, not just your head." It is his body that is walking down the street with her, the body of someone who has just been arrested. . . . That night, as he sits again in the prison cell, there is Sabrina standing proudly by herself in a shaft of light. Yes, she is the beautiful nude he had once seen at the Louvre by the sculptor Aristide Maillol—it was called "Isle de France." . . . A man's bloated body falls from a great height to the street, and crashes on the pavement. Has he just witnessed Father's death? Standing beside him is an old man—it is Prospero—with a white mustache and soft eyes. . . . "Yes," Dwight says to Sabrina the next morning, "we will go to Nicaragua!"

They wait in a grungy, ill-lit restaurant off 23rd Street in New York City. An hour passes after the agreed time, until finally the priest, Father Raymond Dietrich, appears. He is tall and thin, almost emaciated, with sunken eyes and wisps of uncombed hair over a smooth, round skull; he has a stubble of beard, and wears an old leather jacket and paint-spattered jeans. "I suppose," he says with a sigh, "I'm still on Central American time." His voice is quiet like a sign in the sky.

"Can you tell me where the group is going exactly?" Dwight asks.

Father Dietrich pulls a beat-up notebook from his jacket. "We will be five days in Managua for training, and the rest—it will be four weeks—in El Planeta, a village in the *Contra* zone."

"Why the *Contra* zone?"

Father Dietrich smiles to himself. "That's what we do, Dwight. We stay in villages which may come under attack—to be in solidarity with the people." He is holding up his hand, as if he were blessing their donuts and coffee.

* * * * *

Sabrina gazes over a bank of clouds, her lips set. As the plane begins to lose altitude, a line of green-blue haze appears, then sharp-crevassed mountains and the conical shapes of volcanoes—the ground rushes up.

In the airport, the walls are plastered with slogans and posters: the intent faces of the young and old reading books—the literacy campaign; a row of houses under palm trees—the rural housing project; a group of citizen soldiers—the Popular Army. "NICARAGUA READS!" "LAND FOR ALL THE PEASANTS!" "HERE NO ONE SURRENDERS!" "THE REVOLUTION LIVES—THE REVOLUTION IS FOREVER!" Is this actually happening? Dwight copies the exact language of the slogans into a notebook.

An elderly woman appears in a conservative if stylish suit, her lips pursed, her eyes squinting. Sabrina introduces him to her mother, Elvira. They stand awkwardly facing each other; her mother begins to cry as Sabrina looks away. Outside, the chauffeur—his name, Sabrina tells him, is Manuel—holds open the door of the family Rolls Royce. They drive off through the streets of Managua, skirting potholes, as the city sprawls for miles with no apparent center, with milling crowds, cracked buildings, garbage piled up against the walls.

They pass palm trees, farms, and villages which are little better than collections of huts. Five hours later, they drive up to a pillared mansion set against a copse of oaks and elms which looks like Bennington Hall at Georgy Elect. The servants run out to greet them. Maids and valets scurry about; waiters obsequiously serve them; they ride horses about the estate; with the other families of Sabrina's class, they attend elaborate dinner parties and receptions—is this any different from his life at home?

He plays the young suitor, offering ingratiating observations, allusions to his studies at Harvard University, to his famous father, only tentatively to the "strained relations between the United States and Nicaragua." He catches their knowing smiles, the buzz of social acceptance. On Sunday, while a priest intones a Latin benediction and Elvira weeps, they lay a wreath over the grave of Sabrina's father, who still roams the countryside shooting at the rebels with his rifle as if they were rabbits.

On Monday, they insist, over the objections of Sabrina's mother—"Why, for God's sake, don't you let Manuel drive you?"—on taking a bus back to Managua. Eight hours later, covered with sweat, they arrive at a sprawling, one-storey building with a wraparound verandah. There, standing as if they had just seen him an hour ago, is the gaunt figure of Father Dietrich. As they enter the building, he holds up his hand and says, "Yes," as if it were a benediction. Later they see scrawled on one of the walls a quote from *Matthew*, "Let your Yes mean Yes, and your No mean No."

They sit in their first meeting "discerning" why they have come. A middle-aged Black woman speaks first: "My name is Ellen Ferris. I'm the sexton of an Episcopal church of Philadelphia." She compresses a smile which never parts her lips, then stares as if she were listening to what no one else can hear: "I am making this trip, I will follow in His steps, I will see the beauty and the sorrow of the things He saw."

"I'm Harold Mosley. I'm a seminarian from Detroit"—a new beard, a gold earring, a huge cross dangling from his neck. "Well, I am going for kicks. No, seriously, I'm going because in this moment being in Nicaragua is the most meaningful thing I can do."

A slight man in his forties, in jeans and a farmer's straw hat: "I'm Jeff Kanin"—a pure New York accent. "You could describe me as a Jewish Buddhist, a psychologist who's become fed up with the whole middle-class therapy trip."

Next is Manuela Fernández, who wears a pink CSP t-shirt stretched across her huge bosom which shows a line of ordinary people holding hands against some unknown oppression: "I am here with the Lord's help, because without the Lord, we are nothing, nothing at all!"

The group turns to a young woman with dramatic blond hair. A brief pause, an intake of air—she pulls down her skirt over her shapely legs: "Hi, I'm Caroline Swenson. I'm finally here! For years, I searched my feelings through acting, but now that I'm studying for the ministry, I can see my whole life as a vehicle for His grace. No one, no one wanted me to go—my mother, my friends—they all tried to stop me. I need to tell you—I'm afraid, I'm very afraid about this whole trip!" The group pitches forward as if to catch her.

"Don't worry," Harold Mosley says. "If anyone starts shooting, we'll run away together." General nervous laughter—of course, Dwight says to himself, he's gay.

"I'm going, I'm going," Caroline continues in a faltering voice which gradually gains strength, "because I want to drink the faith, the faith I know I will find in the Nicaraguan people."

Is the play over? Dwight waits a few seconds to show the proper respect. "I am Dwight Lockwood. I'm going because my friend, Sabrina Montenegro, is Nicaraguan, and I'm North American, and it is time now for me to be here in her country, and share that experience with others"—it sounds so flat.

"I am Sabrina Montenego. To what Dwight has told you, and to what you all have told me, I add my 'yes.'"

Father Dietrich will follow him into his room and sit on the side of his bed. He will tell Dwight that his lover has died of AIDS, or has left him, or has been killed in the war, as piece by piece he slowly removes his clothes until he is wearing only a loin cloth. . . .

Father Dietrich turns to him, "Go down to the river, and wash yourself clean!"

The group visits a clinic and rehabilitation center run by a *Señora*
Padilla, a middle-aged woman who is constantly blinking her eyes
to stay awake. She tells them that the clinic lacks the funds for even
the most minimal medical treatments. The patients or residents
seem suspended in time—a middle-aged woman with an artificial
arm, a young man with no motor control on his left side, another
with a pained, cross-eyed look. As they leave in their minibus, *Señora*
Padilla is standing in the doorway watching them. . . . Dwight writes
in his notebook, "Wars seem to end only for those who haven't
lost something. The shot, the grenade, the mortar happen so fast,
and then become timeless, leaving their victims scarred and suspended forever."

The group stays in a low, concrete-block building topped with
a wooden cross. They have their first dinner of rice, beans, and tor-
tillas—it is cooked by their designated "mother," Carmen Gomez.
Night falls. Dwight is given a cot between Jeff Kanin and Harold
Mosley. They undress, go to bed, fall immediately to sleep—Dwight
sits up with a flashlight reading a Nicaraguan fairy tale which slowly
begins to inhabit the shadows of the room: a lamb and a jackal,
named Jack, somehow strike up a friendship—or is it a love affair?—
they play together, they go for long walks in the woods. But then, as
Dwight reads, "One day Jack turns on the lamb and takes him by the
throat with his huge jaws. The lamb is bewildered—what is his friend
doing? The jackal bites down. For the last time, the lamb looks longingly into Jack's eyes. 'It was all my fault,' he says. 'I should never
have tempted you to do evil, and now it is too late,' and the lamb
dies." Slowly the dawn begins to pour light into their window.

He wakes up in the middle of the night as the jackal is about to
bite into his throat—if they were suddenly surrounded by the *Contras,* what would he do? They stand menacing him, Sabrina, Father
Dietrich. Suddenly, the words come to him: "We are Northamerican
journalists who are observing *la situación;* I am the son of former

Secretary of Defense Bradford Lockwood, who, as you know, supported the *Contras* . . ."

Father Dietrich leads the group to a church in a poor quarter of Managua. On the walls, murals depict the Nicaraguan people as the early Christians facing the Romans—a twelve-year-old boy stands before the rifles and machine-guns of a squad of soldiers dressed in togas. They sit in the pews as the priest reads the text of the day—it is the story of the loaves and fishes: Jesus preaches before a crowd of hungry poor. He has only a few loaves and fishes, but then the little he has has been magnified, and he can feed the multitude. The priest asks, "My brethren, what does this passage mean?" He scans their faces. "It means that our Lord knew that His spiritual message was not enough. Today there are those in our country who still separate the body and the spirit, but we know what that means. That is the religion of exploitation, is it not, my friends? So it is our task, as has been shown by our Lord, to feed the hungry, clothe the naked, and house the homeless. These are the tasks of our religion, and of the Revolution."

The congregation sits head bowed, then advances one by one, including Sabrina, to take the communion. She tells him, "It is your body that makes the commitment, it is your body, my darling, not just your head."

At the Council for the Disappeared, *Señora* Valdéz, a middle-aged woman, pale and intense, stands before them. Behind her, lining the concrete walls, are framed black-and-white photographs; underneath are names: Alfonso Morales, Elvira Aragon, Sigmondo Alverez, Eduardo Valdéz. . . . "These are the disappeared who were tortured, or raped, then dropped, sometimes still alive, from planes into the ocean, or buried deep in the jungle, or who, years later, were still in the clutches of the police. These are people who, for their parents or loved ones, never died."

She points to the photo of a young man—Eduardo Valdéz: "Yes, you may have guessed, this is my son. They brought me to the police station and made me watch while they gouged out his eyes, and then they defiled him, they defiled him! My son, my son, how could they make him suffer like this? . . . My son . . . and now, I do not know, I do not even know when or if he died, or what . . ."

Father Dietrich holds up his hand: "*Señora*, that's enough, enough!"

". . . We know that many North Americans do not support us and that your government supplies and trains the *Contras*; and we also know that we have *compañeros*, such as *Solidaridad Cristiana por la Paz*, who fight by our side." Yes, in his Harvard dorm, in his world of privilege, including Father who, more than anyone else, is responsible for all this. . . . Eduardo Valdéz, surrounded by his defilers, stares at him from the wall. Slowly the group files out of the office, as *Señora* Valdéz stands watching them.

At dinner, he cannot look at Sabrina; after a brief service, he turns toward the men's bedroom. He catches a look from her, but still he says nothing. Two, three hours, he lies in his cot next to the bodies of Jeff Kanin and Harold Mosley, as he tries to read the story again of the jackal and the lamb, which now fades out of his mind. He gets up, dresses, and wanders out into the street.

He comes to a moonlit plaza with, on one side, an equestrian bronze statue of a general with a drawn sword, and on the other, a dark cathedral. Inside is a cavernous vault lined with cubicles of painted Marys with wax tears, of saints with hearts bound by barbed wire. He sits in a pew—"What did you expect?" Father laughs—then he walks out of the cathedral into a dark rain.

On a side street, a nightclub pulses music, its neon sign fusing into the damp air—the "Casablanca." He squints into the gloom: five, six women sit at a bar, a couple of men. One of the women turns, rises slowly to greet him. She is perhaps twenty, in a clinging red dress; her lips are painted, her eyebrows extended with liner, her expression blank. "Will you invite me for a drink? . . . Would you like to dance with me?" Dwight pays her a Nicaraguan's weekly wages. Someone drops a coin into the jukebox; tinny American music plays; as they dance, she presses her body against his.

He asks her, "What is your name? . . . Are you from Managua?. . . Do you work here regularly?" She answers, "Dolores. . . . *Si*. . . . *Si*." He catches himself and Dolores at odd angles in the mirrors behind the bar, and in the eyes of the others watching them.

"Come, you can taste me, and then, if I please you, you can enjoy me for the entire evening. . . . Here, come with me"—she takes his hand, and guides him up a flight of stairs and down a hall as he mutely follows her.

A single bulb hangs from the ceiling of a shabby bedroom. Dolores is removing her blouse, her skirt, her brassiere, her pants. She lies with her lush, naked body waiting for him on the bed. Black water rises up and floods into his mouth! He has just time to shout, "I must go, I must go!" He fumbles in his pocket, throws some money on the bed, and runs down the stairs, then past the people at the bar, and into the street.

He sits up hour after hour in his cot. . . . "The jackal's tongue is flashing over its teeth, its tail swishing back and forth as it stalks through the jungle looking for its prey." From the other side of a sheet of glass, Father Dietrich says, "Didn't you know the world is transparent?" As the glass vaporizes, he begins to take off his clothes—Dwight sees his ribs, his thin legs, the angularity of his pelvis. Father Dietrich turns away, and wades into a river which swirls in circles around his body, until he has disappeared.

"What happened last night? Why can you not say to me, I think about what we hear, I am upset? Yes, I knew that, Dwight, I was upset, also, but we are here together in Nicaragua!" Sabrina begins to cry. "I am here with you!"

". . . I'm sorry. . . . I handled it so badly."

She shakes her head and stares. That day they visit a labor union, a housing project, a government human rights committee. As they walk toward their bedrooms, he says, "I'm not very good at this."

"No, you are not, my Dwight."

"I'm just learning. . . . I'm sorry. . . . Forgive me." She passes her hand over his eyes as if he were blind, and then he sees—she is smiling.

When Father Dietrich finally appears, his breath smells of alcohol; his round forehead is beaded with sweat. "Listen, my friends, I've asked you to come because we need to discern about our trip to the north. Yesterday, thirty miles down the road from El Planeta, the *Contras* killed twelve villagers, including a pregnant woman, after, I have to tell you this, they had raped her and her two daughters. I've talked to our friends in the government—now they tell me they cannot guarantee our safety. I said to them we'd take the same chances as our Nicaraguan *compañeros*—if that's what you still want to do."

"I didn't realize"—Caroline Swenson's eyes are bulging—"I thought there might be some danger, but, I mean, things have gotten so much worse. I've tried, I've tried to overcome my fears, but I can't. If I didn't come back, my mother . . ."

"It's all right, Caroline." Father Dietrich takes her hand. Caroline's body suddenly loses all its tension. It's as if Dwight were watching them on stage—and yet isn't it real? Father Dietrich says, "These are free choices of the Spirit."

Caroline drops her eyes—a beat in the script?—then looks up and smiles. "I'll go!"

A long pause. . . . Harold Mosley smooths his slick hair. "I came to do this, so I'm going—I only wish I could have read about it instead."

"Of course," Ellen Ferris says, "this is why He has sent me."

Jeff Kanin says, "I think we'll just have to take our chances," and smiles to himself as if he were contemplating some Buddhist conundrum. Dwight records each response in his notebook. . . . Of course, he will go. Sabrina says, "Yes."

As he turns his head in a slow arc, Father Dietrich takes in the faces of the group. "So then we are agreed? Well then, if it's okay with everyone, I thought tomorrow we might go to the beach, and in the evening we're all invited to a party."

"Way to go!" Harold Mosley says.

Jeff Kanin chuckles, then says, "Finally!"

Dwight walks through the gutted streets of Managua, past a crumpled wall, a ruined church, a strange formation of stones. A blast must have turned these stones into a monument to "the fallen of Nicaragua"—he will touch it, feel its shape. He makes the first contact, but then withdraws his hand as if it were polluted. He turns—a huge jackal is stalking him. "My father, my father," he says to the jackal, "was Bradford Lockwood. He was the Secretary of Defense, and, as you know, a strong supporter of the *Contras* . . ."

The minibus traverses a flat landscape with its horizon broken here and there with volcanic cones; then it is winding up a thin mountainous road. From a guardrail, the group peers into a smoking, sulphurous pit fifty, a hundred feet below. "From here," Father Dietrich tells them, "Somoza's *Guardía* threw political prisoners into the molten lava." They are dragging Dwight toward the rim—they are sweating, cursing, enraged by their own cruelty! He is shouting, "We are Northamerican journalist, we are observing *la situación*. We have the protection of the American embassy. My father, my father, Bradford Lockwood, was the Secretary of Defense, he was a strong supporter of the *Contras* . . ."

When they reach the beach, a few white clouds float in a depthless sky; volcanoes rise from the other side of the shimmering blue water. Father Dietrich and Harold Mosley, who stands before him in a skimpy bathing suit, have decided to swim across—"How about it, Dwight?"

"It is too far," Sabrina whispers to him. "Why must you do this?"

"It'll only take an hour or two."

"It is too dangerous. You . . ."

"Oh, it's perfectly safe!"

"Do what you wish!" Sabrina turns away.

Then he is swimming in deliciously cool water as they head toward a line of barely discernible palm trees on the far shore. No matter how long they swim, it seems constantly to be receding. He loses track of time, but then they have reached the other side and are wading in water alive with bubbles which rise from the bottom, emitting puffs of sulphurous steam.

They check in with each other. No, he is not tired—they begin swimming back across the bay. Suddenly the sun has disappeared and the sky turned grey, then black; a stiff wind is sending gun-metal waves into his face. He is still swimming with Father Dietrich and Harold, but after a moment's inattention—how could this have happened?—he's lost them.

Now banks of waves rise up in front of him. Rain wets his face, thunder sounds. Jagged lines of lightning strike the water. Both his legs—they're cramped! He chokes, he struggles, as if someone—who is it?—is it Father pushing him down? He's sinking into a dark swirl of water. What if he dies? He's going down, ten, fifteen, twenty feet. There will be no trace of him, nothing—he'll die before he's done anything in the world, a frivolous, meaningless death.

He hears a voice: "Hold your breath. Let out your legs. Relax your muscles. Do not thrash." He follows the commands, repeating them again and again. . . . Slowly, the water passes like a hand down his face, his chest, his sex—he is rising, and then he breaks the surface! He takes in a huge breath; in a minute or two, he tentatively moves his legs—the cramps have gone—and he begins swimming to shore. Why had he almost let himself drown? Who had saved him—whose voice was it? A rock emerges from the water; he realigns his body until it is vertical—his feet touch sand.

He wades onto a deserted beach, and walks along the empty strand lined with waving palm trees. There is the delegation—Father Dietrich, Harold, Jeff, Manuela, Ellen, Caroline—they're all waiting for him. "Thank God!" Father Dietrich opens his arms. Already the sun is poking in between the huge, mounted clouds, the sand is radiant. Sabrina, who must have been searching for him on the shore, runs up crying, "Dwight, I almost lost you, I almost lost you forever!"—she holds him in front of everyone. "Promise me, promise me, you will never do that again!"

"I'm all right. I . . ."

"Never do it again!" . . . In a few minutes, the group piles into the minibus; as they pull away, the sun is setting between two volcanic cones. A thud—they've struck an object in the road. "It's just a dog," the Nicaraguan driver says, and keeps on driving. Out the window, Dwight sees the dog lying on its back in the middle of the road, its legs upright. Its soul lifts off its body and rises into the air, and then, like a satellite, will begin to circle the earth—had it been substituted for his?

Sabrina says, "It's our last night in Managua, *compa*." Her eyes are searching for his as if he were still lost in the waters. The minibus drives to a middle-class *barrio*, to the home of the singer, Federico Martínez. Plates of sandwiches, bottles of rum crowd the tables; guitar music pulses in the air. They drink, he dances with Sabrina, they attempt conversations about *"la situación"* with Federico's revolutionary guests.

In a burst of applause, Carlos Godoy, Nicaragua's most famous singer, makes his entrance. He is handsome and self-assured, an Elton John, an Elvis Presley—like the heroes of Georgy Elect. As Godoy sings a selection from his *People's Mass*, he seems somehow transcendent, but then starts a satirical song about the literacy campaign. Martínez joins him—"If we can't read, if we can't write, at least we can fight." Together they improvise new choruses, slipping in little asides about each other, about Father Dietrich, about the Nicaraguan President Daniel Ortega, about President Reagan and his agent, Colonel Oliver North.

They pause—will Father Dietrich sing a song? He shakes his head and stares at the floor. They call his name—*"Raymundo"*— *"Raymundo"*—again and again, making runs on their guitars, improvising a song about him. Still he makes no response. Then Carlos Godoy asks him quietly, as a courtesy to his host, to sing one song. Deliberately, Father Dietrich picks up a guitar. His delicate hands caress the strings, his eyes half closed, as his smooth forehead incubates the song. Everything stops—the animals, the flowers, the trees—to listen to the pure tones from his throat, while the plucked strings catch a wind rustling through the branches. It is a ballad from Appalachia of misunderstanding, of love and death. The tragedy is irredeemable—all that remains is his song in a world of desolation, lost love, the aching heart. Where is this song in him? Why, Dwight asks, does he have it, why him?

Why can't I just listen without such self-concern? After a hush which follows the last note, Godoy hugs *Raymundo* as if to welcome him back.

Dwight sits with Sabrina on a bench in a little garden of black flowers at the back of their house. "Tomorrow, we'll be going into the war zone, so I wanted to tell you something."

She waits. "I wanted to tell you . . . so you know everything . . . that my father . . . my father sexually abused me, and . . . I wanted you to know. He did it for many years, until I finally made him stop." He clenches and unclenches his fists. "That is why . . ." He can't say anything more.

The jackal and the lamb are looking at each other—the jackal is licking his lips—what will happen now? Sabrina sits a long time nodding her head. "It was something your father, he did this to you. This is a terrible thing, but you did not do this!"

"But . . ."

"No, no, you did not do this. We go now to the *Contra* zone, and I am glad you tell me, but we will return, and we will live our lives with what we have. These are *our* lives, it can be so much more than the things others do to us. . . . I love you, Dwight, you know that!"

He walks under a threatening sky, while the wind howls, pushing in windows, tossing whole trees into the streets. He walks, it seems, interminably; then he looks behind him—for the moment, there is no jackal, no one is following him. . . . He wakes up with a question: "Does the lamb play music?"

The last morning in their "home," Sabrina makes a gracious farewell speech in Spanish, occasionally glancing to Dwight, as if under his leave. Their "mother," Carmen, responds with a speech to their "new Northamerican friends" that matches Sabrina's. The Gomez family stands stoically waiting for the group to leave, knowing they will never see them again.

"Dwight," Sabrina draws him aside, "where we are going is dangerous. You are foolhardy sometimes, or maybe," she pauses a moment, "I know now, you are perhaps too wanting to die. Promise me you will be careful."

Their minibus passes the shacks and shanties of gutted villages. Children with ulcerated feet and bloated bellies stare at them from the doorways. It was in these villages, Father Dietrich tells them, that hundreds were massacred—their voices cry out, mixing their shadows with the dust and the unremitting sunlight. The countryside is thick with vegetation, with a play of shadow and light, and a symphony of bird cries—perfect cover for the *Contras*—the group falls silent. A sharp crack. The minibus swerves, almost crashes into a tree, stops, lists to one side like a panting beast. The driver gets out and confers with Father Dietrich, who tells the group, "We've struck a rock, the front axle is broken." He laughs, "Welcome to Nicaragua!"

Father Dietrich arranges on the car radio to have the minibus towed; an hour later, they're standing up in the back of an army truck—he starts the group singing "Which Side Are You On?," "If I Had a Hammer," "They Call Him Ron with the Neutron Bomb"— as they climb through sheets of rain into hill country. Sometimes the shoulder completely disappears and the truck skirts a sheer drop. Dwight stands, his hand on the truck's rim, the other holding Sabrina.

The sun has already set and the night fallen as the truck pulls into El Planeta. Three men with AKs are waiting for them on the road. Their flashlights pick up clusters of shacks, sometimes topped by tin roofs, sometimes thatch, with glistening plastic bags covering cracks in the walls which obliquely reflect the moonlight. Out of the dark, an AK slung on her shoulder, a woman appears, perhaps forty years old, with a pale, determined face. Father Dietrich introduces Roberta Sánchez, *"la responsable* in El Planeta." She is coughing as she guides the group over a puddle-strewn path to an abandoned school, a half-shell of cinder blocks, plasterboard, and thatch.

Dwight lays his mattress and sleeping bag next to Sabrina's. Explosions sound in the distance—Sabrina's body stiffens; during the night as they lie on the floor, she presses her body up against his. Roberta Sánchez appears with a flashlight. "Don't be alarmed, these are rockets, the *"Cuarenta Bocas"* ("Forty Mouths") which now are about ten kilometers away. We will tell you if the *Contras* get any closer." . . . Dwight is sitting in a seminar room at Harvard discussing the war with Father: "No, my boy, to actually *be* here is simply an indulgence—you should know, if you don't already, that you cannot decide policy by personal feelings!"

The group's awake, coughing, sneezing, rolling up their sleeping bags. Sabrina says, "We got through the first night, *compa*."

"You okay?" he asks Jeff.

"Of course. We Buddhists are used to sleeping on hard surfaces; that's our encounter with the world. . . . We better check out Manuela."

She's propped up against a wall gasping for breath; Ellen Ferris is offering her water as if the gesture were part of the mass. "This is nothing, nothing. I'm used to this. I'll make it, praise God."

"Do you have medicine?" Dwight asks.

"I have all the medicine I need right here," Manuela says, touching her Bible.

They straggle over to a ditch, carrying rolls of toilet paper. Sabrina squiggles up her nose and laughs; the men and women separate.

In the schoolhouse, the sun pours through the slits in the concrete. Roberta Sánchez stands before them in her army fatigues. "My country," she begins in Spanish, then coughs, a dangerous, hacking cough, "my country is grateful that you have come. This area is almost entirely surrounded by the *Contras*." She coughs again. "Two months ago, they came to El Planeta, entering the town from the northeast. They torched the agricultural station here and killed seven militia, but Radio El Planeta kept on broadcasting during all this fighting. Here no one surrenders—no one!" She coughs again.

"Our *compañero*, Father *Raymundo*, tells me you wish to work. We are very grateful—you can start this very afternoon to help build a *refugio* for the children and the old people."

This time she coughs for a full minute. "Between us, you Northamericans and our embattled people"—she gasps for breath—"are bonds of solidarity which will never be broken. We will fight together, and in the end we will win the victory of justice!"

At the *refugio*, farmers, townspeople, soldiers dig and haul earth. To one side a group mixes concrete, pouring it into wooden molds. He and Sabrina join the line of people hoisting the dried blocks to make the walls. Three older women surround her, exclaiming, praising, touching her hair—*"Que linda!"* "Like silk!" *"Que bonita!"* Sabrina introduces them, "These are my old friends, Consuela, Yolanda, and Marina Luz."

In a few hours, Sabrina's hands blister, then begin to bleed—Dwight runs to the clinic for gauze. When he returns, he finds that a flirtatious *ranchero* has lent Sabrina his leather gloves; his own hands, he laughs, are tougher than the leather. After an awkward moment, he leaves. The sun slowly slips in the sky. There is Father Dietrich sitting on a wooden crate staring; then he returns to work.

Father Dietrich introduces the group to Luis Fuentes, the town doctor, and his wife, Jacinta. He is small and wiry and wears a Seiko wristwatch; Jacinta is white-skinned, delicate, Spanish-featured, clearly a daughter of wealth. The clinic, Dr. Fuentes explains, has only two small rooms, one for patients' beds, the other with an operating table made from an old desk. He shows them the horse stirrups he uses for child delivery, and a makeshift anaesthetic unit, "although with such terrible facilities, I should not operate here at all."

They meet a thick-set woman with heavy breasts in a cheap nylon blouse—"This is Gioconda, my *brigadista*." Dr. Fuentes lowers his voice after she has left the room—"Truly, she is a wonderful woman, but she has been trained by the government for only six weeks." The group stops at the bed of an old woman whose foot he has amputated; Carlos, a boy of ten, who has been blinded in both eyes; a man shot in the head, whose wound he has dressed, but whom, he tells the group, he must now let die.

As Dwight, Sabrina, and Jeff wander about the town, they see a frumpy old woman sitting on a porch in a broken rocking chair. Her hair is unbrushed, leaving patches of baldness. Jeff whispers in Dwight's ear, "Can't you see the Chinese features? I read that her ancestors came here fifteen thousand years ago across the Bering Strait."

The old woman says, "I was born in Cuá."

"When you came to El Planeta, were you by yourself?"

"I had two sons."

"What were their names?"

"I had two sons."

"And now?" She doesn't move her head.

Jeff shakes his head. "I think we'd better go."

Sabrina puts her hand on her heart, and then touches the old woman on the head. "Thank you for speaking to us."

The old woman doesn't move.

They meet a mother of four whose husband was killed last year, a storekeeper, the government agricultural agent, a soldier who strikes a heroic pose with his AK before Sabrina's camera. The smell of charcoal and fat drifts in the air. An old man pisses behind a house; a hard-faced *ranchero* rides by; birds chatter; two or three radios play the lilting anthem, *"Nicaragua, Nicaraguita . . ."* Sabrina says to him in Spanish without a preliminary hello, "They are so brave. We need to write this for a newspaper or maybe a magazine. I know you are taking notes—and I am taking pictures—and then we can tell the others in your country the situation here."

"Alright," Dwight says, "we'll do it." He writes in his notebook, "This is El Planeta, which is like the tree crashing soundlessly in the forest because no one hears it."

Mothers, old men, sometimes children, tell them their stories of burnt farms and homes, of rapes and executions. Sabrina fixes them in the viewfinder of her camera, while Dwight scribbles in his notebook. . . . Father Dietrich is sitting with them at the end of a wooden table outside the Darling: "Now you see how it is here. If our Lord is spirit, is not His people His crucified body, does He not suffer when His people suffers?" His eyes stare out from deep hollows. How long, Dwight asks, will He be with us? Father Dietrich blesses their food, "Help us, Father, to do Thy will," and then recedes into circles of space.

Suddenly the loudspeakers announce, "Stage Two"—almost full alert. Roberta Sánchez assigns each member of the group a noncombatant job in case of attack: Dwight gets the clinic; Harold and Jeff, the fire unit; Sabrina and the other women, the only half-built *refugio*.

That night he and Sabrina make the nightly *vigilancia* with Roberta and two silent men with Indian features, all armed with AKs. In the dark, they hear her incessant coughing, the sounds of distant explosions. The jackal flits in and out between the trees looking for its prey; overhead the planets circle like hawks and eagles. Roberta Sánchez knocks on doors, and greets the villagers sitting silently in the dark. In each house, they offer them coffee, and then ask Dwight and Sabrina questions—"Isn't it dangerous for you to oppose your government?" "If the *Contras* are beaten, will the United States just invade Nicaragua?" "Is President Reagan really as crazy as he sounds?"

Dwight answers, "No, it is not dangerous. Sometimes we are arrested but then in a day or two we are released." "No, I do not know what the U.S. government will do."

Sabrina says, "Yes, President Reagan is as crazy as he sounds," and gives a crazy look, and everyone laughs.

"Even crazier," Dwight says, and they all laugh again.

In one house, as they are leaving, someone takes his hand, and fixes him with his eyes: "When you return to your country, you tell your people what it is really like here!"

At two-thirty, they return to the schoolhouse—bodies are strewn all over the floor—he and Sabrina crawl into their sleeping bags. What language is he speaking—is it Spanish, French, German, Russian?—faces stare at him without understanding. . . . The jackal is singing, "Are you sleeping, are you sleeping, Brother Dwight, Brother Dwight?"

He wakes up in the dark—"Yes," he whispers to himself, "this is the real world, not Father's take on it, not its appearance in books, or in courses at Harvard." When he wakes up again, Sabrina is no longer lying next to him. He walks into the town—there she is standing in the middle of a dirt street, her body defined in the sunlight, her curls luminous in the sun—yes, she is *"Isle de France,"* here in Nicaragua.

After four days of sweat and dust, they will finally bathe. Accompanied by two soldiers carrying AKs, the group takes a path which ends before a river lined with palm trees which sway in arcs over the water. Though Sabrina can't swim, she wades into the river with the other women who soap themselves under their clothes. She calls to Dwight, "This is fun, *compa!*" She splashes around, then holds Dwight in her arms for just a moment before she glances at the others. When the soldiers aren't watching Sabrina or Caroline, they're checking the thick green of the farther bank.

"Isn't this just a vacation?" he writes in his notebook. "Aren't we just here like any tourists in Cancún or Puerto Vallarta? If the sun sprinkles the waters with a little danger, isn't that just an added spice, like skiing or scuba diving?" Father smirks.

The "Forty Mouths," which begin about one in the morning, now sound so much closer. Townspeople spool barbed wire around the radio station, the granary, the clinic. People living in the countryside are moving into the town. A soldier leads a class for the boys on how to fire a rifle—they posture for their friends and for the girls—the girls giggle and gossip among themselves about the boys.

The loudspeaker announces that the *Contras* have hit a nearby village! When Dwight reaches the clinic, the victims are just starting to stagger in: a soldier with a gunshot wound which oozes blood from his chest, a little girl with a charred leg, an old woman blinded by smoke. Luis instructs Dwight how to clean the wounds: "One must be careful not to tear the flesh." "Yes, use alcohol, but not directly—like this." The patient twists in pain, while looking up into his eyes.

Gioconda draws Dwight aside. "The soldier on the cot—he is rapidly losing blood. He will not live more than a few minutes." The soldier's pressure is falling—the bottle of plasma hangs over his body like a ticking clock. His ravings become quieter, more coherent; his wife and his father-in-law wait; another soldier, presumably from his unit, stands stiffly outside with his AK, as if on guard. Dwight sees the soldier's face lose animation, his muscles relax. His wife throws herself against him weeping. "So that is how it happens," Dwight will write in his notebook, "as simply, as quietly as this."

Luis stands outside the clinic smoking; Gioconda brings him a cup of coffee. He is staring at some shacks in the middle distance. "There was no way I could have saved him; in Managua, they might have, but here our facilities are so poor." He turns to Dwight, his voice now almost shouting, "What does it matter if this little village survives? And yet we fight for it. That is why we are alive, to choose carefully what we give our lives for!"

Full Alert! The world does not stop and wait, even for a moment—the loudspeaker's on continuously, giving the siren codes, the latest movements of the *Contras*. The villagers lay more barbed wire, dig trenches, work on the *refugio*.

Night falls. Dwight stretches out next to Sabrina; the minutes slowly pass, as the darkness swirls around them in malignant currents. He leaves her curled body around his empty sleeping bag, and joins the next *vigilancia*. Roberta and the two soldiers say nothing; even when Dwight questions them, they answer in monosyllables. The four make their rounds, the silence broken only by Roberta's cough, as they drink cup after cup of coffee. In the huts and houses, the adults stay awake; the children sleep, their inert bodies curled up in little cribs or on the laps of their parents. When Dwight returns to the abandoned school and the group, the loudspeaker is quietly playing Carlos Godoy's *People's Mass*.

Suddenly, the sirens are blasting! Deafening noise! The ground quakes, as if a huge dog had taken them by the scruff of their necks and was shaking them. Explosions all around! Dwight grabs Sabrina and pulls her down to the dirt floor. The explosions continue as they lie waiting for the ground to crack. Then the explosions stop.

They sit up and glance about the room—the air is thick with dust—"Everyone all right? Anyone hurt?" The loudspeaker's on—

it's Roberta Sánchez: "*Compañeros, compañeras*, El Planeta has just been attacked by mortars. No *Contras* have been sighted. Seven people have been killed, maybe more. There are many wounded, we do not know how many. Another, another five are dead!" Dwight glances at his watch—it's four thirteen. Sabrina's breath comes in pants. By the light of the flashlights, he sees Father Dietrich's completely calm face. Suddenly Dwight says to the group in a voice he does not recognize, "Now you must all go quickly to your posts and check in!"

Sabrina and the other women run to the *refugio*, Harold and Jeff to the fire station, Dwight to the clinic. A sharp smell of phosphorus hangs in the air; at the edge of the village, fire lights up a line of trees. The wounded are limping in, or are being carried by their relatives; some are screaming with pain; some are holding their wounds to staunch the pulsing blood. Gioconda quickly sorts them out—those who must be treated quickly, those who must wait, those who will die.

After how many hours—Dwight applies sponges and bandages as more and more villagers reach the clinic. Finally, the sirens are blasting the "all clear." More hours of treatment, and then a ten-minute break—Dwight can run to the *refugio*. Sabrina stands outside the still unfinished building with Ellen and Caroline; the old people are just leaving, blinking their eyes in the sunlight; most of the children have already run back to their homes.

Sabrina looks at his blood-stained clothes, and shakes her head—"Oh, Dwight!" A little girl sidles up to her. "Concepción, Concepción, this is Dwight, *mi compañero*." Concepción tries to hide between Sabrina's legs—Sabrina picks her up and smooths her hair; the child closes her eyes.

"I've checked on the possibility of our going back," Father Dietrich tells the group. "Right now parts of the road to Managua are either torn up or will have to be cleared of mines. The government says that Popular Army units are coming, but for the next couple of days we'll have to remain here—everyone all right with that?"

"This is where the Lord has sent us," Ellen Ferris says.

"This is where we are," Jeff Kanin says, and smiles to himself.

"Walking around the streets of Detroit," Harold Mosley says, "is going to feel pretty safe. I never thought Detroit would feel safe."

"Years from now," Sabrina says, looking at Dwight, "when I am an old woman, I will think of you here in my country, as now we are here together in the Darling."

The radio music stops for a special announcement: "At eight o'clock this morning, the government of Honduras demanded an emergency session of the United Nations Security Council to protest a violation of its borders by the Sandinista government of Nicaragua . . ."

"Can you believe this?" Jeff asks.

The group turns to Dwight—by his silence is he silently protecting Father, or what he stood for? A moment later, they hear, "A U.S. fleet from Panama is sailing toward Nicaragua. . . ."

"You know," Jeff says to him, "things like this do happen. Except this time we happen to be *where* it's happening."

"I'd like to turn in my ticket," Harold says.

Dwight says, "We thought there was a purpose in being part of this."

Jeff turns on him with cold anger. "But now that you've shown us how brave you are, you'd be out of here, if you could, *wouldn't you—wouldn't* you!"

"No, I wouldn't!"

"You make me sick!"

Dwight turns on him, and in just that moment he catches a look from Father Dietrich—the searching eyes at Emmaus. He asks quietly, "Why, Jeff?"

"I'm just tired. . . . I'm just tired." Jeff shrugs, his face twists up, and he begins to cry; then he runs out the door.

Another night on full alert. The loudspeaker reports an attack on Las Manos, a nearby village—an occasional thud of mortars, the distant crackling of small arms. At three o'clock, the alert goes off.

Dawn comes up over the town, birds trill high in the trees. They breakfast at the Darling, pat the pigs, slip them pieces of tortilla.

At ten, Luis tells Dwight he's received a radio call from Las Manos. The *brigadista* there has more wounded than she can handle and is out of antibiotics. Luis is going—would Dwight want to help? Luis has secured some soldiers to be on the truck. Father Dietrich will be coming—the town has asked him to perform a funeral Mass.

"It's only twelve miles, and we'll have some soldiers," Dwight tells Sabrina. "I'll be back by tonight."

"I want to be with you when you do these things—I will come with you."

The two soldiers are silent as they scan the impenetrable green on either side of the road. The truck inches its way past a section where the road has partially fallen into a ravine; then they must ford a stream, and twice they dig the truck wheels out of mud.

Finally, when they reach Las Manos, they're met by half a dozen soldiers—three are bandaged. They hug Father Dietrich, are formal with Dwight and Luis, call Sabrina "*señorita*." A smell of wet ash mixed with that of a sickly syrup fills the air; houses are still smoldering; villagers wander shocked and listless through the dirt streets.

At the town's destroyed agricultural cooperative, a corrugated metal silo is broken in half, its contents spilled on the ground—that's the source of the smell. An ill-shaven old man with eyes staring out of holes in his skull—he's the *responsable*—tells them it was here that the militia stopped the *Contras*. He shows them patches of purplish red on the ground, which even the rain hasn't washed away. Dwight and Sabrina take photos and notes for their article, which now they have decided to submit to the *New York Times Magazine*—Dwight tells her he has a contact there through one of Father's old associates.

At the makeshift health station, they meet with Milagros, the *brigadista*. After her training, Luis had told them, she was in the field for eighteen months; once she was captured and raped by the *Contras* before she escaped. The woman is plain-faced, pudgy, perhaps thirty, with crudely applied lipstick. When Sabrina asks to take her picture, she fluffs her hair and turns away to put on still more lipstick.

Outside the health station, he sees a ragged line of perhaps forty people waiting for treatment. Luis and Milagros prepare syringes to inject the penicillin. Dwight shows Sabrina how to wash wounds and apply tourniquets and bandages—Sabrina gets right into the work—the line of people shuffles forward.

At four, Milagros takes them over to a diminutive wooden church. Father Dietrich stands in a simple white surplice. He is surrounded by his many friends in the village he has come to know over the last three years.

Then he is standing at the pulpit with raised, open hands: "The poor," he says, "is the body of Christ. The people's suffering is His suffering. Only if you give yourself for others, will you find your own soul. 'What you do for the least of them, you do for me'—this is the meaning of the Revolution. This is a revolution which must take place in our hearts and in the world, or the crucifixion of our Lord will never end."

He stands before them, the light from a window obscuring his form as he holds the bread and the wine. "This is my body, this is my blood." The people shuffle forward, an old woman, a soldier, a farmer, Milagros, a child, Sabrina. . . .

"And now I speak for our sister, María Gomez Muñoz, the beloved wife of Daniél and the mother of Ramón, Teresa, and Vidaluz, whom everyone in Las Manos knew as a pious and pure woman. . . .

"And now I speak for our brother, Ignasio Cardoza, who, like our Lord, was a carpenter, and who built the houses of Los Manos with his own hands. . . .

"And now I speak for Tina María Mendoza, who will never even be a child on this earth, but whose spirit will live forever. . . .

"Those who have fallen are still with us; they are still in our hearts. María Gomez Muñoz"—the crowd responds, *"Presente!"*

"Ignasio Cardoza"—*"Presente!"*

"Tina María Mendoza"—"*Presente!*"

"Concepción Nováles Hernández"—"*Presente!*"

The names go on, ten, twenty, thirty, of the people of Las Manos. . . . "And now I speak for our enemies, those who hate us and have caused our suffering. I speak of those who fought us here in Las Manos, and of those, yes, of those who killed our loved ones. We forgive them, we forgive them in our hearts, and we ask the Lord to receive them and to forgive them, even as we ask that He forgive us. Amen."

"Amen," says the crowd.

After still more hours of work at the health station, Luis tells them they should stay overnight rather than risk the trip in the dark. "Okay," Father Dietrich smiles, "but then I wouldn't mind taking a dip." He turns to a soldier, "Can we go to the river? Manuel, what do you think—is it safe?"

". . . Yes, Father, if that is what you wish."

Luis looks displeased, but says nothing.

Sabrina's hair is glowing with sunlight—Dwight asks, "Want to come? It'll be just for a few minutes."

"Is it really safe? . . . We don't need to go."

Manuel points to his AK—"At your service, *Señorita*." He is thin, with a small mustache and sweet eyes. As the four walk to the river, he tells them that he comes from San Francisco de los Cedros; he has a wife and two children; they have just received a small plot of land from the government.

The sun, still over the treeline, cavorts in the water. Manuel picks up a smooth rock and skips it all the way to the other bank; birds trill for the end of the day. Father Dietrich stands looking out at the river. "I'm not going in," Sabrina says.

"Hurry, please, hurry!" Manuel says. Dwight begins to take off his shirt.

A sharp crack—Manuel falls, clutching his shoulder. Sabrina screams. From nowhere, appear six or seven men—they're dressed in fatigues, carry carbines and rifles with grenades and special launchers.

Dwight grabs Sabrina—an accident happens so fast, a bird is snatched from flight by the branch of a tree. . . . "Pay attention," a voice says to Dwight, "pay attention to what's happening, don't disappear as you often do." . . . It's happening to someone else. . . . "Pay attention!"

The *Contra* leader, a thin, dour man with a mustache, turns on Father Dietrich. "We know who *you* are; you have been here many times before; you are with the Sandinistas and only pretend to be a priest." One of the *Contras* kicks Manuel, who groans in the dust. The *Contra* laughs and kicks him again, this time in the face—a tooth flies out. Sabrina yells in Spanish, "Stop it, stop it!" The *Contra* stops kicking Manuel, who manages to stagger to his feet. His shoulder is soaked with blood.

Father Dietrich says, "We are norteamericanos, from *Los Estados Unidos*—I demand you release us."

"You demand—you son of the great whore!" The *Contra* leader punches him in the stomach. Father Dietrich pales. Several *Contras*, looking nervously about, begin to push them along the river bank; no one appears from the town.

"Take me," Father Dietrich says, "I am the one who made them come." Is he trying to die? The leader punches him again, this time in the eye; Sabrina lets out a muffled scream. Dwight half carries Manuel who is now barely able to walk. The *Contras* push them further along the bank—the eyes of the jackal stare out amidst the trees. Hidden in a small cove, with crudely painted over U.S. Navy markings, are two motor launches.

The *Contras* shove them into one of the boats—will they rape Sabrina? Dwight's eyes meet with hers—she's holding up.

Their boat travels upstream, maybe two-thirds of a mile; then the engine conks out. A *Contra* swears, "Boat from hell, there's no more gas!" They drift over to the farther bank. The other boat moves on; they sit on the bank talking among themselves. They seem so young, just boys—what are they doing, raping, murdering?—except for the leader and one other, a man perhaps thirty, heavyset, with a beard and squinting eyes, a carbine across his knees.

Dwight asks the *Contra's* name. He shakes his head. Dwight asks, "When do the others return?"

"In a half hour, no more."

"And then what happens?"

"I think they will kill you, quickly, if you are lucky; artistically, if you are not."

Dwight pretends not to understand.

Father Dietrich sits with his head bowed—has he fallen into one of his depressions? Dwight asks Sabrina, "Are you all right?"

"Do not worry about me."

Manuel sits holding his shoulder; he's sweating, his teeth are clenched in pain. "Bad luck, bad luck," he mutters incessantly. More time passes. Dwight asks Sabrina again, "Are you all right?"

"I need to tell you now, because it is possible we do not return. I love you, Dwight. I want you so much . . ." The *Contra* tells her to shut up.

Will Father Dietrich send them a sign? Will somehow he create a miracle? He continues looking depressed. The *Contra* sits with the carbine across his knees; Manuel holds his bleeding shoulder, rocking in pain.

A fish breaks out of the water, and falls back. Dwight whispers to Sabrina, "It'll work out, *compa*."

The other boat appears with a tank of gas, and they motor to the *Contra* camp. Hundreds of men mill about holding their rifles, some shirtless, some in fatigues, some with straw farmers' hats. When a soldier tries to grab Sabrina's arm, she fiercely shakes it free. Someone is jabbing Dwight from behind with a rifle butt.

They arrive at a big tent which has several folding tables with field radios. Adjutants stand around giving Sabrina lascivious looks. A *Contra* approaches them, a big beefy man with a beard and slow, ironic eyes—he tells them his name is Comandante Raven. He looks at Sabrina and extends his hand; she refuses it.

"Who are you reporting to?" the *Contra* leader asks.

Now Dwight speaks: "We are Northamerican journalists. We are here to observe *la situación*. We have the protection of the U.S. embassy. We demand that you release us, and that you release our guide, Manuel. I am the son of the former Secretary of Defense, Bradford Lockwood, who, you will remember, was a good friend of the *Contras*. You have my identification. You can verify this with the American embassy."

Comandante Raven listens until the end, then he laughs. "You Northamerican pigs will say anything to save yourselves. As for this piece of trash," he points to Manuel, "we will kill him, and as for you, *Señorita*, we have better things in mind."

Dwight says, "If you harm any of us, I want you to know what will happen. Next week in our Congress, there is a major vote on *Contra* aid—can you risk that? If you harm us, someone will pay for it, and that person will be you, do you understand, Comandante Raven? I appeal to your humanity to release us, but I also appeal to your self-interest."

Raven says, "I make no deals with you sons-of-whores. You are spies, and this piece of trash," he kicks Manuel, "will die slowly and painfully."

He turns to Sabrina, who backs away. Dwight steps in front of him; Raven hits him in the face. He feels nothing. "If you touch her, you will have to kill me first!" He puts up his fists. Raven laughs, then signals to have them taken away. Dwight says, "Our guide goes with us."

"For the moment," Raven says.

Dwight says, "We want water and we want medical attention for him under the Geneva Convention."

Raven signals to the guard to take them away.

As they wait in a tent, Sabrina's hand is over her mouth; she is blinking her eyes, as she occasionally glances at him, though she says nothing. Father Dietrich seems to be praying. In an hour, a canteen of water arrives; a little later, an old U.S. Army sulfa pack, which they put on Manuel, who now is feverish. Dietrich starts singing, and soon they're singing together, "They Call Him Ron with the Neutron Bomb."

"Will they come for us in the morning?" Sabrina asks. Dwight shakes his head, then hears the echo from an old 1960s record; he takes Sabrina's hand as they sit together in the tent as if forever. Manuel sleeps, his head burning. Father Dietrich talks now about his childhood in Tennessee, his alcoholic father, his troubled choice to become a priest. Outside the tent, two guards stand with carbines.

Night falls—they lie on the ground and try to sleep. Manuel is raving, drifting in and out of consciousness; Father Dietrich mumbles parts of the Mass. "This is where I need to be," Dwight whispers to himself in the dark. Sabrina miraculously sleeps. . . . Hawks and eagles wheel in the sky. . . . The jackal visits him in the night: "What did you expect? Now you see what you get from your little heroics."

Night gives way to dawn and the chirping birds, which flit through the trees. Father Dietrich tells Dwight, "Now it is in the hands of God, but then," he smiles, "it is always in the hands of God." He has a terrible black eye. At ten, Comandante Raven calls them in: "You will be released as a courtesy, *Señor* Lockwood, and the northamericans in your company."

"And our guard, Manuel?"

"He must be considered a prisoner of war."

Dwight responds, "If we are released, Manuel is released with us; otherwise we will not leave, and you will be kidnapping American citizens, and the son of a United States Secretary of Defense, at a time, let me remind you, Comandante Raven, when *Contra* aid is being considered by our Congress."

Raven shrugs. "Anyway, he will die before he returns."

Released on the Honduran side, they begin the trek back to Las Manos. After only perhaps a hundred yards, Manuel collapses. Dwight tells Father Dietrich, "Help me put him on my back." He carries him for over an hour. When he can bear the weight no longer, Father Dietrich carries him, but in only a few hundred yards he is exhausted. Then Dwight takes him still again.

Manuel has turned pale—is this more dangerous than the fever? Sabrina wets his forehead with water from her canteen, and rips a piece from her blouse to hold against the wound, which is bleeding again. They sit down to rest. Suddenly, Father Dietrich shouts, "If we don't get him back soon, he'll die!" Dwight picks him up again.

After several more hours, they reach the section of the river across from Las Manos. Dwight guides Manuel's body to the other bank, and swims back. He leads Sabrina to the water. "Now take a deep breath, and we will start. I will be holding you, and swimming to the other shore."

It is the same voice which instructed him as he was sinking in the bay! Sabrina lies in the water, takes a deep breath, and then their two bodies are moving together diagonally across the river. On the other side, Dwight picks up Manuel and puts him on his back, and with Father Dietrich and Sabrina, they reach Las Manos and the clinic.

He is still carrying Manuel. The gnats on the river swarm in his eyes as he bears the impossibly heavy body; his feet are slipping into the silt—no, he is carrying Father Dietrich! He wakes up in the clinic in Las Manos. He sinks back into sleep. He shouts, "Raymundo Dietrich!" The crowd responds, *"Presente!"* "Raymundo Dietrich!"—*"Presente! Presente! Presente!"*

The people push their leader to the top of a hill overlooking the village—it is not Father Dietrich, but a simple peasant. He stands for a moment, his back to the sun, his hands extended in exhortation; on one side is a huge rock with the image of a face. Then the peasant—or is it himself?—is sliding slowly to the bottom of the hill and into the river. Underneath the surface lurk hungry pigs.

When they wake up, Luis apologizes for not greeting them properly when they arrived, but, nodding in Manuel's direction, he'd had some work to do. He'd removed the bullet from his shoulder, and given him a shot of penicillin and several blood transfusions—"He's still not out of danger, but he'll make it." Luis had figured out what had happened from the bloodstained sand and had immediately radioed the U.S. embassy in Managua, which apparently had contacted Comandante Raven, and confirmed Dwight's identity.

As Dwight and Sabrina walk with Father Dietrich through Las Manos, the children are playing with their tops, the women are cooking; woodsmoke hangs in the air. Dwight says to him, only half in jest, "When you leave here, you should tour American campuses, be a singer—you could be a star in no time, your voice is so beautiful."

He smiles, shakes his head. "No, I want the world to take me. I want to be more objective, less self-concerned."

At El Planeta, Ellen, Jeff, Caroline, Manuela, and Harold are all waiting for them at the roadhead—they give them a big cheer as if they had just been released from prison. That night the loudspeaker puts El Planeta on semi-alert, but the following day a Popular Army column clears the road to Managua.

El Planeta throws the group a goodbye party at the church, with cookies and soft drinks. Roberta Sánchez is there, Gioconda, farmers, *rancheros*, endless numbers of children, including Concepción, who nuzzles Sabrina, the old woman at the *refugio*, the old man bent over his stick. Roberta, with her terrible cough, makes a speech of appreciation for all their "northamerican comrades," and then they are all standing together holding hands—as if in the drawing on Manuela's pink t-shirt.

In Managua, they sleep at a motel near the airport. Before going back to his room, Dwight sits on Sabrina's bed. "I want, I want so much to marry you," he says. "It may be we will always be apart. . . . I want you so much . . ."

". . . How could we? . . ."

"My father—I told you—he has polluted me forever. . . . Whenever I think of my body, I think of him, and I am full of terror." Tension now is in his arms, his throat, almost strangling him. As he cries, she holds him, then rocks him back and forth. "I will always love you, Dwight. I know we cannot make love, and I will always, always want you . . ." She is crying, and then she is silent. . . . Then she says, "Just hold me, and be with me always."

THE WITNESS

As they walk through Cambridge, the houses seem like toys set on the street by some giant, bare-footed child, the people like small, purposeless dolls. "Yes," Sabrina says, "we will write the article for the *New York Times Magazine*, but after that what will we do with all this?"

". . . I really don't know."

"My Dwight, it is as if someone says, 'Who shall go for us?'"

They stand waiting for a red light, and then cross the street. . . . "All right, all right then, we could organize the students here to raise money for the poor in Nicaragua—we could do that—and, also, we could work to help the poor in East Boston."

"Yes," Sabrina says, as if she were Father Dietrich holding out his hands, welcoming them to Nicaragua.

"The medicines," Dwight goes on, "we could get them free from the hospitals and doctors' offices—they must have hundreds of samples they don't use, and then we could bring them down and give them to the Nicaraguan clinics."

"Yes!"

"And, and once we'd raised the funds, we could fly medical students down to work in the clinics."

"Yes, yes!" And now she laughs.

"And in East Boston, we could set up free classes in computer programming for the unemployed, and the students could staff a day-care center for the children—what do you think?"

"Oh, Dwight!" They sit up in her dorm working on the plan until almost dawn. As he rises to leave, Sabrina is staring into his eyes like a cat, her body with "its soft fall and swell/ Awake for ever in a sweet unrest." Time stops, but then he has already reached the door. He walks into the still darkened streets.

Dwight recruits a "management group" to put the plan into operation: a student responsible for securing the medicine, another for hospital arrangements, a third for day care, and to help with the general management, a sophomore, named Todd Jacobs—Dwight says to Sabrina that he has a Geiger counter in his brain which registers intelligence, and suddenly with Todd Jacobs it had begun to click.

To recruit the students, Dwight proposes they organize a gigantic march ending in Harvard Yard. "Boss, let's lead it with a drum," Todd says, and then he laughs, "if that doesn't seem too pushy. And then we can have tables at the end to sign up the marchers, and we should put up posters all over the campus so when we have this march we get the troops." From Sabrina's photographs, they make a recruiting poster which shows the children of Nicaragua— Concepción, from the *refugio*; Carlos, who was blinded; Dolores, who lost her leg.

As the parade passes their dorms, the students join in, until there are almost three hundred marching to the sound of Todd's drum. Within hours, they've signed up a full complement of volunteers—"Boss," Todd says, "I think we're in business!"

Now Dwight is inexplicably in front of a group of students who sit or stand on the grass of Harvard Yard waiting for him to speak. As he walks step by step to the megaphone, the distance shortens by a half, a quarter, an eighth . . . will he ever reach it? . . . "Pillow'd upon my fair Love's ripening breast/ To feel for ever its soft fall and swell. . . . And so live ever . . ." He takes up the megaphone and begins to speak: "It is not our decision, if we choose to help the poor. If we truly know their plight, if we sound the depths of our common humanity, we must respond to their needs. We can turn away, we can refuse to look, we can choose to be deaf to their cries, but if we see, if we hear, we must stand up and be counted! We are the privileged; the people who need our help are not. It is ours in this life to give. Let us do what must be done! Let us *stand up and be counted!"*

The students are actually cheering as if he were running for office. Sabrina stands up and shakes her fist, "We can do it! We can do it!" Sabrina is looking at him, her eyes wide, her face glowing—is this what she has been waiting for? No, not just for him to make love, but for this?

With maps of Cambridge—they've numbered blocks for each contingent—the students disperse to make their door-to-door calls to solicit money and volunteers; later, they will write to their wealthy parents. The gap between his words and their acts has been bridged, not on a stage, or in the pages of a book, but in the world where, yes, he has begun to act.

Their article appears in the *New York Times Magazine*, with Sabrina's photographs—where's Father?—shouldn't the pictures be of him? Dwight receives congratulations from his professors, and an invitation to speak at the Student Forum to recruit even more students for "Stand Up and Be Counted." This is the name they choose, as they work night after night, planning and organizing—yes, he can work without sleep, just as he did on the watches in Nicaragua.

During the Christmas break, after still another late-nighter to stuff the boxes and suitcases, Dwight and Sabrina rent a car to take down their first shipment of medicines. They drive through the country asleep under its mute blanket of snow, stopping at little restaurants and country stores with shingles, not signs, with barrels and shelves and small lamps; in the lobbies of the hotels hang antique chandeliers. When they tell the owners and shopkeepers what they're doing with Stand Up and Be Counted, they hear, "God bless you!," "You're doing the Lord's work!," "Praise be the Lord!," but does anyone know that the Sandinistas are about to be voted out of power; does anyone even know where Nicaragua is? When they go up to their rooms, they see on the beds hand-sewn quilts and Bibles on the dressers. During the night, as he lies sleeplessly in bed, a huge serpent slithers past, its tongue darting in and out.

They drive through the level plains of Mexico, then past the snow peaked mountains, the jungles of Guatemala, El Salvador, Honduras. Then once again they are in the chaotic, pitted streets of Managua, with the crowds of poor, the smell of garbage—the din and stink of imminent failure.

As they pull up in front of the clinic, *Señora* Padilla greets them. "Yes, it is good to see you, and, God bless you, you have the medicines?" While she watches, they unpack the thousands of samples— a few pills will cure a killing case of diarrhea; a shot of penicillin, a serious infection—the effort on their side now seems so small, the effect on the other so large.

Sabrina photographs children in the clinic with bloated bellies and stick-like arms; an old man, only forty-nine years old, dying from cancer; a retching, pregnant woman suffering from anemia; a young man in the rehabilitation section who sits waiting for his artificial leg; a woman dazed and disorganized who simply stares into space. . . . Thirteen or fourteen years old, Dwight is wandering into one of Father's glittering parties—Father is raising his glass for his assembled guests, "For brilliant pebbles," "For Oliver North!" Where is Mother? She is kneeling in an empty room before a small crucifix; she is holding out her hands to receive the stigmata.

"Yes, these are the medicines we will need in the next six months," *Señora* Padilla tells them. "These will be the duties of the fourth-year medical students, as soon as you are able to bring them down." Dwight records each detail in his notebook, as Sabrina takes the pictures. Finally they are standing at the door waiting to leave; *Señora* Padilla, blank-faced with fatigue, is rubbing her eyes.

They drive into the countryside to pay a quick visit to Sabrina's mother—she bustles about her mansion, ordering the servants, making the endless arrangements for her vacuous life. They stroll about the estate, which will soon be restored to its full pre-revolutionary opulence—"It is what your father would have wanted." They meet with Elvira's friends, and say nothing of what they are doing. Again, they are waited on by maids, served by liveried waiters in a life as timeless as Sabrina's memory. At night, Sabrina's father

continues patrolling his land with his rifle, shooting at the Sandinistas like rabbits.

They drive on to El Planeta, which now seems, if anything, even
poorer. There at the clinic is Luis Fuentes still complaining about
his inadequately trained help and the lack of support from "our
government." He is grateful, of course, for the medicines they have
brought, and looks forward to receiving the first medical students—
"It will certainly be an improvement," he says, glancing at Gioconda
in the next room, "over the help I've had here."

In a still lowered voice, he explains, "Jacinta would be here to
greet you, except she is under treatment for certain emotional problems in Managua. . . . It has been difficult here for her."

"Yes, I can understand," Dwight says. "And what about Roberta
Sánchez?"

"You did not know?—she died two weeks ago, of tuberculosis."

They walk through El Planeta—the walls of the *refugio* are still
unfinished; the half-crazed old woman still sits aimlessly on her
porch; the children play in the streets, but a new government will
soon be coming in. When they greet their old acquaintances, for
just a moment their eyes light up, but then sink into a stare; he
and Sabrina are no longer part of their time, as if they were silently
passing them on a road. At night, a ghostly Roberta Sánchez, her
AK slung over her shoulder, guides them among the trees and huts;
they greet the families sitting up with their sleeping children, crack
jokes about the "Gipper" and Oliver North, while jackals stalk in
the woods. . . . On a blackboard, Dwight has written his senior thesis,
but when he returns to defend it before the now assembled committee, a young fop with a cigarette and a lascivious leer is already
erasing it.

They make the long trip back to Cambridge with their empty
crates and suitcases, their "To Do" lists, their notes and rolls of film.
They read to each other from an anthology of Nicaraguan revolutionary poetry—the voices of generations who had fought in the
streets and in the mountains. They hear the last words of those
hiding from the *Guardía* patrols, giving each other courage before

the silent moment of greatest danger. Whole families had been lost—brothers, sisters, husbands, wives—sometimes after months or years in jails and torture cells, with others "disappeared" and so forever set adrift, always with the vision that at the end they would achieve the Revolution, the new society. How much they had sacrificed; how, if they were restored to life, could they bear to see the Nicaragua of today? "Was it all for nothing?" he asks in his journal. "If it did not register in history, was all that effort genuinely useless, was it all for nothing?"

In Cambridge, Dwight writes a press release on the first shipment of medicine, then on each new program of Stand Up and Be Counted, which, augmented by Sabrina's expert photos, become stories in the *Boston Globe*, and through his father's old connections, in the *Post* and *Times*. One story claims Dwight has the same "organizational genius as his deceased, but well remembered father." Another praises the effort as "still another example of the generosity of Americans which is known around the world."

At meetings of Stand Up, students gaze at him with what seems to be, yes, reverence. As he walks with Sabrina, the houses in Cambridge are witnesses to what he has done. . . . Father Dietrich, who is lying in a loin cloth in a hospital bed—or is it in an alcoholic ward?—says in a dream that he is watching him every night on television. He growls at himself, "I've got to stop this!"

Stand Up spreads to dozens of other campuses around the country, while at night, Roberta Sánchez lies coughing herself to death, and Jacinta inhabits shadows on the walls of her hospital in Managua. Despite the endless meetings and conference calls, the web site, the speeches, the flyers—he is still sleeping only a few hours a night—Dwight keeps up his straight A average.

Having met all his requirements in Economics and Political Science, Dwight takes an optional course called "The Philosophy of the West." It starts in ancient Sumer with the *Epic of Gilgamesh*, an ancient king, who, afraid of death, roams through the world seeking the secret of eternal life, only to find himself in his own city, mortal and committed to do what he can in this life. Then the course takes up the ideal world of Plato, then Aristotle, and the message of Christian thought, ending with the major philosophers of the modern period.

Each philosopher, Dwight notes, has a position as if he were a delegate to an international conference. There is Plato who believes in an eternal soul, Aristotle who does not, Descartes who does, Hume who does not, Kant who seems to, and Hegel . . . Dwight plucks petals from the flower—"She loves me, she loves me not, she loves me . . ." He marks down their positions on God, on eternal ideas, on history.

That's it, "The Philosophy of the West," and yet underneath it, like an underground river, is something he cannot define, or put on a chart. Is there a hidden message, a deeper reality beneath the outward positions? What does it mean when Plato hints that God, unlike the kingly Jehovah, may not have created the world all at once, but is creating it in every moment, as the professor at the CIA had once hinted? Or that God is within each person? Or that God permeates the world as it continually struggles to realize itself? Has he God within him? If the world is realizing itself in each moment, is he part of its creation?

. . . He is swimming in a river as the current carries him far out to sea. Above, stars signal to each other back and forth. In a moment, they will dispatch a meteorite—will it be a message or an attack? He finishes "The Philosophy of the West," "Econometric Analysis," "Europe in the Post-War Period," and "Media and Political Thought." Next year, he will enter graduate school in Economics—"Excellent, my boy, excellent!"—and, of course, he will continue to run Stand Up and Be Counted. And Sabrina—yes, it had been her work with him in the clinic in Nicaragua which had gotten her started—will begin medical school.

* * * * *

After only a record two and a half years, with a Ph.D. and with his thesis, "The International Monetary Fund and the Third World," Dwight decides that he will enter the U.S. Foreign Service. "You can't stay with Stand Up and Be Counted your whole life," Father says. "What is it after all"—he smirks—"it's just a student activity."

He'll have to leave to Todd Jacobs the management of Stand Up—Todd, of course, will be more than capable of handling it. "If that's what you want to do, boss, I'm okay with it."

"Yes, maybe this is where your life is headed," Sabrina says, as she looks down at the floor. He stops in the middle of the street, but then begins again to walk. His Harvard Ph.D. in Economics, his summer internships at the CIA, the International Monetary Fund, and the Foreign Relations Committee of the U.S. Senate, which have "broadened his experience"—yes, these years have netted him not only degrees and honors, but also a "solid body of supporters" who will champion him for a middle-range position at the Department of State. Of course, he will always have behind him the former associates of his father—the future stretches out in front of him like a paved road.

At his interview with the State Department, Dwight enters a paneled room—there, waiting for him in their impeccable suits, is Ramsay ("The Rod") Hensley, his former boss at the CIA; Cyril Adams, another of Father's "old friends"; and a new face, Albert Johnson, a young Black man. The ritual begins.

First, the soft convivial chatter—it's as if his acceptance has already been confirmed. But then Albert Johnson asks, "Do you think U.S. policy was wrong-headed in Nicaragua?" A sudden stab in his stomach—was it the article he had written for the *Times*? Was it his arrest? Had they agreed Johnson would ask the tough questions, or is he doing this on his own?

He looks Johnson straight in the eyes. "I think the Sandinistas posed no danger to us, and, for the Nicaraguans, they provided badly needed social services." He gives meaningful glances to the other two members of the panel. "I tried to report this as objectively as I could in an article in the *Times*. I thought it was important that I report honestly what I had observed."

After an awkward pause, Ambassador Hensley says, "Yes, an interesting piece." And then, "In the end, isn't this what we want, officers who give us objective intelligence—isn't that what we're still fighting for here?"—the ranking person on the panel, then at the end of his career, paying off his debt to Father.

"Yes, the trips to Nicaragua caused some consternation," Ambassador Hensley admits to him privately as they sit over *cappuccinos* and *pain au chocolat* at a little French bistro off Massachusetts Avenue, "but your enthusiasm for reform, Dwight, is to be commended. Personally, I found the Sandinistas inept rather than dangerous, and a bit corrupt, as we certainly are learning now. . . . I must confess, your arrest almost scotched it for you, but it could be construed, and, indeed, with a little prompting on my part, it was written up as a childish if somewhat embarrassing enthusiasm. But your superb work at the Agency and then the IMF and Foreign Relations Committee, and, of course, Stand Up and Be Counted—what a stunning achievement! I told the people in Personnel that no matter what your peccadillos, I would personally vouch for you." Dwight repeats to himself, "I am the son of the former Secretary of Defense, Bradford Lockwood, who, you will remember, was a good friend of the *Contras*."

Two months later, he receives his security clearance, and then a notice that he should report for work as a middle-grade officer. "Boss, we'll miss you," Todd says, then gives his little laugh. "No, I mean it."

It is the mystic Meister Eckhart he is reading now, as Dwight sits up in bed or in coffee shops and restaurants. "The soul," he writes in his journal, "is a manifestation of God who pervades the whole world, who, Eckhart says, is the life in the dark matter, and the formless shadow which animates all being. If I am truly open, then will I be its vehicle?" In a dream, dressed in a transparent gown, Sabrina says, "The body is like a shadow, and yet it is what creates the soul." Then her gown is slowly dissolving into the air.

That night, he calls her up, and then takes a commuter plane to Boston. Sabrina listens, nods her head. "It is right that you think about these things, but in the end, the language—it does not matter, Dwight, no, it is the deed, the commitment of your life, my little hero." . . . Each time he leaves, there is the same awkward moment, as she stands waiting for him, and he can do nothing. He writes in his journal, "If the soul is the life of the body, and if the body is polluted, as mine is polluted, what of the soul—is it polluted as well?"

At the hospital, where Sabrina is beginning her first internship, she dissects muscles, bones, nerves. She stands behind a machine— is it an MRI, a neural scanner?—which displays as data what once was spirit. Light filters under the curtains; Sabrina rises from the sheets like a goddess from the sea, and with just a glance at him, flies out the window over the waters. . . . He wakes up, again alone in Mother's house, only a brief cab ride from the State Department where, this morning, he will report to work.

From the first day, the "son of Brad Lockwood" senses the special reception, the aura of expectation—"We know we can count on you, Dwight." Of course, at such moments, his superiors do not mention Father, but isn't he the person they are counting on?

His first assignment is to the UN Political Office, where he will write speeches, draft position papers. Clearly, with the collapse of the Soviet Union, the atmosphere has changed—what will the United States do with its new position as the world's uncontested superpower?

After briefings, after reviewing the work of decades in the files, he enters into a life which is little different from Father's: the conferences with their felt-covered tables, the wainscoting, chandeliers; the delegates testing out their positions, shaping their resolutions; the embassy parties with their swell of conversation, soft music, and subtle diplomacy, which now he must sound for every nuance, and report to his government. It is as if he were relearning an ur-language, more basic than English, one genetically deposited into his system. At night, he revisits Proust's *Remembrance of Things Past*—yes, the receptions of Madame de Guermantes, and those in his own home as a child, mimic the receptions and conferences he is attending now, as if time were not really lost.

After just a few months, the speeches become repetitive, his work mechanical. Everyone, including himself, dresses alike, despite the fact that one delegate comes from Nairobi, or another from Tehran, or from London. What if they entered the conference hall in a loin cloth, or came charging in with a spear on a camel, or sauntered in with a bowler, a three-piece suit, a watch chain, and the spats of the last century? His colleagues sit next to him doodling on their ubiquitous pads—sexual symbols, geometric boxes, irrelevant phrases— while they dutifully attend the conferences, take notes, prepare the next remarks.

At night, drink in hand, he makes the rounds of the embassies: "Hello, Elhadji," "Ah, Abdullah," "Hello, Singh," "Kim," "Pierre," "Mrs. Amesworth, so good to see you . . ." Then an occasional moment, "Yes, I can discuss it with my colleagues, but I should think we could accept some compromise along these lines. Could we possibly see a text tomorrow?" Soft music in the background, an orchestra of three or four totally disinterested Blacks, the rows of drinks on the linen-covered table. Later, writing up his report, "The new Guinean *chargé* still sees the world along Marxist lines, but with the usual African nationalist twist."

He begins to entertain at Mother's home, to hire the mandatory group of musicians and servants to man the tables and circulate the *hors d'oeuvres*. "Of course," Mother says, "it is your house as well," who also uses it for her own receptions, as she continues to immerse herself in the endless sociability of her previous life. At his receptions, as at hers, he hears the soft swell of music and talk, except now it is his world, as sure an inheritance as a landed estate. Hadn't he known even as a child that pleasure and work would merge in this seamless fabric of sociability—aren't these parties a simulacrum of the tainted world in which he is now establishing himself?

"Dwight,"—he sits with his colleagues at a coffee break in the State Department cafeteria—"isn't life like buying a ticket, and then you take the trip, and you just see whatever is there to see?"

"No," he says with an ironic laugh, "it's like putting in a request for the funds to buy the ticket, and then waiting for months, only to find out that the request has been denied, or lost." He draws the predictable laugh—is this any different from Georgy Elect? His colleagues cultivate him, even as he cultivates them. Father sits at the head of the table, agentive, egocentric, and, yes, just as bored as he is.

"Necessary," Dwight says aloud to himself, as he sits alone in his office, "though not my strong suit." His colleagues will live out their lives in a kind of colloidal suspension, becoming less sensitive to their endless compromises, and to the tedium of years, rising slowly in the ranks, amassing their benefits.

He arranges for private briefings with his superiors, and works late into the night, reading all the relevant reports, mastering every "jot and tittle." In departmental meetings, he becomes the dependable reference, while he speaks with the requisite charm and precision. . . . No, nothing has changed—despite the demise of the Soviet Union, the world of diplomacy continues its unbroken history of hundreds of years—"Ah, yes, I should think, given the time constraints, we might offer the Chinese just a slight concession to whet their appetite." One night, Henry James meets him at a reception, and remarks, "A diplomat? How curious. I should have thought . . ."

Months pass, until the speeches again become real. In the clichés and the orotund phrases, in the expression of people whose first tongue is none of the UN's official languages, is a groping for a better world. No, Father had not heard that, but only the posing and posturing—a confirmation of his own cynicism.

"With this resolution," the delegate from Mali proclaims in French, "we, the people of Africa, affirm our faith in the future of our continent. We hold . . ." Even if the delegate himself is from the privileged class, and, as Biographic Intelligence reports, has a mistress in Chevy Chase, and is involved in diamond smuggling, even if what he says cannot happen, yet hope needs to be articulated, like a mass—if not for the priests, then for the people?

"Mr. Chairman, the people of the United States share with the peoples of all the member states the aspiration for a better life. Our aim is to work together to fulfill this aspiration. The means we will employ . . ." The delegate, using Dwight's words, then describes the rather meager contribution which the United States will make. . . . Increasingly in demand, Dwight sits up writing such speeches night after night, while he garners commendations for his file. "Is it possible," he asks himself in his journal, and then when he talks to Sabrina on the phone, "to lie continuously and yet maintain at least the option someday of telling the truth?"

"Now is the time you learn how it works, my darling. And then, there will be a time when you must leave."

"When will that be?"

"Before you start to enjoy all this, if you are not *already* enjoying it too much." In just a few months, she will begin her residency at Boston General Hospital, and after that, will she insist on living with him?

"Yes," Ambassador Hensley says, at his retirement party, "Brad would already be proud of you." The old man, drink in hand, with his white mustache, and famous pince-nez, which he reputedly wore even as a young diplomat, asks Dwight and Sabrina to join him as he makes the rounds of his guests. "So nice of you to come." "I am indeed honored." "Do say hello to your charming wife." "Please commend me to President Ortiz . . ."

He delights in introducing Dwight "who now is taking up the mantel of service which his father not so many years ago had to put down." Does he look worthy of the comment? Does Sabrina appear lovely, and satisfy any doubts about himself? Isn't he still too pretty, his lips too red, his eyes too blue, his skin too fair? Isn't he just using her, as Father used Mother—isn't that what he's doing?

"Once," Hensley says, recounting one of his stories, "when I was the ambassador in Moscow, I accompanied President Reagan to Reykjavik. That was the time, you'll remember, the President had his famous confrontation with Nikita Khrushchev. 'The point, sir,' I suggested the President say, 'is not what the Soviet Union threatens, but what would be left of your country if you even *attempted* to carry out these threats!' At that point, I should tell you that the United States possessed a missile advantage of almost seven to one, and Khrushchev knew it. Reagan memorized my lines and when he had used them, Khrushchev looked at the President out of the corner of his eye, and laughed, 'Very good,' and walked on, as his aides paced nervously a few steps behind him. It was delicious," Hensley recounts to still another group of guests, already deep into his memoirs, and with a contract from Random House, and the first intimations of cancer.

Sabrina chats in Spanish with the Bolivian chargé—is she flirting? She smiles, she arches an eyebrow, raises a shoulder—yes, she is flirting. . . . The lines extending from her fingers are those of a spider or a scorpion. "No," Sabrina tells him after the party, "I am seeing no one—who has any time for this!"

Mother stands upright, composed, like a painted masthead extended over the sea. She is dressed in a Bergdorf Goodman suit, her coiffeur impeccable, her chin tilted. She is the perfect social being, and yet she is telling him not that she has consented to chair still another socially prominent charity, or take yet another cruise, but that she has decided to become a nun in a silent order. "The Sisters of Mercy," she explains, "has clinics in the Third World; after my paramedical training, Dwight, I will work wherever I am assigned."

"Mother. . . ?"

"I have made up my mind." A little boy, he sits with her in the family pew at St. Paul's as she listens to the sermon and stares with quickened breath. "Didn't you always know," she says, "that the life I had with your father meant nothing to me, but that I had made my promise to God, and once in the bond of matrimony, and with your father's child. . . ?"

"Yes, I think I knew."

She kneels in front of the crucifix as now the light streams into her palms. "I will leave everything to you, though, of course, it does not really matter." If only he had been able to enter into her silence; would she have told him—would she have known herself? Her lips etch a thin smile. "I know, Dwight, you will have little need of it, but maybe it will prove to be helpful in your work."

A quarter of the estate goes to the Sisters of Mercy—"Would you like to give more?" Another quarter will create an endowment for Stand Up and Be Counted—of course, Todd will be ecstatic; and the rest, including the Georgetown house, will be left to him. . . . As Mother goes through her last days, her manner is silently submissive, as if she had already taken the vows of her new order. Beside her new divine husband, does he still matter so little? He closes his eyes—a bird wheels in the air; no, beyond his question, it flies into the reaches of the selfless sky!

She takes only a small suitcase as they drive in the family limousine to the airport; then he watches the plane take off for Portland, Oregon. She sends him a brochure, a few letters, which describe her training and the strict routine of her new life, which ritually close with a biblical blessing. He calls or writes her regularly, but after only a few months, the order imposes its regime of silence, and he must stop.

Six months later, he receives notification from the Sisters of Mercy that Mother has been assigned as a paramedic to a clinic in Southern Sudan. Dwight finds the river on which it is located, the Bahr-el-Ghazal. The clinic picks up the victims, the Sudanese desk officer tells him, of the periodic famines and the civil wars which wrack the country. . . . "Is the work dangerous?"

The Sudanese desk officer shakes his head, "Your mother is a brave woman, Mr. Lockwood." That night he sits in a canoe winding down a river as bloated corpses pass. As he wakes up, he is asking her still again, "Why didn't you protect me?"

After still more months of speech writing, and endless attendance at conferences, he receives his new assignment—the embassy in Moscow; Sabrina will just be starting a second residency at Boston General Hospital. In the next two years, he will, of course, write her letters, but no longer will there be their periodic visits, when at the end she is looking into his eyes, and he can do nothing.

She flies down from Boston for his last day, and with the weather fair, they pack a picnic to spend the afternoon in Rock Creek Park. The trees spread their trellises over the river, birds turn in magic circles. Nearby, British diplomats, dressed in three-piece suits, entertain a mixed delegation of Africans and Europeans.

"Ah, Dwight," Sabrina says, glancing at the diplomats, "I think the position of your government can only be considered as absurd."

"Really?"

"Indeed, we have no other alternative than to declare war."

"Before tea?"

Throughout the afternoon, he and Sabrina sit gazing into the stream, listening to the buzz of several languages, the inflected compliments, the subtle laughter, the clink of wine glasses as if such sounds, ingrained in his memory, were as natural as the wind rustling the trees. That evening, as they sit in the cab to the airport—she is on duty at eight the next morning—he sees again the longing in her eyes, but now it is as if it were his.

"Dwight, I love you. I don't want this—that we will not see each other."

"I . . . It's as if the world were subtly inserting a glass between us—I can see you, but we cannot be together."

"Do you *want* to be with me? . . . You can be with me if you want—you know that!"

He is still nodding his head, he can still feel her soft lips on his, as she boards the plane. The next morning, he taxis again to the airport, and is then injected into a bank of grey clouds, which, as he flies over the Atlantic, never lifts.

"In St. Petersburg," he writes to Sabrina, "I was met by a staffer from the embassy named Broderick, who reminded me in his diffidence and deference, and his cynical, insinuating undertone, of García, a young servant whom we had employed in the house when I was a boy." The subtle signals pass back and forth, the off-looks, the presumptuous allusions; Dwight brushes him off as Sabrina fixes Dwight with her longing eyes.

"In just a few hours I was projected into another world, as the Russian phrases passed into my mind—*pazhah'lsta* (please), *spasee'ba* (thank you), *do'braye oo'tra* (good morning)—are you remembering all this?—and then the whole language (which I won't write). As Goethe says, a new language is like gaining a new soul, although, needless to say, I am still trying to understand my old one."

He hops into a cab, which makes its way down one of the grand boulevards. "You must come to St. Petersburg, which is like a dream of the past. It is all laid out on a river, the Neva, with canals and brilliant boulevards, with such clarity of design, as if the city were created in a single burst of imagination. Italian baroque buildings with pillars and porticoes, four to five stories, painted in oranges, greens, and blues, under a limitless sky—these were the town houses for the wealthy who in the last century would sweep in for the season in their splendid coaches. Today there are potholes, crumbling masonry, garbage piled up against the walls, little stalls in the once magnificent boulevards, so that I must close my eyes for time to slip, and see it as it was.

"On the city tour, our guide was a young woman named Anna, only eighteen years old, who spoke in a very careful English, with each word laboriously pronounced and often with an extra syllable, like *pleaz ah* for please. She repeated each instruction three or four times: '*Pleaz ah*, do not forget we meet again at four o'clock, four o'clock this afternoon, if you will remember, at the bus at four o'clock, when we will leave, so *pleaz ah*, not to be late, at four o'clock, when we will leave.' She was charming and vulnerable, being so young and with so much responsibility. One young man on our tour was smitten with her, and followed her dreamily around the streets."

Sabrina's first letter arrives at the consulate general in St. Petersburg: "Who is this lady you describe as Anna, and the young man who follows her dreamily around in the streets? I can only guess. I have already contacted the—what is the name?—the KGB?—and made arrangements for you to be followed.

"I miss you already, even though we were already apart, but Russia seems so much farther away, another world. I look into the future—yes, I can do that, I am Madame Montenegro—and I can see you always in a different country, speaking a different language, which only you can speak, while I write my wistful letters, and the time of our lives ticks away.

"Today, I operated on a woman with a blocked uterus. It was not a complicated operation, but in Nicaragua, perhaps even in Russia, she would have died. That is why I am here. That is the story I tell myself to mask the truth—not because we cannot live together. But is that true? Don't we love each other?"

As he enters the embassy's Economics Section as the Deputy Director, he again catches the tone of those who deal with a rising star: "I think you'll find this assignment rewarding, Dwight." "You've come at a good time—plenty of new developments here." "Glad you're on board."

Then he meets Gregory Downs, head of the section. Downs wears black-framed glasses, under which is a seemingly perpetual scowl. "Yes, glad you could finally make it."

"The country desk had asked me to spend my first week meeting with the Petersburg people before going on to Moscow."

"Yes, yes, they always do that."

"Well, I'm here . . ."

"I suggest at this juncture, Lockwood, a briefing is in order."

He writes to Sabrina, "The job seems interesting enough, but with my grouchy section chief, it's going to be a long two years. The economy is plunging each day as Russia is being transformed into a third world country. It is clear, although I have been in Moscow only a few days, that we are not helping the situation with our insistence on immediate privatization, a balanced budget, high interest rates—the whole IMF program. How I am going to deal with this, I suspect, will not be easy.

"Let me tell you about some of the Russians I've met so far. On the train to Moscow, I started up a conversation with Dimitri, a university student, who is hoping to study in the United States, at Columbia University, which, he informed me with widening eyes, is in New York City! 'Americans have so much, so much money,' he told me, 'they can do whatever they want!' He knows all the

American rock and movie stars. Yes, when he was in school, he had learned about injustice in America, the ill-treatment of Blacks, the exploitation of the poor, but, of course, now he knows that was all Soviet propaganda, and even if it wasn't, what does it matter?

"Then there was Sergei Rubin, a young Jew, who I met through a Harvard connection, who had just produced a program for the BBC in English on Boris Pasternak. Sergei works at half a dozen jobs scratching together enough funds to help his parents. His dream is to study in France, but, of course, there is no money. His father is a chemist, and is also the Russian language's principal translator of Jorge Luis Borges, but makes practically nothing; his mother is an engineer, but is presently out of work. They live in a tiny flat in a dingy high rise on the outskirts of Moscow. At Sergei's home— the Rubins graciously invited me for dinner on my second night in Moscow—we discussed Proust and Rimbaud and Borges and, yes, Allen Ginsberg, until two in the morning."

"Why didn't you answer my letter? Of course, I am interested in your new position and in the people you are meeting, but I am worried about us, about how we are going to live like this. I could become completely involved in my work, I could try to forget you, or like a Hindu, I could live in the world and think of myself suspended in space, but I won't. No, I won't do it!"

"Of course, I cannot just write to you as if I were only observing Russia. I miss you, Sabrina, that's what I'd wanted to tell you, while I cover my loneliness with this letter like an old cloak." The letter ends, he shrugs, he stares at a wall. As he lies in bed, a filthy rat emerges from a hole, and then is crawling over his blankets. In the morning, he sits in a café reading four newspapers, so he will be current for a forthcoming meeting with the head of the British economic section.

"I want to think we are connected by letters, that we can talk to each other this way, but can we? Will we not drift apart? You are my life—how can I let this happen?

"All right, all right, I'll stop.

"Today I visited Todd Jacobs at Stand Up. I think you would be very pleased at how well he is keeping our programs going. He gave me a little tour of the office, smiling, giggling, making his little self-disparaging remarks. Stand Up continues much as we left it. Todd said, 'Tell the boss hello.'

"I walked about the streets of Cambridge, and through Harvard Yard, and thought of us here together, as when we had first met at the Pamplona Café, and you were attracted by this talkative waitress from Nicaragua. . . ."

Sergei's eyes hold the possibility of love, rather than adventure or exploitation, but then he is so enmeshed in his family, so much a Jewish son, possibly so embarrassed, and so unsure, if this is what he really wants. No, Dwight says to himself, no, he won't even think of it! . . . Each time he passes him in the embassy halls, Broderick is a prostitute leaning against a lamppost puffing a cigarette, waiting for his business.

He will do nothing, not here, with Sergei, with Broderick, not with anyone, specially not in Russia. Already he has heard stories of officers compromised by the KGB, then confronted the next morning with the photographs and the threat of blackmail. No, Sabrina, although that is not the reason—he will do nothing.

"The world has not changed for the intellectuals, like Sergei or his father, who even in the old regime were somewhat alienated or detached, but it has for the entrepreneurs and oligarchs, who now like rapists gain immense profits by their violent takeovers. The model for them is the United States, far more than Europe, though a United States a hundred years ago, of robber barons and instant millionaires. But even for the people in the street, America is the dream of wealth—you see American ads everywhere, often in English—'Test the West,' 'Smoke Marlboros,' 'Wear Levis.' "

Now must he tag something affectionate to the letter? Inside himself—is nothing. Is she right, are they losing each other, will they just drift apart? At night, a bear walks through his room, tearing down books from his shelves, ripping out clothes from his closet, coming closer and closer to his bed. In the morning, he carefully dresses, sits in a cafe, taking notes for a report on the latest devaluation of the ruble.

"These days, Sabrina, I'm reading an anthology of Russian poets of the last seventy years. They write the poetry of the 'soul,' almost as if these Russians had found a particular way to define that something whose metaphysics still seem so distant for me. Theirs is the soul in agony, as if their very pain sharpens its definition. So many of them lived tortured lives, mostly because of the times, which eventually could kill them directly, but more often silenced them or made their lives tragic, as they did the poetess Akhmatova, who says to death, 'You will come anyway, so why not now?'"

. . . Like an orbiting weapon, the young man finds him along a line already traced in the sky, and, with just a little adjustment, changes his speed so that they are orbiting together. The young man's hand moves over his body, the other over the round of his forehead. . . . "Why not now? I mumbled to myself as I woke up to finish this letter. Now, if I am lucky, I will drift back into sleep for an hour or two while the moon and stars complete their arcs in the sky, and the dawn slowly rises over still another day."

"Dwight, are you all right? I worry about you. I know I need to be with you, and I am so far away. Tell me you are all right!"

"A few weeks ago, the government inexplicably decreed that all rubles issued before a certain date will be worthless unless turned in within twenty-four hours, and has set limits on the number which can be converted, unless, of course, the bribe that one offers is sufficient to pay off the inspector. The maneuver, which, in effect, will devalue the ruble by almost forty percent, seems clearly aimed at making money unfairly off the already strapped population, and has caused a furor in the Parliament. The President, who seems completely in the clutch of the oligarchs, denies having given the decree, and blames the crisis on some hapless subaltern."

"Where are you? Are you still here on this planet? Do I mean anything to you? Yes, Russia is far away, but you seem even further."

"Can't I tell you what is happening here, what I am working on? Aren't you even interested? Yes, it may seem dry, or technical, as if you would tell me the muscles you would need to slice through to reach a cancerous organ. But isn't this the detail we need to understand the sufferings of the world, and to try to heal them? For me, when I look outside the banks, there are long lines of anxious people dutifully converting their rubles. I need to ask, isn't there anything the United States can do? For you, when you operate, it is to relieve pain, extend life. We must operate on the world as we find it, with all its technicalities as necessary ingredients. It is not what the romantics thought, Wordsworth or Shelley, or even Marx, that in one lyrical burst of revolution the world could be transformed, although when I say this I think of Him at Emmaus looking at me across a table, and saying, 'Do what is in your heart.'"

"What can I say? If that is what you want to tell me, I must listen. Of course, you are right. I will be patient. I know that this is your work, and that it must be done. I must learn not to be selfish."

As they sit over drinks in the bistro, Sergei gazes at Dwight with his dark eyes and wistful manner. He writes, "At night, as I walk home, I see the long lines of ruined people crouching in Red Square selling their last possessions, family ikons, jewelry, clothing; they are wrapped against the chill in patched blankets, sometimes sleeping under the stars with newspapers stuffed in their jackets. This is the end of the revolution, just as it was in Nicaragua, 'not with a bang but a whimper.'"

As he goes to bed, Sabrina is watching him with her longing eyes. He looks out the window—the dawn has barely begun on a new day, as he prepares for his meeting with Greg Downs.

Downs perches on Dwight's desk sucking on a cigarette, blowing its rotten smoke into the air. "So what is the subject of our little meeting?" Downs asks.

"It is our policy regarding the economic reforms."

"And you have some problem?"

"Let me state it as simply as I can."

"Yes, please do, so I can understand it."

". . . If the West continues to hustle Russia into privatization, the country will sell off its still remaining assets to the only bidders around, the oligarchs and the gangsters, at a fraction of their worth, and it will be left with nothing for effective state action, including, of course, its social programs."

"Bravo, Dwight! Only I would advise you to keep this view mostly to yourself, as it will do you no good here. We are, as you may have observed, committed to the path we have already taken."

"Which is. . . ?"

"Oh, you know, but you want me to indict myself in your moral court—you see, I read your little piece about Nicaragua. . . . Well, yes, our policy, which you so desperately want to hear: we favor privatization as quickly as possible, first, to cut ties with the communist past; second, to allow privatization to work; third, to provide maximum opportunities for Western investment—are you taking notes? Does it make any difference what I tell you?"

"I try to imagine what life is like in Moscow. It is cold enough here in Boston. On the streets, I see old men wrapped in blankets, leaning against the stone buildings. In the slums, there is no heat; if people are sick, there is no medical attention. Poverty here, as in the Third World, or as I can now imagine in Russia, is the major health problem.

"As I walk home from work, I see you on the street. As I return to my little apartment, you are there in the soft chair reading. As I go to bed, I see your form—I have a lurid imagination!

"Is it better simply to report, as you do, my day-to-day work? Shall I just put all my longing out of my mind, and 'make the best of it'?"

"Today I wrote a report to Downs, who, no doubt, will trash it, about the retail economy in Moscow, where all but the most basic goods are out of the reach of the majority, buttressed, of course, with endless statistics. Yes, I am here in Russia at an historical moment, but then what am I doing? I have not come into life to be a voyeur. If I stay in this business, I will have no role but to be a witness, and worse, one who is not even allowed to testify.

"Today I am going over the head of my boss, Greg Downs, to speak directly with the Ambassador. I needed to talk to you first." . . . He wanders through the stone streets, listening to his own footsteps, until he notices he is being followed. He begins to run but cannot outpace the two toughs behind him. Now one is on top of him, and begins to penetrate, as the sky cracks open, and he ascends into the void, and begins to orbit the earth. . . . The next morning, he stares at the letter, and forgets to sign it.

Sabrina telegrams, "DO WHAT IS IN YOUR HEART!"

Ambassador Pruitt, another old friend of Father, opens the meeting: "Greg tells me you have some problem with our privatization policy, Dwight."

"Our aim, as I understand it, is to help secure a democratic society here which is responsible to the people and which cooperates with us in an economic sense—is that the aim?"

Ambassador Pruitt is tapping his pen on the table, "Yes, yes, of course, Dwight."

"Well, then," he continues, "I suspect that in expunging the last traces of Soviet oppression, we are, if I may say so, forcing the government to sell off its assets too quickly, and therefore too cheaply, while fostering a class of rapacious oligarchs and quasi-criminals for whom democracy is a bad word."

Downs is staring at the rug under Pruitt's desk. "Shouldn't we be better off now," Dwight goes on, "in slowing down the pace and encouraging the Russian government to keep its remaining assets so it can continue to provide the needed social services? At the same time, of course, it could be fostering strictly capitalistic ventures."

"I'm glad you haven't omitted these, Dwight."

"Not in the slightest, but, I need to say, that if the economy sinks still further, we risk a swing to the right or to the left which might be far worse than what we have now."

"I trust you have documented these observations. . . . Greg?"

"Should we be taking the position Dwight proposes, we will clearly find ourselves at odds with the Department, not to mention the Administration. As you are no doubt aware, the International Monetary Fund has just recently issued a study, which I put on your desk. . . ."

"Yes, yes, of course, but if Dwight is correct, as I suspect he is, wouldn't it be more, shall we say, in the public interest, if we were to, ah, nudge Washington a bit? We would perhaps have some credibility as we are on the ground, as it were. . . . Greg, we have discussed this issue before—please object if you wish, or is it that you are hesitant, as you are earlier in your career, in being associated with an oppositional point of view?"

"No, not at all."

"Then what is your objection?"

"And so the report went out under Ambassador Pruitt's signature. My life will be appropriately miserable in the Economic Section for my remaining time, but it was worth it. I will ask Pruitt to write a letter for my file to undo any damage Downs may cause by his insinuating, bland praise."

A telegram from Sabrina: "CONGRATULATIONS!" On the signature line: "STAND UP AND BE COUNTED!"

* * * * *

"How many months have gone by—eighteen now? Yesterday, in Red Square, I started talking to an old man with a lovely wistful face. He was selling his ikons just to survive. I bought one (it is against the law to take them out of the country), and paid him what he asked, which was so little, and then I gave the ikon back to him.

"I hardly know how to live in the present. It is almost too much to see the world as it is, neither fiction nor history. I could so easily have been a writer or an historian and merely recorded the events of my time, except then there would have been you, Sabrina, and the real world, and our pact to live and work in it together."

Slowly, as if it were first a faint noise, and then it had grown louder and louder, until it is pounding in his heart—she will come, she will come—in just three weeks! "I can't wait," he writes in his journal, "although I know I must for the time to pass, while my mind, for which time means nothing, contracts the world into an instant."

What is happening? It is Sabrina and not the mute houses he speaks to now, as she listens with her open-eyed yet shy look, as she responds with her slight accent, as she sweeps the landscape like wind on the steppes. But then there is the dark shadow of her in the next room, or by him in her sleeping bag on the floor in Nicaragua, as his muscles tense, and again, he cannot sleep.

Her plane finally touches down in St. Petersburg, and through a plate-glass window, he sees her walking down the gangplank. He runs out of the building, flashes his diplomatic card to a startled guard, and is there when her feet first touch the ground. He hugs her, lifts her up, and for just a moment, before the stab in his stomach, he is alone with joy.

They walk down Nevsky Prospect, past the toppled monuments to Stalin and his lieutenants. They poke into stores, and talk to venders in the streets, as he makes the translations. At night, they attend the opera—she is exquisitely dressed in a red silk gown which must have cost her a month's salary—and hear *The Barber of Seville*—in Russian!

Again and again, he glances back to see her face—behind her image, like that of Mother, is a dark shape, or is it the image of his longing? No, he will not try; why should he submit to the bitterness of his own repression? He kisses her at the door of her hotel room, and after it closes, he stands staring at it in the hallway.

They walk along the beach at the Gulf of Finland. The Russians squat in the dirty sand, reading books, with their gold chains on their necks, their overweight bodies burning with the relentless sun, or in group picnics, strewing the sand with their garbage, stinking up the air with their endless cigarettes. He dives into the water—there is Sabrina's lithe body swimming in the deep. As they rise, she gives him a bubble kiss.

She laughs, takes his hand, she seems without bitterness. Why does she wait for him year after year?

Sabrina says, "Last night, as I lay in bed, I could not sleep—there were so many things I will never forget."

"What?"

She laughs. "You, here, there, in each place we visited."

They take the train for Moscow, as the clear blue skies change to a perpetual gloom. They are constantly stepping into puddles, walking around filled potholes. He puts her up in a gigantic new hotel, called the Ismailovo, which accommodates ten thousand people, and is filled with groups waiting to take off on the new day's excursions. A group leader holds up her umbrella with a little sign at the handle, and leads her pack to a waiting bus. Dwight holds up his hand for a taxi, and Sabrina laughs, "Ah, now the tour begins."

"*Cavarec'te vy pa anglee'skee,*" he coaches her.

She giggles. "You are such a pedant!"

At Zagorsk, they enter a windswept stone church with its round arches and cupolas, its iconographic paintings covering the walls. From every angle the face of God or an august Christ looks down at the humbled believer. They watch the orthodox clergy administer communion to the village women. Only if they are totally passive, their chins tilted, their mouths open, their eyes abased, are they allowed to receive it. The women fall on their knees before the shrines, bowing their heads, or sweeping the ground with their hands prior to making the sign of the Cross. Is this the god Mother worships? Has this god any compassion, or, like Father, is he just a divine ego?

The next day, he takes her to Red Square, then to Lenin's tomb, where they stand almost an hour as the line of people slowly files into the mausoleum. There in the casket are Lenin's body and his willful face perfectly preserved like an Egyptian pharaoh; outside are the busts of Stalin, Brezhnev, Khrushchev. . . . "For these men," Dwight says, "history has been everything. It's as if they had ridden a train over a cliff, and now we are watching it fall into the sea, turning over and over, until it sinks into the depths of time." No, he is not talking to her; he is already writing her one of his letters even before she has left.

The last day they wander through the mazes of the flee market near her hotel, looking at the marioshka dolls, Red Army hats, ikons, t-shirts—a picture of Lenin drinking a bottle of Pepsi, another which says, "The Party is over," chess sets—one side decorated with American stars and stripes, the other with the hammer and sickle. They look at each other—yes, the Revolution with all its promise and ugliness is over. Sabrina buys gifts for her mother, her friends in Boston, her colleagues at the hospital—she calls it the "sack of Moscow."

He loads her luggage into the embassy car. "Years from now," she says, "we will think of this time we spent together."

At the airport, she says, "I don't want to go."

She says, "Do you love me? Think, if you do . . . if we should ever be apart again."

That night, as he sleeps in his bed with Sabrina, a huge bear enters the room and watches him; in the morning, the bed is empty.

The leaves in the park are beginning to fall, the cruel chill already hangs in the air, the threat mounting for the homeless poor. He continues writing his reports on the deepening economic crisis, forming liaisons for American companies and financial institutions, increasing his contacts with the International Monetary Fund and the World Bank. For each meeting, he is meticulously prepared, takes copious notes, leaves a detailed record with succinct summaries for Downs, and when Downs leaves, he heads the Section.

He writes to Sabrina: "I have almost nothing at stake, no image of myself, but of technical perfection. Someone actually referred to me as a 'technocrat'—yes, but they know my name, and they ask themselves, Is it possible that someday he might even outshine his famous father?"

He writes in his journal: "He had lived here as if in exile, with only his reading of the Russian poets, and of Proust and Dostoyevski and Tolstoy, and Meister Eckhart whose voices are the ones he hears now."

. . . He is sitting at a table with Meister Eckhart, who speaks to him: "You have not yet looked into your heart. It is there, the spirit of God, waiting for you, if only you will look. I will not ask you again, I cannot wait still more years."

"Today, as the first snow fell, I revisited the Tolstoy Museum. As one enters, one sees his portrait, the ridges of hard bone over his eyes, a truly frightening figure he must have been on his wedding night, as described by his young wife, Emma, whom he had just gone ahead and raped as if she were an animal.

"I pass by manuscript pages of his novels, with their almost continuous revisions (Emma dutifully copied *War and Peace* six times); portraits also of the models for his characters in *War and Peace* and *Anna Karenina*, and at the end perhaps himself in "The Death of Ivan Ilyich," in which he continues his consciousness past his own death. I think to myself, Will it be like that? Not to end, but to go on thinking after death like a spirit without a body?

"A last round of glittering parties, at the French, Turkish, Indian embassies, held, they tell me, in my honor. I make the rounds, drink in hand, remembering the names, telling little anecdotes, playing the game here for the last time.

"My next assignment—I have just heard the news—will be in Guatemala as chargé and chief political officer." Suddenly, his heart is pounding—for the first time he knows! His pen moves over the paper: "Is there any way you could work in Guatemala, that we could be together, any way at all? I do not want to be apart from you again!"

He writes up his final reports, briefs his successor, packs up his apartment. "My last night, I spent with the Rubins—they prepared a lavish dinner for me, which they could ill afford. Sergei's face was the one I will remember most, eager, smiling, with his young talent, inventive, multilingual, doomed, he believes, to a life of perpetual, distracting care. Afterwards we spoke about literature as if it were a province of the gods, as if Rimbaud, Proust, and Woolf were Apollo, Orpheus, and Athena, magically inhabiting a space lifted out of time.

"In the morning, when I am driven to the airport, all this will be behind me, while the Russians will continue here to live out their lives. I ask myself, How will I put all this together, how will I avoid being just a linguist and a 'technocrat' with the complementary cynicism and detachment of the people in my business, and somehow, out of all this, create a self?

"Soon, soon, my darling, I will see you, and these questions will all be answered—I know they will be, if only we can be together!"

GAZING INTO THE WATER

The Ambassador, Al Henderson, rises from his desk. Again Dwight's penis and testicles are mounted on the seat of a unicycle going over a hill—why does he still have to be haunted by such images? "You've come at a propitious time, Dwight"—yes, he remembers him from Father's receptions. Henderson was a bit younger then—a "company man," Father had told him, addicted to Cuban cigars secretly smuggled through Mexico in a diplomatic pouch. "I probably needn't tell you, as you are undoubtedly exquisitely briefed—you already have gained a reputation in the Department for thoroughness—that now, after so many decades, the civil war is about to end."

"Yes," Dwight smiles, "and can we then become a sleepy little embassy again?"

"I doubt it. . . . No, I'm afraid the work will be taxing."

"I should imagine."

"Our position, as you will see, is to support the growth of democracy here—it's a bit uphill."

"I was browsing just recently in a book on the American revolution, and I ran across a letter that Lafayette wrote to his mother. It begins, *"Chère maman,* when one is twenty-three, and has an army to command, and Lord Cornwallis to oppose, the time that is left is not too much for sleep."

Henderson smiles. "Your predecessor, I should say, was competent and reliable, but a bit of a drudge, so I am, to say the least, quite pleased you will be joining us."

Sabrina will be coming—in just six weeks. "How did you manage to do it? You're wonderful! You're wonderful!" She'll be joining a team of two other Guatemalan doctors at a clinic in a village called San Miguel Acatán. . . . How long before Sabrina arrives?—the clock begins to tick.

"Glad to have you aboard, Dwight." He sits for his first meeting with Roger Channing, the CIA country director.

"From all I've read, we've picked a lovely country to work in."

"Indeed. I think you'll find it compares quite favorably to your Nicaragua."

Dwight smiles—Channing had done his homework. "I've just been reading the files. I'm not sure we have all the information about the important work you're doing here."

"Yes, I can see, you might wonder."

"Well. . . ?"

"The question, Dwight, is do you have a 'need to know'? If I might be so blunt, as *chargé*, you might indeed operate more freely *without* knowing."

"But it would be useful . . ."

"Some matters, Dwight, as I'm sure you'll understand, particularly after you've spent some time here, are a bit, how shall I say, 'sectarian,' and probably best kept to ourselves . . . at the Agency? The embassy handles one side of our relations, quite ably I should add, and the Agency, of course, the other—not a bad balance, as I think you'll find."

"But it might be helpful if . . ."

"I'm referring not to a moral division of labor, which is what you may have in mind, but rather simply to each side maintaining the clarity of its objectives, and its capacity to work without impediment."

". . . For instance, it's not clear from our files, at least, to what extent the special forces of the Guatemalan Army, or some of the irregular units, are keeping you informed of their activities."

"For the most part, closely, I should say."

"And informing the embassy, as well?"

"Ah, Dwight . . ."

"Or, how shall I put it, to what extent you are directing them?"

"That is why, to beg the obvious, we have covert operations, is it not? And why it is probably all for the best that the right hand actually does not know what the left hand is doing."

". . . What if we were to meet, say, once a week and review matters, not officially, as I can see some inhibition here, but strictly, as the French might say, *entre nous*? I think you would find me discreet, and perhaps useful in the long run, were there to be the danger of possible embarrassment, now that the United Nations is negotiating still another settlement and our government, at least officially, is backing them."

"Yes, I can see . . . interesting. . . . I had harbored some suspicion, I'll be frank, in view of that article of yours in the *Times*, that you might be, ah, judgmental, but no, I can see a pragmatic twist."

"Quite so. . . . I'll leave the restaurant to you. Is there one you have in mind—for our next meeting?"

Next he pays a "courtesy call" on the military advisor, a Colonel Steward A. Dodson, R.A. Colonel Dodson looks like a walking refrigerator and has shoulders like a plow; his head is square, his hair is spiked in a crew cut. "A pleasure to meet you, sir. The last time I saw your father—it was some time ago—he was receiving the Distinguished Service Medal from President Reagan at a ceremony on the White House lawn. You were there with your mother, a most beautiful woman, as I remember—my job at the time was to command the honor guard."

"How did you end up in Guatemala?"

"The luck of the draw, I guess. My Spanish is still piss poor, but I've been around—Afghanistan, El Salvador, Serbia, Iraq."

". . . How do you see your mission here?"

"Same as everywhere else, really. Buck up our friends, beat down our enemies." He laughs. "Okay, I'll take it as a serious question. It's to keep a government in power that we can talk to, that uses people in power that we've trained, or who speak our language—not too surprising, huh?"

"But, officially at least, our military mission has been termi-
nated by Congress."

"Welcome to Guatemala!"

That night he is climbing in the Caucasus, except he is naked,
mounted on the unicycle. Stars are streaking in the sky, as he pedals
higher and higher. . . . Then he is walking slowly through a Nicaraguan village strewn with the dead. . . . How long before Sabrina
arrives? As he wakes up, Sabrina is sitting on the bed, smiling
to him.

"Dear Sabrina, I am working late at night—my old habit. But
now I am just waiting for you. Every day I go through the motions
of life, take off information from screens, but know that without
you, it cannot be real, that you are what gives it meaning.

"I know it now, I will love you forever. I don't know what to do
with it, except now to say it, and wait for your coming."

In the Department of Petén, coffee workers seize the offices
of the new Land Fund and occupy the offices of the governor. The
demonstrators are brutally suppressed—sixteen die; the union is
disbanded . . .

Dwight reviews the statistics: falling wages, thousands of
workers laid off; the World Food Organization calculates a hundred
and sixty-two municipalities with acute malnutrition. He puts down
the report, rubs his eyes—three more reports left to read. . . . Despite
a rise in coffee prices, workers' wages are dropping. The money is
being diverted to the major U.S. firms—Proctor & Gamble, Kraft,
Sara Lee, Nestlé. . . . Two more reports. . . .

In the city streets, Dwight hears the faint hum of the Mayan villages, the stomp of naked feet on the earth. On corners selling their
wares, women are still dressed in the ancient fabrics with their geometric play of colors and beads. Sabrina will be working in a clinic,
just like Luis in Nicaragua, or Mother in Southern Sudan—only
two weeks now. . . . A nuclear explosion—Dwight's living room is

filled with radioactive energy. He hits the floor, then begins picking his way toward the bedroom through the rubble and orange-yellow dust to see if Sabrina has survived. His voice echoes—"Are you all right, are you all right?" When he reaches the bedroom, she's gone!

Even while the negotiations are taking place on a new UN settlement, the army patrols continue to terrorize the villagers—stealing their crops, intimidating their customers in the towns, as well as fire bombing, murdering, and raping as before. Nor, Dwight learns through his meetings with Channing and Colonel Dodson, has anything changed on the American side: the School of the Americas is still training the Army and its intelligence interrogators; military aid money is still passing under the table, while the embassy goes on reporting the "upturn toward democracy."

Outside the window, birds with lavish blue wings make nests in the branches. Sunlight is pouring onto the land as if from a pitcher. As his eyes shift down the trunk of the tree, he sees chunks of flesh, a head, a whole torso on a broken branch! Next week, Sabrina is coming. How can he live even these seven days until she comes?

She descends in a silver plane, then stands expectant, radiant—her dark hair and eyes, the sheer grace of her slender body! As he presses her to him, the sun stops in its arc; they look into each other's eyes—tears run down their faces. No, no, he will never live without her again!

He takes her to her hotel; they say nothing—she is a flower, her petals redolent with a fragrance which drowns his senses. Slowly she removes her blouse, her skirt, as they continue to gaze into each others' eyes.

He kisses her, as she undresses him, as he touches her, as they move toward a moment already contained in the present. His eyes close, as she kisses him, as somehow the past is erased, the demons gone, the hawks, the eagles, the malignant comets, as they move closer together, as their bodies rock back and forth, as with a tremendous burst of energy they become one—if only now, if only for this moment—he is free!

They repeat the moment again and again—she will bus down to the capital, or more often, he will drive up to her village. Time passes, but not between them, as if they had gone back to the beginning of time, even before the moment it commenced its relentless ticking, as the world creates itself continuously in each moment.

The world is theirs forever and ever! There is no measure of this blessing, no fitting it into time or space, but it is like the glow of sunshine, the sheen and flash of a fish jumping out of the water, or the pure sound of silence.

No, no, it does not matter that in the depth of almost fatal scars are the memories of Father clutching his body and penetrating his soul. No, it does not matter, if these memories can be dispensed in this moment without time, to be repeated again and again—he is free!

The Mayans speak a living poem, Sabrina tells him—the sounds of birds or animals have become the words, or their motions conveyed in the meter of sounds, the long line of the horizon expressed in a single extended vowel. It is the birth of language, as again and again, it comes into being. He and Sabrina hold out their hands as sunlight falls directly on their palms.

Here the poor live as they lived a thousand years ago, though now in fear, or in greater want, but with no sense of time, as now he has no sense of time, when he is with her. He sits as they file into Sabrina's clinic, as she decides the right medicines, prepares the shots, or operates, if she must. Again, for those hours, he assists, as he did in Nicaragua. It is the body which appears to her, and to him, of a person in time, suffering, needing them, while they, dutiful to the present need, continue their timeless presence with each other.

The village women, heavy-set, wrapped in their geometric weavings, gossip, spin, hug, and weep; the men are solemn and deferential; the children are like the little pigs in Nicaragua at the Darling, always underfoot—everywhere she walks, she is followed by the children, Juanito, María, Carlito, Sofía. . . .

Every week, Dwight brings Sabrina a suitcase of medicine from the embassy clinic, just as they both had brought medicines to their clinics in Nicaragua. Here, too, a few pills can save a child from dying of diarrhea, penicillin can stop an otherwise lethal infection. Sabrina tends the tropical diseases, the injuries from fights and accidents, and from the continuing attacks and bombings by the paramilitaries and the army.

Sabrina shows him the sign, which one day appears tacked on the door of her clinic: "SABRINA MONTENEGRO, DEATH TO THOSE WHO AID THE COMMUNISTS! LEAVE NOW WHILE YOU CAN!"

"How did this get here?"

"I don't know."

"Don't you have security?"

"An old man—Carlos Mendoza. They probably left it during the night—what could he have done?"

In the next few months, as Dwight shuffles back and forth between the embassy and Sabrina's village, the notes multiply. "SABRINA MONTENEGRO, YOUR TIME IS RUNNING OUT!"

"Darling, shouldn't you leave? Is it worth your taking this risk?"

"LEAVE BEFORE IT IS TOO LATE!"

"I think it is time . . ."

"LEAVE, NORTHAMERICAN SCUM, LEAVE NOW!"

"It is too dangerous. You must leave!"

"You know I can save lives here. You know that. The people here are depending on me." She continues applying a bandage, giving a shot, shining a light into an infected eye, sometimes operating, as the line of villagers shuffles into the clinic.

"But what if they mean to do what they say?"

"I can save several times more lives in one hour than my own, Dwight, and, you'll see, everything will work out."

"What kind of math is that?"

"I'm an American citizen now. . . . They threaten, but they wouldn't touch me." She's in the clinic as it implodes like lungs sucking air, and then bursts into orange and yellow light, as Dwight's shadow races toward the doomed building.

"Yes, my darling, I am sure there are people in San Miguel who are in the resistance. That is what I hear, but then . . . I look around, can they be María, José, Ana, Jesús?"

"Do you know?"

"We are not a 'village in resistance,' like some in the other provinces. But then, I suppose, people here have relatives who are in them, and perhaps they have secretly sent them food, or money, or . . . That is not my job, Dwight!"

"But you do know who they are!"

"My job is to care for the sick and the hurt!"

They walk about the village in the dark in the faint hum of cicadas—no electric lights, no billboards, no restaurants or night clubs. Figures move about in the shadows of the "streets," which are no more than the distance between houses, the gravel or dirt for the few vehicles which pass through. In total darkness, like a death, the village waits for the dawn. As they circle the earth, satellites signal back and forth, each one ready to swoop down like a hawk or an eagle.

Dwight presents her with an engagement ring, the one Mother had given him when she became a nun, so she would be free for her new marriage to Christ—as he slips it on her finger, has he encircled her as if he were Father?

"Shall we marry now?" Dwight asks.

"Yes, as soon as this assignment is done . . ."

"Why not now? I want to marry you now!"

"Then yes, my darling, yes!" She laughs, "I accept."

A brush fire runs along the ground.

The UN concludes the new settlement—the repression will end, the opposition will be legalized, a rights commission will hear testimony. . . . Of course, Dwight says to himself, nothing will happen—the embassy knows that, but then why should he be a party to it?

"YOU WILL DIE, AMERICAN WHORE!" . . . "How could I leave?" she asks. "I would be trading one life for all those I could save." He is already planning the ceremony—they will marry in three weeks.

"But the life I am speaking of is yours."

She stares at him.

"Yes, yes," he says, shaking his head, "all souls are equal in God's sight," and he stops. . . . Planets circle the earth, each one the face of a Mayan peasant, with Sabrina's just another face. . . . The two stand tied to posts, like St. Sebastian, as he watches the arrows pierce her twitching body.

He stands before Ambassador Henderson in his office. "Dwight, this report of yours, I must say, leaves something to be desired. It is, how shall I put this, so we do not become bogged down in semantics—it is, uh, too candid. We are, as you are undoubtedly aware, in a most delicate situation here. To beg the obvious, our purpose, as it has been defined for us, is to support the present government. That is the policy, Dwight."

"Yes."

"Then why this report? Frankly, it looks as if it were written by Amnesty International, not an agency of the U.S. government!"

"If anything, it understates the present situation."

"On what do you base that?"

"On the Archbishop's recent report, on the cumulative statistics one can read by attending to published sources, on my contacts with the Agency, with Colonel Dodson. The report suggests the need for us to desist from covert operations which . . ."

Henderson looks up at the ceiling. "That's a long story, as you know."

"I don't think . . ."

"You've simply got to join the team. I hope—I'd been a bit afraid of this—I will not need to say any more."

Dwight walks back to his office and closes the door: "Can I go on like this? How old am I? Thirty—isn't that enough? Haven't I passed the time of experience, of voyeurism? Isn't there a moment, when what I do is *my* responsibility?" Isn't he engaging in a bit of self-drama? "Can't I just wait out my assignment?"

As they lie in bed in Sabrina's cabin, they hear a knock on the door just after dawn—the village just three miles away has been hit! They dress, gather up her medical equipment, and drive off in his car. As it enters the village, they see whole buildings blown away, the school gutted, bodies littering the street. The villagers tell them that the army had come in with bazookas and fired point blank at the huts and buildings, then shot the people who were attempting to flee. Not every one, they say, has been accounted for—six women and two men have disappeared.

Sabrina and the two other Guatemalan doctors treat the wounded: a man with his leg blown away, a woman with deep intestinal bleeding, a child—but when her mother brings her in, wrapped in a shawl, she is already dead. On the faces of the survivors is blank disbelief, the terror of eyes which may never again completely focus. The unaccounted, the "disappeared," linger like faces in clouds or underwater.

When they return to San Miguel, and are moving the wounded into the clinic, there on her *desk* is a crudely scrawled note—"NOW YOU WILL DIE!" The hawks and eagles circle in the air. They are fleeing with no chance of rest, until Dwight sees Sabrina fall—the predatory birds swoop down. . . . There is nothing he can say, she refuses to leave—it is her "duty." He drives back to the embassy.

Can't he just tone down his reports, and wait out the two more years? Yes, there had been some slackening of terror in the wake of the final settlement, but already it is coming back.

He stands in front of a mirror, staring into his own eyes.

He holds her body next to his, her perfume drowning his senses—"Pillow'd upon my fair love's ripening breast/ To feel for ever its soft fall and swell"—her body begins to twitch.

His next report will be due in ten days—after they are married. And then will she finally do what he tells her?

Roger Channing stops him in the embassy hallway, but instead of some sly allusion or Agency tidbit, his body and face have taken on a curious rigidity. "I should tell you, a paramilitary unit, one which operates on its own, has just made a strike on the clinic at San Miguel Atalán—isn't that where Sabrina works? I think you said something about . . ."

"No, no!"

"Frankly, Dwight, in the last few months, with the settlement and all, I've been trying to talk them out of such ventures. I mean, what's the point; this is the kind of p.r. which the government hardly . . ."

Dwight runs down the hall with Channing's voice trailing after him. The Communication Section is just picking up a radio message from the clinic. He puts on the extra set of earphones— Carlita, the nurse, is shouting, her voice full of dread: "The clinic has just been hit by a squad of soldiers with AKs and explosives. Twelve people are dead, maybe more. Twenty, thirty are wounded. The clinic is destroyed!"

"Is Sabrina, is Sabrina all right!"

"I am sorry, Dr. Montenegro has not been counted among the living or the dead. We do not know . . ."

Dwight runs out of the embassy, and jumps into his car, fills up his extra gasoline tank, and drives off into the mountains.

In four hours, he reaches the clinic: again, a gutted building, but now it's Sabrina's! A huge hole is in its side, its metal roof has been blown away; other houses have been hit; there are dozens of people still milling about in the streets; bodies covered with blankets are piled up against the crumpled walls of the school.

"Where is Sabrina, Sabrina Montenegro! Do you know where she is? Dr. Montenegro, do you know. . . ?"

"She was taken."

". . . I was running, I did not see."

"I think they put her in a military car."

"Yes, it was in a car . . ."

As soon as the embassy opens, he calls in to tell them to approach the Guatemalan government for her release. He waits, he calls again. The government knows nothing. The raid, they say, was done by a paramilitary unit over which they had no control. He gets

Channing on the line. "I'm sorry, Dwight, but it's out of our hands. For all we know, they may have already killed her, and are covering it up."

Channing's lying—what does he know?

As he drives back to the capital, Sabrina is in a prison or a detention house, her eyes glittering, unfocused; hands from an Army uniform reach around her body, drawing her in—are they burning her body with cigarette butts, are they penetrating her?

He calls Elvira, her mother in Nicaragua. She shouts at him over the crackling phone: "What did you expect? It is all your doing! You twisted her mind with your communist politics! You exposed her to this danger! It was for you, for your own selfish reasons! You put her life at risk! You are nothing but a stupid, stupid Northamerican communist! What do you know about our countries here? What do you know? Nothing, nothing . . ."

He puts down the receiver as Elvira's voice becomes just a thin noise; and then the phone clicks. As he lies in bed, Sabrina slowly removes her skirt, her blouse—there is nothing underneath, only her severed head. Her face explodes into a swarm of maggots!

When he passes Channing in the hall of the embassy, Channing cannot even look him in the face—"Dwight, for Christ sake! We're all sorry, but Jesus, *I* didn't do it! The *Agency* didn't do it. I told you, it was some paramilitary kooks who must have gotten to her, some group out of our control altogether, or . . . hell, I don't know—we don't know *everything*!"

"Then how did you know about the raid before the radio broadcast?"

"I didn't. . . . I think you must have gotten the sequence mixed up."

Dwight stares at him, shaking his head, at Colonel Dodson, at Ambassador Henderson, who says simply, "I'm truly sorry, Dwight. I know how you must feel." . . . Each day he will go to work, read the intelligence traffic, the communiqués, have his meetings. No one talks to him, except one of the code clerks, a young woman from Terre Haute, Indiana, who says she's heard his fiancée has been taken, and asks, "Do you want to talk about it and share your feelings?"

"No!"—had she taken some course called "Sympathy 101"? Was he rude to her? Did Channing actually order it? Or did he just know it was happening, and then do nothing?

The clinic at San Miguel Atalán closes down—one of the Guatemalan doctors had been killed, the other has already moved to the capital. Dwight keeps Sabrina's clothes, her papers, occasionally reading one of her medical reports, or the death threats he had collected—"SABRINA MONTENEGRO, YOUR TIME IS RUNNING OUT!" . . . "LEAVE BEFORE IT IS TOO LATE!" . . . "NOW YOU WILL DIE!" . . . Or he will run the soft tissue of a blouse or a scarf over his hands, even putting them into her shoes, his wrists bent to imitate her high heels, and then he will pretend to walk on the ground, as if she were alive. Is she still in their custody? Or have they buried her body in a common pit, or thrown it from a plane over the ocean? Naked, her body falls through the air, her hair flayed, her legs extended, as she twists and turns, her glittering eyes staring into the rushing air.

Ambassador Henderson calls him in. "Take some time off. We can survive, Dwight. I know that all this has been a shock for you." . . . He walks through the streets of Guatemala City, as the Mayan villagers wait expectantly. He had been part of it, just as much as Channing, or Henderson, or Dodson; they are no more to be blamed than he is. When will he begin to resume his bland reports, his meetings with American corporate representatives, his *entre nous* lunches with Channing, his "be advised" encounters with Colonel Dodson?

As he lies in bed, she is a dark shadow. In the morning, when he awakes, she is there, she is there beside him in the bed! As he dresses, she is there watching him! She is there as he leaves his apartment, as he walks down the street!

"I hope now," he tells Ambassador Henderson, "I will be allowed to write the truth of what is happening here."

Henderson stares off into space. "Of course, I know how you feel, Dwight; it's completely understandable, given what has happened, but then we must be professionals here. What does that mean? It means, if I may say so, to separate one's personal feelings from one's professional responsibility. That is what we must do, if we are to do our jobs." Father's form, his face, merges with Henderson, until Dwight must squint his eyes to see him.

"But isn't the truth ultimately what we must base our policy on?"

Henderson sighs. "And 'the truth shall make you free?'" He smiles to himself. "I know how you feel, believe me. But then, this is not an ideal world, but one," he takes a deep breath, "where policy is imperfect, the best we can come up with, and our reports, if that policy is to make sense, must be in sync with it. . . . You do see that, don't you, Dwight? Think about it."

Dwight shakes his head.

Henderson pauses a moment. "I respect your integrity, I do. If it's another assignment you want, I'll write the appropriate report, that you are leaving because of a personal tragedy, so that your career will . . ."

"No!"

He pays one more visit to Channing: "Roger, if you ever learn anything about Sabrina, have the goodness to tell me," and sees for one moment a face basking in its own bittersweet ambiguity, and its power to lie.

Of course, he knew! Was it this ultimate sense of power that he could watch even Sabrina killed in the "exercise of his duties" that had twisted his face into this simpering mask?

A week later Dwight flies back to Washington for his final debriefing, for the inevitable signing of forms, by which he will acknowledge that he is still subject to the nation's security laws, . . . He looks over his shoulder—Sabrina is sitting right beside him in the plane!

As he ascends into the clouds, Guatemala lies below like a tortured body.

At the State Department, as bureaucrats behind their desks go through the litany of questions, Dwight answers in monosyllables, signs more papers, then leaves the Department for the last time, and "retires" to his Georgetown home.

In the next weeks, he calls the embassy every few days, but there is no information. He notes a growing impatience, mixed with feigned care. "No, I'm terribly sorry, Dwight, but we still don't know anything." "We're still trying to find out, but I must tell you, I think at this point . . ." At night, he hears the hum of cicadas in Sabrina's village, sees her tortured face. He sees her again and again in the police station, surrounded by her torturers, as they stick their cigarette butts into her flesh, or move their grotesque bodies over her, as her body heaves up and down. Will she ever die? Is that what it means to be 'disappeared'?

He calls the clinic in Southern Sudan, and speaks with a Brother Antonius, and through the static receives permission for Mother to break her silence so he can tell her what has happened. He hears "the will of God," "so sorry for you, Dwight" . . . "I cannot tell you." She is crying—had it been the will of God that Sabrina had been taken, that Father had violated him? He puts down the receiver.

He sits reading St. John of the Cross, who writes of his love of Christ: "Where have you hidden away?/ Never a crumb of comfort day or night . . . if you should meet my love,/ my one love, tell him how/ I'm heartsick, fevered, and fast sinking now. . . . Oh shorten the long days/ of burning thirst—no other love allays them./ Let my eyes see your face. . . ."

He has to stop! He puts down the book. "Our bed: in roses laid . . . patrols of lions ranging all around . . ."

A card from Todd Jacobs: "I've just heard about Sabrina. I want you to know that Rachel and I love you, Dwight, and we will never forget our sister, Sabrina. Think of us now forever as your family."

Will he appear on a television program called "Conversations with Thoughtful Men and Women"?

Had he agreed to speak? What is he doing in the studio? There is Bill Moyers with his steel-framed glasses, his earnest, inquiring face. Dwight says, "I arrived in Guatemala City already briefed about the situation in that country, that hundreds of thousands of Guatemalans had died in a brutal conflict stretching over decades."

Moyers: "How did you view the U.S. role there?"

Lockwood: "As complicitous."

Moyers: "In what way?"

Lockwood: "It was our task to promote a government there which would reflect the will of the people. Instead, we violated our trust by supporting a brutal military regime, and by economic policies which robbed the people . . ." He goes on describing the situation in more and more detail until Moyers stops him.

Moyers: "And your fiancée, Sabrina Montenegro, she, I understand, was killed . . ."

Lockwood: "Yes, she was disappeared, and the United States government knew it was happening and did nothing to protect her!" Father shouts, "That's enough, Dwight! You don't want to burn up your credit if you should ever want to work for the government again. Your personal life, however engaging, isn't the point, is it?"

He stoops to the ground in the back of his house, then begins digging with his hands until they are bloody. He kneels with his eyes closed; then he covers her over with earth.

When he lies in bed, she is beside him; when he walks in the street, she is there by his side. She is always with him, with her staring, tortured eyes, until he cries, "Stop! Be with me, be with me forever, but not like this!"

She will not leave him—he reaches his hand to touch her body, and feels it covered in a dark liquid. She twists and turns, as her torturers continue to violate her—how long can he endure it?

The season changes from a dank, rainy winter to a bright spring. One night, as they lie in bed, Sabrina turns and asks, as she had when they had come back from Nicaragua, "What will we do now?"

He gets up and paces up and down, as he used to when they had worked together on Stand Up and Be Counted. "Yes," she says, "it is time now."

That morning he phones Todd Jacobs that he is ready to return as chair of Stand Up and Be Counted. "O.K., boss." With the next call, he books a flight to Boston.

MEETING WITH THE PUBLICANS

He wakes up in Cambridge in a hotel room—there, lying next to him in the bed, is Sabrina. What can he do but dress, then sit staring into the dark? He goes to his briefcase, takes out the files of Stand Up and Be Counted. In the mirror, Sabrina is staring at him; from her body flows a thick, black stream which spreads over the rug. "I'm going to a meeting now, Sabrina!" Suddenly, his breath is sucked from his lungs.

He tells Todd again he is ready to take charge—Todd seems to be treating him as if he were suffering from a fatal disease. But then Todd says, "I was thinking, if it's not too out of line, well, maybe we could get a larger endowment from your mother's estate, although I better apologize for what I guess"—Todd widens his eyes—"is my impetuous remark."

He shakes his head. "I want to review the operation thoroughly, and then draw up a new plan." There in the office is Sabrina listening to them.

That night in his hotel, he lies with the dead at the bottom of the ocean; above him, the waves ebb and flow. Still holding his breath, he listens to the voice instructing him what to do. He begins to rise through the water, which passes over his face, his body, until he breaks the surface and can breathe. Slowly he realigns his body, then walks onto the shore through a dense fog.

As he lies at the base of a forest, light sifts down tall trees only to be lost in deep shadows. One by one, the trees fall. But then, they begin to rise again as they angle into the sky. At the convergence of the risen trees is a concentrated, if irregular, white knot—it is the shape of the light he had seen in the prison window after the demonstration with Sabrina. What could it mean—is it a sign?

He sits in the little office of Stand Up reading reports, jotting down notes, making lists. Todd sucks in his breath, opens doors for him, fetches his umbrella, hands him files. The programs of Stand Up which Todd has maintained all these years still seem valuable, but now slightly yellowed with age—Todd could be wearing a three-piece suit, and speaking into a telephone mounted on a wooden panel.

Dwight explains his plan: "Stand Up will become a service agency, providing fund-raising and organizational expertise for socially involved non-profits, as well as dispensing funds for their programs." Todd sits blinking his eyes. "Once we work out the plan, we'll start arranging meetings with groups in different cities—first, of course, in Boston, and then in cities all around the country."

"Sabrina," he asks her, now back in his hotel, "is that all right, is it?" He walks with her around Cambridge in that time when Stand Up was still a quickening idea—no, it is not the Sabrina who is with him now, but "the talkative waitress from Nicaragua." He tries to talk to her—again Sabrina stares at him with her tortured eyes.

He and Todd rent a larger office, hire new staff, and for months train themselves to do the job they have set for themselves, taking a course in computer science, arranging for day-long briefings by the heads of other non-profits in the Boston-Cambridge area, working out the details of the new organization. Then they are flying to one city after another to meet with the local agencies, making their first contacts—in Cleveland, a social worker named Christie Balka; in Chicago, a day-care center administrator named Aishah Anderson; in Detroit, an AIDS activist named Enrique Cruz:

"Enrique," Dwight asks him, "if you could imagine a wish list of services, a list which reaches the whole AIDS community here, what would it look like? Spend whatever time it takes to spell it out, and then we can help you prioritize your services and set up reasonable schedules."

"You really mean this, man?"

Dwight smiles, "We'll be here."

"Like you're going to have to be here every day for a week or two, because that's what it's going to take to even *begin* to nail down all this shit. Hey, like you're not planning to take off on the next plane?"

"We'll be here, as long as it takes."

"And then you're going to help us pay for all this?"

"Yes, we'll provide some funds directly, and then we'll help you raise the rest."

Enrique is dark, almost black, with an ugly scar on his neck; he carries his papers in a backpack. He tells Dwight that he is HIV positive, but is taking the "cocktail" of medicines. He brings in more and more of the AIDS workers, as together they lay out plans for a shelter, an expansion of counseling services, a public education program, while Dwight and Todd help plan the fund-raising, the community rallies, the door-to-door campaigns like the ones he and Todd and yes, Sabrina first organized in Cambridge.

Again and again, he and Todd pack up their bags and briefcases, and make the next trip—on the plane, there is Sabrina sitting next to him, waiting for what he will do next for Stand Up and Be Counted.

He and Todd meet with the staff of operating organizations in their grubby urban offices, or with the foundations and sponsoring corporations in their lush board and conference rooms—immediately, the intense talking begins as if Dwight were an emissary from a foreign country. He writes in his journal, "The vivid faces of the poor, their spirited but inaccurate language contrast with the colorless style of the rich and powerful, with its lost social grace and its measured compassion."

Stand Up extends itself around the country—a day-care center in Boston, vocational training in New York, a refuge for the homeless in Chicago—now all clearly defined, with numbers, flow charts, computerized programs—"Is that all right, is it?" he keeps asking Sabrina, who stares into space, but can't he now begin to see just the slightest softening in her tortured eyes? Father smirks, "Of course, this is distinctly not the work *I* would have chosen."

Todd says, "I know the foundation is growing, but stay with me, man, and I'll grow with it." It's as if he had woken Todd from a deep sleep. "I used to think my job was just to keep going what you had started—guess not." He gives his little laugh. "Do you see this computer program I just picked up? It's beautiful—it organizes any contribution alphabetically, and then by location, amount, type of donor—clever stuff, huh? Someday, we'll just flip a switch and go home."

Sometimes he brings Rachel on their trips—"She's never been to Florida; is it okay?" She is a small, dumpy woman, who wears a wig in public, who reads mystery novels on the plane, and smiles sweetly, and, Dwight suspects, is sharp-tongued and querulous at home. She and Todd had met in an orthodox synagogue in Crown Point in Brooklyn when they were still in high school—did he woo her with bouquets of flowers and his shy looks?

With Todd and Rachel, time recedes to a Russian *shtetel* in the last century. She is cooking, sewing, tending their little store in the village, or feeding the chickens in the barnyard, while Todd sits all day in the *schule*, rocking back and forth, head bowed, intoning the intricacies of the law. They had been childless due to an early curable case of uterine cancer—their unborn son with lovelocks and soulful eyes stares at Dwight from under his skullcap. Todd takes Rachel's bag, helps her into the cab, holds her hand as they walk onto the plane as if she were his mother.

In the office, Todd is endlessly intelligent, as if for three thousand years he had been a flashlight moving down history's dark streets. He invents whole systems of organization, intricate patterns of reporting and record keeping, matching Dwight's pace, as they open up one city after another—a vocational training center in Des Moines, an immigrant placement office in El Paso, an AIDS program in Seattle. . . .

* * * * *

After two years, Dwight decides to locate the national office for Stand Up to Washington, D.C., and moves back into his Georgetown home. As he walks through the abandoned rooms, as he stands before Mother's portrait in the living room, he asks sententiously, "Is this where my life has come—has it been to return to this?" "Pitiful," Father says.

As the federal government increasingly diverts the resources of the country toward a series of international police actions and withdraws from social services, Stand Up attempts to fill in some of the gaps. Now supported by major foundations, it funds a burgeoning number of programs. As the years go by, Dwight and Todd watch Stand Up grow into a huge national organization.

His Georgetown house becomes the animated scene of a renewed social life. Again, the chauffeur-driven cars deposit their charges in front of his door; soft music fills the air; the tables, manned by liveried servants, offer the drinks and *hors d'oeuvres*. Again, the clink of glasses, the soft symphony of talk, the carefully maintained balance between the casual and purposeful, while Sabrina stands nearby, her eyes no longer glittering with torture, but softer, assuring, the eyes he remembers. Here he cements his connections with the Washington-based foundations, and possibly sympathetic figures in the Administration, and maintains his association, initiated in Moscow and Guatemala City, with the World Bank and the International Monetary Fund.

A new language has arrived in Washington. Rather than the old elliptical pseudo-British style, it seeks the metaphor of the obvious: "It would be like running down two streets at once," "like playing the game left-handed," "like calling it quits when the game has just started," or, in refusing to help, "The color of change isn't always green." The language is corporate, although, when turned toward the public, can also be colored with phrases from the Pentecostal churches. Anyone entering the government must learn it like diplomats assigned to a new country taking a crash course in Urdu or Swahili. Now corporations or government agencies are "cultures" or "architectures," programs are "robust," policies are "synchronous," or sometimes, even in the same speech, "fulfilling our mission under God."

Old friends of Father, using the new language, reappear like ghosts. "Stand Up certainly seems in sync with the Administration—yes, we're all part of the same culture."

"Yes," Dwight says in the quiet glow and clink of glasses, "my father would certainly have appreciated a remark like that."

"I knew you'd be following our line, Dwight."

"Yes, Schofield, thank you, and you might well consider Stand Up in your corner, if you think of the alternative—I'm speaking, of course, of government programs. What we are offering is a very different model, a robust citizen group direct from the heartland which can accomplish many of the same objectives."

"What exactly do you want?"

"Ah," Dwight laughs, "don't tempt the hungry man. No, seriously, what would be useful is a modest federal appropriation, nothing embarrassingly high—I think I understand your position here."

"We need, I can see, to discuss this at some length."

"At your office, perhaps?"

The *hors d'oeuvres* come around again. "No," Dwight says, "I must pass."

"Are you watching your waistline? No, not you. . . . Didn't you used to play soccer at Harvard? Do I remember that right? My son was on the team."

"Yes, quite correct. Of course, I remember Allenby. Once . . ."

"I think I was at that game, at that game when you were playing Haverford, and it was you who set up Allenby's goal—I remember it quite well."

"Remarkable!"

"Well, yes, certainly we should talk!"

He pauses in front of the mirror—the ambiguous mask he had seen from childhood staring back still inexplicably his, though now with a slight wrinkling of the brow, a recession of the eyes, a tightening around the lips. The image lifts away from the mirror, and behind it is no image at all, but an intricate machinery of purpose and calculation, like the revealed workings of a computer, which notes the guest list, the catering, and, of course, the possibilities of gain for Stand Up and Be Counted in each conversation.

As Sabrina watches over his shoulder, he writes, "I sit down each day with the publicans and discuss the latest tax, the most recent war. Who would have guessed what I really thought? No matter what the motive, is there a price to be paid for each departure from the truth? How separable are means and ends? Shouldn't I hire an attorney now, or should I wait for some angel to write an *amicus* brief for my Maker?"

As head of Stand Up and Be Counted, Dwight is chosen to join a citizen advisory group for the Department of Health and Human Services, and selected as an advisor for the International Monetary Fund. From HHS, he will arrange federal subventions for his domestic programs; and from the World Bank and Fund, he will negotiate support for Stand Up's Developing World Division, as its programs now achieve a semi-public status.

In his press conferences and media interviews, he still carries the aura of his famous father, who, as the *Times* points out, "would have thrived in the new Administration." He appears as the advocate of a "revitalized private sector," "a new culture of civic responsibility." Even his language, although occasionally witty in private, has the bland anonymity of the public servant—yes, he is a "technocrat," even now, in this rise of his celebrity.

Father still makes his disparaging remarks—yes, even now, even after Dwight has "proven himself," but then how much he had learned from him, how much he owes him. Without him wouldn't he have been "just a writer?" "Ah, Dwight, this is not a time to be expressing yourself, but rather serving your cause, whatever that may be." Whoever said *Father* was a "technocrat"? No, not him—he was a "personality." And himself?—he stops in the middle of the street, and stares until a new rush of traffic forces him to cross to the other side and resume his walk down Pennsylvania Avenue for still another meeting.

At a cocktail party, he asks Denise Charcot, the younger sister of the French ambassador, if she will attend with him the opening of the Matisse show. For just a moment he catches a puzzled look in Sabrina's eyes, but he has to have a life, doesn't he? Denise has startled blue eyes, a languorous figure, and is clearly intrigued by his career, and by his beauty, which, yes, is still an objective commodity, as is hers. As Sabrina watches, Denise sits in her designer gown, intermittently crossing and uncrossing her legs, as if they were the hands of a clock.

"No, Sabrina, I will do nothing. . . . How could you even begin to doubt me?"

"Do what you want!"

After taking off so many hours, he calculates he will have to work until three or four in the morning, and yet he will have made his appearance, registered again in the public memory. . . . In several canvases by Matisse, Denise sits by an open window gazing out at the sea, her eyes like the sky, with the drifting clouds overhead, the soft wash of waves below her balcony.

"Ah, Dwight, where shall we dine tonight?"

"Whichever restaurant will meet the demands of your exacting taste."

"Then not in this city—shall we fly to Paris?"

"Perhaps we should make the reservations now."

They dine, they banter as the ritual of *haute cuisine* consumes the hours—he tightens as the moment comes for his refusal of further intimacy. "At the end," he writes in his journal, "there was nothing, just this vacuity."

Mildred Hewitt, the eldest daughter of the head of C.O.I., a huge oil conglomerate, encourages him to ask for her company. Nothing more will happen, he assures Sabrina, or so he reads into the discreet distinction she consistently maintains between beauty and sensuality, as they make the rounds of receptions and openings. Or he will sit, as he did years ago with Mother, in the drawing rooms of Bergdorf Goodman as Mildred consults her designer and negotiates the world of line and fabric; or he will "shop" with her at Southby's to furnish her home with exorbitantly priced antiques, or review the latest Washington gossip:

"Tell me, Dwight, do you think Mansefield has really allied himself with Connor and his crew?"

"I should think so, but it is clearly an alliance of convenience, hardly a bond or a friendship."

"What will come on it?"

"It is a queasy alliance at best."

"And the appearance of Boyd Herrick and Alice Phelps at the Altons last week—how would you comment on that?" He will see her staring eyes, the downturned mouth, the gaze of one watching life pass. What can he give her more than his occasional company? Has his love for Sabrina consumed all his feelings, and left him merely pleasant, as vacuous as the passing hours?

His other feminine companions—Denise, Charlene, Suprya, Madeleine, and still more—allude to engagements to which he might take them, a play or performance, and eventually to situations suggesting more intimacy; he smiles, diffuses, parries, and, if he encounters too much insistence, too evident frustration, he drops the association, as the gossip swirls around him of a secret liaison, sometimes even of a gay lover, with this actor, or poet, or even a government official. He emerges in the more sophisticated columns as an enigma. Who knows his private life—does he have one—beyond the public schedule of his social appearances?

Then to return home, now decorated in an expensive, tasteful, yet impersonal manner as the site for his receptions, and, after still more work at his desk—his servant, Manuel, has been asleep for hours—to lie in bed with Sabrina, now eager to talk—"Did the work go well today, Dwight? . . . What did you think of the new lady, if I may ask? Why must you see them—what is it you want?"

"Nothing, darling, I want nothing! You know that!" He stares into her eyes—he feels behind his head, the softness of her hand, then the touch of her body.

In the press, in the always growing collective story about him, Sabrina becomes "the dark-eyed Nicaraguan beauty, who was tragically murdered in Guatemala." He is "the founder of Stand Up and Be Counted" and, of course, "the son of former Secretary of Defense Bradford Lockwood, a towering figure in the Reagan and Bush Administrations," and so still another example, fulfilling the deep hope, or defusing the anxiety, of Washington families that their momentary fame can be transmitted as reliably as wealth through the generations. Yes, he has become a "part of the Washington scene," an accepted member, to be spoken of knowingly with allusions hinting at an unrealized intimacy.

He writes in his journal, "What a spectacle it must be to Him! Has anyone ever imagined that God might be so thoroughly bored?"

Sabrina stands by, a look of disgust on her face. "Does it matter, Dwight? What you are *doing* in the world—isn't that the point? Isn't Stand Up and Be Counted the reason you are alive?"

In the hours just before dawn, he sits up reading the poetry of Chandler Ellis, a former career ambassador—of course, Dwight had heard his name during his time in the State Department as Ellis had filled one demanding position after another. Ellis had written his poetry privately for twenty-five years before seeking publication. Now, he has extended his work to epic length, to the depiction of mythic wars, finding in the midst of chaos the stopping of time in his heroes' fleeting consciousness.

At a reading at the Library of Congress, Ellis offers selections from his *The Alzheimer War*: it is a conflict in which each side possesses digital weapons which eliminate information from their opponents' computers, and then from their brains, leaving them disorganized with only chaotic fragments of their previous lives. It is not weapons which kill in *The Alzheimer War,* but ultimately anxiety as both sides struggle to keep conscious of their identities. . . . Dwight had written nothing himself, except his journal, which, in any case, will never be published, or his letters to Sabrina, which he had found after she had disappeared—wasn't this still another way he had followed Father's orders? No, there is no record of himself, of his private consciousness, so different—will anyone except Sabrina ever know—from his public persona?

He introduces himself to Ellis after the reading. "You may not need to hear this, but your poetry continues in my mind as only the poetry of a few others do."

"Don't tell me their names," Ellis laughs.

"Ah yes, you know, of course, the famous law firm of Homer, Virgil, St. John Perse, and Ellis."

"No, no, I'm afraid you'll find me only a junior partner, or rather, just a clerk."

Dwight suggests that perhaps Chandler might like to join him for a brandy at the Cosmos Club, and in the succeeding months, they see each other every few weeks. He writes in his journal, "If one looked for Chandler, not only would one not find his personality in his diplomatic career—another 'technocrat'?—but not even in his poems. Perhaps they contain more about himself than he knows, or could otherwise say, yet what emerges in the corpus of his work is not revelation, not the portrait of the poet, but a fearsome act of self-abnegation. But then, who is Homer, or Virgil—aren't these transmitters of a higher consciousness, and so, like God, without personality?"

Chandler maintains a home in the British West Indies, and occasionally invites Dwight to spend a few days. They take long strolls on the endless, deserted strands where the land, the sea, and the sky juxtapose their infinity, where flowers fill the air with their lush perfume, sheep graze in the grasslands punctuated by palm trees, and spiders on the leaves of trees display the most intricate geometry. They sit in restaurants on the piers eating braised grouper or dolphin, drinking the local Pinot Grigio. Chandler makes no effort at intimacy, nor any allusion to a private life. Can a man be just a poet, Dwight asks himself, and not a person? Is he, himself, cordial and impersonal, however charming, or well-informed, equally without a private life?

"'Shall I compare thee to a summer's day?'" Sabrina laughs. "'Thou art more lovely and more temperate.'"

"That's what I should be saying to you," Dwight answers.

"You did once! You did once, my darling!" Outside the sliding panels of his bedroom, the palm trees blow in the early morning wind, as do the bushes, the clouds, and the sea itself, in a symphony of motion, as Dwight checks the time for his return flight.

Back in Washington, he sits up in bed reading Chandler's new poem, dedicated to "the world consciousness of my friend, Dwight Lockwood": "Time's winged chariot, or is it stasis?/ Linear time, what could it yield?/ Timeless contemplation?/ Oh, to look into the face of time, and see not my own reflection,/ but beneath, a darkened mass."

He places the poem in a file jacket—"Ellis, Chandler, Poetry." No, he had not written it. No "eternal lines to time," no pen had "glean'd my teeming brain." "What's the purpose of dabbling in the arts," Father asks, "just to create some illusion that you are bigger than your task, or that the future can be secured with the stroke of a pen?"

In the Alpine Society, he meets Heinrich van Hippel, a Nobel laureate in physics. Born, like him, in the sixties, Heinrich had come from Amsterdam to study quantum mechanics at MIT. "It was, I found, a distressing if still rewarding set of contradictions between waves and particles, with a proliferation or even chaos of parameters, dimensions, and models."

Dwight waits the mandatory length of time, as if he understood what he had heard—for years, while he was studying Economics at Harvard, he and van Hippel had been only a few miles apart. "I understand you have proposed a scheme for the creation of our present world. Is there a definite beginning to your scheme, and a definite end?"

"Who knows, perhaps the world is eternal, but physics," van Hippel laughs, "is quite ephemeral. Yes, I have worked through to a new if still somewhat tentative model like a dyke against the sea which, I must confess, might not survive the next storm." Father's "brilliant pebbles," now endowed with their own intelligence, unite in formal dances called atoms or molecules, then murderously swoop down on their enemies.

"If I were to show you my work," Heinrich says on one of their coffee dates, "what could it possibly mean to you? Of course, I cannot do that. I am isolated from you, and from most others, with only a handful of people with whom I can talk—mostly, of course, through virtual journals."

Dwight smiles. "Then why, pray tell me, are we meeting like this?"

"Because somehow, Dwight, I can talk to you, not about my particles, if that is what they are, if they are not just information, or modeled bits in my computer. What are they, I ask myself—are they anything *real* at all? Do we still know what that word means? No, no, I would rather talk to you about the world, I almost wish to say, the real world you live in, but it is certainly a different one, one I miss, or have missed, and would wish to know." He laughs. "Tell me what's happening."

"Shall I tell you about Stand Up and Be Counted?"

"I believe that is the subject, although I understand there is still a larger world which it does not fully comprehend."

"Indeed, although it manages to occupy at least fourteen hours of my day, so I must confess there are days in which there is no other."

"Tell me how have you negotiated those magical agreements I just read about in the *Times* with the pharmaceutical companies?"

Their conversations, which eventually range from current events to epic poetry, from the United States to Africa and Asia, and yes, even to quantum mechanics, occur more often than not on some mountain top, be it in the Alps, the Rockies, or the Himalayas, where Dwight and Heinrich, laboring past their exhaustion with ice picks, boots, and digitally controlled gas masks, scale heights and then look out over the clouds covering the lower peaks. The change in scale—the whole earth shimmering below—makes such conversations appropriate, as Heinrich describes the first milliseconds of creation, or rather the continuous creation of the world which is occurring, he says, even now in remote galaxies. . . . Father shouts, "Come down off that stupid mountain!" "Does it matter," Dwight writes in his journal, "that for Plotinus or for Meister Eckhart the continuous creation of the world was a vision, and for physicists like van Hippel it is sustained in fact, although now, as he points out, we do not even know what facts are?"

Van Hippel looks up from his table at the Pamplona, as Sabrina, after touching Dwight's cheek, disappears into the kitchen to fetch their *espressos*. He wakes up and stares into the dark: If only he could reverse time, if only Sabrina could really be here at the Pamplona, and their lives be all in front of them, if only he could turn a switch, say a few magic words, or so intrigue a God that He might act on his behalf—if only . . . Sabrina is caressing him as if he were a small child, or rather, a furry kitten being licked by its mother. As he wakes up again, he is crying—had Heinrich seen him? No, he is in a bed by himself in his own house. He shakes his head; he checks his schedule—this morning he will meet with Stand Up's mid-Atlantic office.

* * * * *

For Dwight's forty-fifth birthday, Todd and Rachel Jacobs present him with a quilt—Rachel had made it herself, piecing each fabric together on her antiquated sewing machine. He holds it against his head, as if he were already asleep. Like the Rubins' home in Moscow, here he can relax, eat home-cooked meals—"Are you comfortable, would you like another helping?"—and not program every nerve to respond with a brilliant or, at the very worst, a merely appropriate response.

As he sits in one of the overstuffed chairs, Rachel tells him stories she has heard about her great-grandfather and the life of the *Talmud*—again and again, he is back in the little Russian village, the sun just setting with the horizontal lines of light illuminating her face, the same light in the lidded eyes of scholars as they sit in the *schule*. The rabbis, the disputations, the simple life of the village, the menacing Cossacks—it is as if he were a child being told a fairy tale. He writes, "If not a mystic vision, what can stop time? Only this, a lost village, an ancient text, a life repeated generation after generation, and yet I have chosen a life more like a train which, in its scheduled passage, allows each such village only momentary recognition."

On his field trips for Stand Up's international "clients," Dwight sees again the bloated bellies and ulcerated feet of the children of the poor, the scarce food, the pitiful medical facilities, now in dozens of countries, whether it be in Bolivia, Uganda, or Malaysia. Thousands die every year for want of food, or nets to screen out the flies, or simple medicines. He had written once—yes, it was his Harvard dissertation—about the role of the International Monetary Fund in the Third World, its self-serving policies, its depression of the living standards of the common people in favor of its "clients," the financial community. What had he done himself to raise these standards? How few resources Stand Up commands, but a policy change in the Fund, yes, that could make a difference. Shouldn't he say something, now that he is an advisor? He turns to Sabrina, who tells him, "If you have something to say, my darling, yes, of course, you should say it."

Dwight dutifully schedules his first address before the IMF Board of delegates. They sit in the auditorium as he advances step by step to the podium—the distance shortens by a half, a quarter, an eighth, "Pillow'd upon my fair love's ripening breast . . . And so live ever . . . And so live ever . . . or else . . ." until he is standing before the group.

After the customary greetings, the expected quips about the ephemeral market, the play of currencies, he comes to the point of his talk: "The evidence is in, and compels us to recognize that the Fund needs now to return to its original policies advanced by our founder, John Maynard Keynes. Perhaps, in returning to this vision, the Fund might attempt, initially in a test case or two, to apply less stringent requirements during times of financial stress, by allowing lower borrowing rates, and by supporting governmental programs to increase spending power in the less fortunate classes. . . ."

A sprinkling of applause—the speech had been given, but then in the next few days, the Fund launches still another program of the kind he had just spoken against. At another meeting of the Board, he brings up the idea again, and receives the same reaction, although Sigmund Harris, the ranking Democrat on the Senate Foreign Relations Committee, who had been sitting in, and some country reps from countries as disparate as Russia and Bolivia, support him. Over the next year, he regularly repeats his position, and becomes a "voice," which draws increasing, if still intermittent, support.

He is running with his briefcase to make an old-fashioned train pulling out of a station with Sabrina waiting for him in one of its coaches—the train is always just a few feet in front of him. Still running to catch up, he sees rising before him a glass skyscraper in the midst of a great city. "What is the meaning of the glass building?" he asks in his journal. "Is it a symbol of future fulfillment, or just the frailty of my own ideas?"

"The policies I have been proposing for the IMF," he tells Mildred Hewitt, as they sit over drinks at Washington's exclusive La Fontaine Club, "apply as well to the national economy. Decreasing jobs and diminishing governmental programs are plunging parts of the population in this country to practically third world levels."

Mildred sighs. "Dwight, why do we need to speak of such matters now? Tonight we have seen an excellent play, we can count our blessings, and tomorrow morning you will return, I know, to your seemingly endless work. The world, believe me, will be just as wretched as it is now—you needn't worry that overnight it will correct itself without you."

"No, nothing," he says to himself, as he leaves her home in Georgetown to find his car for the brief ride back to his home. He sits up writing in bed: "Will events simply overtake these futile conversations? Has he simply come to the middle of a yet unspent life, is he just living out the years until the bones of his face poke through his skin?" Sabrina, who is lying in the bed beside him, shakes her head, "No, no, my darling."

In the morning, he sits reading the *New York Times*: continuing wars in the Middle East, the competition for oil around the Caspian and South China Seas, the ongoing threats of a nuclear exchange in Kashmir, the weaponization of outer space, the increasing financial instability. . . . He puts down the paper: the threats seem so immense, his efforts at Stand Up so feeble—he sits five, ten minutes unable to move. Then he turns to Sabrina, and laughs, "Why don't we just give up, and walk hand-in-hand off the Potomac Bridge?"

"No, my darling, have another cup of coffee."

He calls for Manuel, who brings the second cup, and, still in his robe, he begins to review the communications and paperwork which have accumulated in the last six hours. He checks his palm pilot—a meeting with the Undersecretary of Defense on using Stand Up as a supplemental resource during the occupation of Syria; a meeting, at the Congressman's request, with Derrick Braendel from Indiana; a late dinner with Denise Charcot at Le Corbusier. . . . "Is this a life?" he asks Sabrina.

"I think it was what you said you wanted."

"It never ends."

Sabrina snaps, "It does, believe me!"

Suddenly he is shouting, beside himself in a rage—"I don't need this, I don't need this!"

"Nor do I need you, not any more!" As she turns away, he rushes toward her, only to grasp air. Then her hand is on his cheek—"Darling, darling, I love you—I'm so sorry!"

He checks out Congressman Braendel on the Web: working class—his father a steel worker; before he was thirty, he became the "boy mayor" of Gary; after eight years as mayor, a successful run for the House. His voting record—Dwight scans its fifteen-year history—"liberal," on the political edge—and so discountable, and yet, hadn't he supported every measure Dwight believes in?

Braendel rises from his desk: he is a wiry little man with a bald head, with none of the Alpha-dog look of the typical American politician. When Dwight shakes his hand, it feels like metal. "I asked for this meeting, Dr. Lockwood, because I admire Stand Up and Be Counted."

"Yes, thank you." Long pause.

"Will you take coffee?"

"Of course," Dwight answers, "you've made an offer I simply can't refuse."

There are four empty cups on Braendel's desk. "Like you," he begins, "I work directly with the poor in my district." He explains he has hundreds of his workers going door-to-door signing up the voters, explaining his programs, meeting their local needs, as if he were an old-fashioned ward boss. Last year, he processed ten thousand individual requests, and took his district by seventy-nine percent. "I think I have a model which can translate from my district to the country as a whole."

Looking directly into his eyes, Braendel says, "Dr. Lockwood, for the next election, I will be making a bid for president. If I win, I will put forward a series of bills which will turn this government around."

". . . How will you do that?"

"From being a servant of the corporations to being a servant of the people." Then Braendel goes through his proposed legislative program, one bill after another—universal health care, increased federal aid to education, federally funded vocational training, inverse taxation for those below the poverty line . . .

Dwight sits blinking his eyes. "Remarkable!"

"Dr. Lockwood, what I want to ask you is this, "Can I count on your support?"

"Ah, I must say, it's a bold move. . . . How do you estimate your chances?"

"It depends on my support, particularly in the beginning."

The little determined man sits in front of him. Dwight glances at his watch, congratulates him on the decision to run, reaches for his briefcase—"Of course, I'll have to give the matter considerable thought."

"Ridiculous!" he says aloud. "Why should I even be thinking about this?" He paces up and down in his office. "If I came out for Braendel"—he stops in the middle of the floor—"if I broke my non-partisan stance, it would kill immediately any chance of further funding from the Administration and, of course, from the corporations. . . . My arrest and that article I wrote on Nicaragua for the *Times*—yes, I was granted absolution, because of my 'immaturity,' because of my father, yes, because of Father, to enter the diplomatic corps, but now"—he begins again to pace—"aren't the stakes so much higher, aren't so many more people dependent on me? How could I possibly take the risk?"

Braendel's face is intent, motivated, impersonal, all business—not unlike his own—is this really happening? Dwight laughs—he is in some cosmic harmony with a yet unknown world, and in that moment, perhaps a fatal one, he says aloud, "Yes, I'll back him!" He sets up a brief meeting, and promises Braendel to work on his presidential campaign—when he shakes his hand, it *is* like iron. "Good God," Father says, "you are even more foolish than I thought!"

In the next few weeks, he opens up for Braendel his entire set of contacts—non-profits, wealthy individuals—"deep pockets," foundations, corporations, as well as members of Congress. The communications from Braendel's office, which at first arrive once or twice a week, become more frequent. Dwight now regularly attends Derrick's staff meetings, as if he were a member. When Derrick begins his speaking tour, he invites Dwight to join him.

As he advances to the podium in Albany, he sees spread out before him not an audience, but an electorate. He repeats his little ritual: he will have gone the first half, then a quarter, then an eighth . . . but never reach the goal. "Pillow'd upon my fair love's ripening breast . . . my fair love's ripening breast" . . .

After the mandatory greetings, he proclaims, "Now it is *our* time to remake the world, not in the specter of our disappointing past, but in the vision of our fondest hopes. It is not required of us to settle for less. By acting now, by choosing a man for president, not for the corporations, but of the people, by the people, and for the people, we can help create a world to meet our deepest needs and to achieve our fondest hopes. I give you the next President of the United States, Derrick Braendel!"

The crowd responds; Derrick looks him in the eye, shakes his hand, then mounts the podium—has this little man any chance at all of winning the nomination, much less the election? Has he made a fatal mistake? Sabrina is smiling at him—"Oh, Dwight, how could you be wrong?"

Over the next few months, he appears with Derrick on several television talk shows, and flies to a dozen cities to meet with him— at a Kiwanis club, a chapter of the World Affairs Council, a community council, a rally of the poor. In each city, Braendel insists on learning the local facts, and meeting the community leaders himself. He peppers his speeches with references to "an unfair city tax in Richmond," "the lack of day-care facilities in Detroit," "the harmful teacher-student ratio in the Cleveland schools." In each community, his well-organized supporters go house-to-house soliciting support, signing up the unregistered voters. Working with networks of not-for-profit organizations millions of voters are registered, all committed to Derrick Braendel.

Though the media coverage is, of course, meager, and, for the most part, biased, like an underground river, the campaign begins to pick up support, and in three or four months, as the country sinks further into a new recession, Braendel's ratings shoot up. He now appears to be sweeping over the landscape.

On one trip, Braendel tells him that his websites are being electronically gutted, his most prominent supporters are being selectively investigated for tax fraud, and his office in the Rayburn Building has been bugged. Despite such harassment, his campaign contributions are increasing, as corporations and "deep pocket" donors attempt to cover themselves in the still unlikely event that Braendel might actually win the nomination, and then the presidency?—could the little man do it, is such a thing even conceivable?

Month by month, as Dwight works on the campaign, funding for Stand Up dwindles, and he must scramble to keep its programs in operation as the dreary winter lurches into the new year. As Todd mumbles under his breath, he must cut staff and programs, until in just six months he has only a fraction of his operation left—has he just deliberately destroyed the best thing he ever had? Todd says, "It was your decision, Boss." What was he thinking? Was he just indulging his fantasies, was he just being perverse, was he just bored? The papers carry stories of the latest terrorist attacks and a new U.S. military thrust into Saudi Arabia, but then Derrick's office calls to tell him Braendel has just carried the Indiana primary. Braendel takes a second, a third state—Ohio, Alabama, and then, California.

Outside San Miguel Atalán, the ground suddenly gives way and after a moment of dread, he and Sabrina stand atop a high peak under the stars, as meteors streak the sky. "These are the hands of clocks," Dwight says. Sabrina smiles, her teeth points of light. Behind them, more shadow than image, stands Derrick Braendel.

He continues to rise in the polls, and to take even more primaries. As his potential running mate, he chooses a fence-mending southerner, Senator Allen Barton, and at the convention in Detroit, he wins a slim plurality and the nomination. From Jakarta, where he is on a fact-finding trip for the International Monetary Fund, Dwight sends him a telecom—"CONGRATULATIONS!," signed "STAND UP AND BE COUNTED."

As the presidential race begins in earnest, Derrick continues to gain support. Dwight writes in his journal, "His determined face—principled, ambitious, almost anonymous—seems more like a force of history than the face of a person."

The dollar experiences a huge devaluation in relation to the Euro. Dwight sits having cocktails at the Cosmos Club with Senator Harris. As he raises his glass, Dwight says, "Diminished taxes, an imbalanced trade, a bloated military budget, a still deepening national debt—what did they expect?"

"A textbook of bad economics," Sig agrees. On the walls are former secretaries of state, ambassadors, foreign statesmen; down the hall is an old-fashioned billiards room where the balls continue to clack generations after the last player has left.

"Yes, I can't believe that the dollar will survive yet another round of debts."

"You'd think that the Administration would have been watching the store a little more closely, and yet, the immediacies of greed seem to have overwhelmed its discretion. Consider, for example, the most recent scandal involving our sainted Secretary of Defense."

"Indeed," Dwight says, as he sips his drink. "I think the attacks, now scattered, should focus, and slippage give way to plummet. Is 'plummet' the word we seek?"

"Speaking of plummet, another drink?" He signals to the waiter. "Dwight, I wanted to ask you—have you ever thought of directing the Fund? I've thought for some time now that our putting up an American would make a statement, both of support and, if it were you, it would signal a bold new turn in policy. As you know, Suringar is again speaking fondly of returning to his farm near Utrecht—I think after this latest attack on the dollar, he means it this time—so there might be a possibility. Your image, I needn't tell you, is just what the Fund is looking for—compassionate, competent, American, but clearly internationalist."

"I never imagined . . . I would have to be nominated by the Administration, which . . ." Had Sig rehearsed this little speech?

"Yes, of course, but there *is* the election. . . . Don't think of me as the devil tempting you with the kingdoms of the world."

"No, Sig, as a good friend."

The next day, Dwight calls him up. "I think, yes, if we win in November, you could bruit my name about—I think Stand Up could survive without me."

He walks through the streets of Washington during one of the stifling days of early fall. "Before the war," Father had told him, "the

Brits used to offer their diplomats hardship allowances for working in this town"—shouldn't he be wearing a pith helmet? Yes, he had done enough. Each effort for Stand Up seemed now a repetition— "Stand Up can run itself, or Todd can run it for me," he says aloud. Hadn't he already made the gamble—government and most corporate support for Stand Up had now almost completely dried up. "Have I purposely mined my own road—*was* I just bored?" He flips on the television: Derrick is still trailing with only six weeks to go.

Then, with still another sharp drop in the economy, Derrick starts edging closer. The polls suddenly catch up with the fact that millions of voters they had never bothered to contact had been registered by Braendel's workers in his "People's Campaign." In the last two weeks, corporate money begins pouring in. Even the newspapers, radio stations, and CNN take up the growing momentum, and in the final week, Derrick's victory, though close, seems secure.

November 2nd, and by ten o'clock at night, Braendel has lost. But then the media begin reporting cases in which voting machines in areas favoring Braendel have been stripped of their information— yes, as in Chandler's *The Alzheimer War*. Dwight sits, like everyone in the country, glued to the television as the stories multiply, until it becomes clear that there has been a massive attempt at fraud.

Braendel refuses to concede and takes to the streets, as his organizers create demonstrations at the Washington Mall and in cities all around the country as hundreds of thousands parade with their signs—"We won't take it!" "One, two, three, four; the Republicans are out the door." "Victory, or civil war!" Challenges follow in the courts, and finally, after weeks of litigation, and with the evidence overwhelming, the Supreme Court unexpectedly declares Braendel the winner! Sabrina sits up in bed smiling.

THE MONEY CHANGERS

At the victory reception, Derrick embraces him—"I couldn't have done it without supporters like you." His body is a metal machine, or is it a ticking clock? What is Dwight hearing? At still another reception, which he watches on television, someone is offering Braendel a drink—is it poison?

A week, two weeks, go by, as the walls of Dwight's office at Stand Up close in tighter and tighter. Finally, he receives the call from President-elect Braendel—"Dwight, the United States will officially nominate you to be the next Managing Director of the International Monetary Fund. Our friend, Sig Harris, tells me that Dwight Lockwood would be the ideal candidate—what do you say? Lee Ashworth—he'll be my Secretary of State—thinks you'll be perfect. . . . Can I count on you?"

". . . Of course, I'm flattered."

"Well, what do you say?"

"Could I think it over for a day?"

"Sure, take your time."

Sabrina touches his lips, then seals her approval with her smile—hadn't he already agreed to do it? Dwight gathers Todd and the rest of the Washington staff to announce his decision. Todd makes a little joke, looks down at the floor, then sticks out his hand. "I've guess I've said this a few times before—we're going to miss you, Boss."

He writes in his journal, "How did I think my life would end? In a study alone with my thoughts, with a still unfinished manuscript, or this—the insistent, consuming demands of a position which finally resolves the conflict between art and life—is this what I wanted? Did I have any choice?" Three months later, in a pro forma vote, he is elected Managing Director.

As he enters the IMF building for his first day of work, there is John Maynard Keynes perched on the edge of his desk. He's wearing a three-piece suit, yes, and with a watch chain, as if he were about to address a class at Cambridge. He turns to Dwight with a quizzical expression: "One of the things I seem to remember was our effort at the end of the war to provide the peoples of the world financial support as they strove to improve their lot. Now as I review the operation of the Fund, I'm afraid my original vision has been quite lost—in the shuffle, as it were."

"Yes, yes, I'm handling it now," Dwight says aloud. He checks the recent correspondence, studies the portfolio of loans over the last forty years, reviews current staff studies, calls in analysts and regional directors. His meetings now with the financially powerful G7 group will be crucial, as they hold a controlling fifty-three percent of the voting rights.

"Can we agree to test the new policy for the next two years?" he asks the French representative, M. Lefèvre, who has already gone on record speaking against it.

"Ah, you really mean to do this."

"We will simply be testing a policy, not installing it. Once we have the results, you will, of course, have the option of discontinuing it, or," he smiles, "of continuing it."

Just as M. Lefèvre seems about to raise the same objections, he notices Maillol's *"Isle de France,"* which is standing in Dwight's office on a small pedestal in a cylinder of overhead light. Lefèvre sits smiling at the statue, and says nothing. . . . Finally, as if almost to himself, he mutters, "Well, yes, why not?"

After conferring with each representative of the G7 group, Dwight gains a limited acceptance for temporarily dropping the "Washington consensus." He then calls a formal meeting of the Fund's Board of Governors to pass on his "experiment." He scans the delegates' faces—white, brown, black—the majority from the developing world, whose weightless votes hardly count. He looks up—no predatory birds soar overhead; he clears his throat, and begins, thanking the delegates for their support, providing a few expected anecdotes, before getting to the substance: "The world economy is in a crisis, which demands that we test a new approach. We cannot rely on the same measures which we have employed for the last four decades. Today I ask your approval for a period of two years to undergo an experiment. I ask for a suspension of disbelief, if that is your present feeling, but more, I ask for your wholehearted support as we put this policy into practice and test its worth. . . ."

"Yes, indeed," Keynes intones, and then almost coyly bats his eyelids. A polite applause catches here and there in the audience like the beginnings of a fire, then dies. Little groups of delegates stand chattering in the aisles. On the formal vote, a number of delegates from the third world actually abstain, but Dwight gains the votes he needs from the G7 delegates to launch the plan. . . . The next day, *The Wall Street Journal* reads, "Lockwood's clearly proven administrative abilities provide some hope that his experiment, whatever its merits, may succeed in achieving at least a portion of its promise."

Jan Suringar, the outgoing director, stops him in the hall. "Before I leave, I should like to provide you with one last bit of advice."

"I fully appreciate the advice you have already . . ."

"To be blunt, in your position, Dr. Lockwood, you will need to employ a bodyguard. Let me recommend my Bill Miller—he's proven his worth over many years."

"Do you really believe a bodyguard is necessary? I wouldn't have thought . . ."

"Trust me, he is. . . . You can ask a member of my staff to call Mr. Miller in for an interview at your convenience."

That afternoon there stands before him a hulk of a man, with a face which seems less features than muscle, with straight brown hair which spikes over his forehead, eyes which flit back and forth. Dwight, of course, has already reviewed his file: in his late thirties, an ex-Marine, a graduate of the University of Nebraska, with fifteen years of experience, and a series of commendations. "Sure, that's my job," Miller says, "but maybe I should spell it out: I'm your bodyguard, but I'm also around if you need me for anything else— remember, you can always count on me, okay? Course, you've got my résumé—what else? I have a wife, named Emily, and two children, named Leo and Violet—we all live in Chevy Chase. . . . Oh, you should also know—I don't know why, but I'm proud of it—a million years ago, I played left tackle for the University of Nebraska and won a Mid-West Best Player Award. . . . I guess—it's your reputation— you'll probably want to know what I read. Old mysteries, I'm afraid. Tony Hillerman's my favorite, and then, ah, John Grisham?"

"Do you like television?"

"Oh, you wouldn't want to know the junk I see; not you, Dr. Lockwood."

Dwight sits with Bill and Sabrina on the plane to Dakar—Senegal will be the first "client" state he will visit for the "Lockwood Plan." Bill says, "I've been here before—it can get a bit nasty. You okay with that, Dr. Lockwood?" As Dwight takes notes on a staff report, Bill sits across the aisle reading a beat-up copy of Tony Hillerman.

At the airport, the Economics Minister stands waiting for them. After what must be the customary, effusive French greeting, they are ushered into a limousine which will take them to the ministry. As they enter the city, the road is blocked by a crowd of motley dressed young people with signs, bullhorns, and placards. Some of the demonstrators are hooded in shrouds, or wear lion or bear masks; others have painted their faces in lurid reds and greens. "One, two, three, four, the IMF's a fucking whore! One, two, three, four, the IMF is out the door!" Dwight feels the skin on his face contract as the demonstrators press against the police, who, armed with tear gas, clubs, water cannons, and guns, now surround the car. Bill, seated next to Dwight, nervously scans the crowd, his hand on his '45.

Dwight stares at the screen of his hand-held computer which shows the very scene he is in: a city whose buildings and streets look like the interior of the computer itself, with its chips and circuits.

Taken by the Senegalese security police from a helicopter, the scale diminishes, as the helicopter swoops down to become the crowd of demonstrators with their signs and drums.

Dwight opens the car door and steps out. "God, don't do that!" Bill shouts, but then they are surrounded by the demonstrators. Bill is standing by his side, as Dwight shouts in French: "I am Dwight Lockwood—I am the new managing director of the International Monetary Fund."

"Why are you exposing yourself?" Sabrina snaps. "Are you still trying to die?" The horns blow, the chants go on for a minute or two more, but then the crowd quiets. "I am here in Dakar not to continue policies of the Fund which you rightly point out have created distress in your country. No, I am here to return the Fund to its original purpose—to reduce the economic stress of market changes and to put money into the hands of the poor." Is anyone listening?

"When I took office, I asked the directors of the Fund for two years to institute a new program, and I was granted those two years. I asked this of your country representative on the Fund, and now I ask this of you. Give me these two years. All I ask is that you give this new policy a chance. Our aim is to help. And we will. We will!" The crowd does not clap or cheer, but one young man in a lion mask shakes his hand.

In each country—Colombia, the Philippines, Malaysia, he is protected not by the police but ultimately by the protestors themselves. In each country, the central bank representatives are virtually the same, dressed in the same suits, speaking the same language. They are diffident, guarded—each assumes that Dwight's pronouncements will make no difference, that the policies of the Fund will remain unaltered—*bien entendue*. They are the publicans—the Roman soldiers dressed in togas and short swords who protect them against the mob.

Day after day, in the right-wing press and in some pointed private correspondence, he is an "agitator, no better than the mob of anarchists and wild-eyed idealists who applaud him in the streets." "How can such a man gain the confidence of the international financial community?" "The streets may be reduced to chaos, but at the apex of the financial world there needs to be order and good sense."

He orders his chief staff aide, a young blond woman named Barbara Helmholtz, to do a quick study for his critics of the first trial countries. After a week, she stands in front of his desk with a portfolio: "We've gone through the indices. Truth is, Dr. Lockwood, so far we are having only a marginal effect." She is strikingly beautiful as they sit in his office drawing up a new set of conditions for the IMF to advance funds. She arches her back as she tilts her head to suggest stricter auditing procedures, the threat of the suspension of loans unless they are met—no, he will do nothing.

At an embassy reception in Washington, he tells Chandler Ellis, "The more I work at this job, the more the world seems reduced to economic data—even the demonstrations seem like digital creations, just as you depict in your poems."

"'The Epic of Dwight Lockwood,'" Chandler quips, and then recedes into the swish and swirl of the party—had he actually spoken to Chandler? At another turn, Sabrina is standing by the bar—each time a hooded waiter fills her glass, she drinks it down.

Dwight weaves his way through his guests, greeting each one by name, crafting his comments to indicate that no, he has not become a tool of the Left, no, he has not deserted his establishment friends—the new policy is just an experiment, and its continuation will rely upon evaluations which are just now coming in—no, he is not yet ready to report the results. The music plays, the talk continues, until the party winds down to the moment when a few distinguished guests, who had come, despite his "alliance with the streets," signal it is over—he can measure his diminished prestige to the minute by how soon they leave.

After the guests have fallen asleep in chairs, on couches, and on the floor, alley cats emerge out of holes and crannies, and then are standing at the bar drinking down their cocktails. Again as he stands before her, he asks Sabrina to marry him; her gown falls away and on her bare back are the lurid red circles. . . . A buzzer is sounding—it's five o'clock. After Manuel brings in his coffee and he's read the papers, he will review Todd Jacobs' monthly report on Stand Up and Be Counted.

With a small majority in Congress, President Braendel proposes the first shift toward more progressive taxation in forty years. In the next months, the little man stands in a hundred venues raising his fist, initiating his program which now draws comparison with Roosevelt's "hundred days." Yes, the little man had come through—he had matched his promises with action.

From the press, his policies draw a sniping incredulity, punctuated by phrases like "leftist," "liberal," "off the page," "twentieth century." In interviews, Dwight, taking the stance of an independent expert, finds the policies "refreshing," "constructive," a "breath of fresh air after years of stagnant thinking." "Isn't it clear," he asks a crowd in Dallas, "after over a decade of failed policies, we need to reassert the responsibility of the federal government for the welfare of our citizens?"—the cameras just stare at him as if they were as incredulous as the people behind them.

A summons from the White House: Derrick sits not behind his desk, but directly across from him leaning forward in his chair. "How can our domestic programs be further in sync with your policies at the Fund?"

Dwight smiles. "Or ours with yours?"

"I'm glad we're working together," Derrick says, and for a moment this engine becomes sweet, almost flirtatious—"You are everything I had hoped for"—as if he were a sixteen-year-old on his first date. The moment passes—once again, he is all business.

They discuss the effects of the Fund's programs on the international economy, as well as its domestic effects, then an outbreak of violence in Kashmir as once again the armies of India and Pakistan mass at the border, the tension over oil in the Caspian Sea, the move of the European Union and China to compete with the United States in putting their own weapons into outer space. . . . A *tour d'horizon*, it covers every aspect of U.S. foreign policy, rather than focusing on international economics. At the end, his eyes widen: "I can't tell you how much I've enjoyed this, Dwight. You are always such a pleasure to talk to. This job—what can I say—it's what I always wanted, and now I feel so alone, as if I will never talk to anyone again as a human being." He stands up, puts out his hand.

Dwight is released into the saturated Washington air. Yes, for those thirty-two minutes, he'd had the "ear of the President." The crickets chirp, flowers slowly open; Sabrina, in her high heels, walks a few feet in front of him. . . . He is again in front of Derrick as ideas spring up like Heinrich's atoms: they collide, cohere, form molecules, then organize into organisms, societies, planets, solar systems. He writes in his journal, "Can the immanent God be reduced to a set of mathematical formulas which subtly guide each particle into increasing complexity? Is the world we know, even with all its imperfections, the work of divine providence?" Yes, these would have been just the questions to ask Derrick. . . . Bill says, "Let me take your coat, boss."

The phone rings—it's Barbara Helmholtz: "We've got a crisis which demands an immediate response. The Senegalese economy has collapsed overnight, and without immediate help, several million people will be without any resources—the crisis is spreading to other countries!" For the next seven hours, he is on the phone, he is dictating e-mails, and in digital meetings with colleagues in half a dozen financial institutions, as piece by piece he constructs a response. As he walks home at one o'clock that night, the pillared buildings of the city, which line the boulevards, shine in the darkness—Washington could be ancient Egypt, and these the pillared streets of Luxor or Thebes—the nearest star falls below the horizon. As he goes on walking, he is in the streets of Dakar as they begin again to fill with demonstrators in lion masks and painted faces—his semen has penetrated into thousands of homes—the young toughs are his children.

Another vapid reception, and then a long dinner with Mildred in which she continually presses him for details of his conversations with economic ministers, with officials in the U.S. government.

"Mildred, this is what I talk about all day; can't you see I need to speak of something else, anything?" She moves closer to him and places her hand on his thigh. He gets up, and makes himself a drink; can he go on seeing her after this?

Soon he will take a break to climb in the Andes with Heinrich and now, of course, Bill—"Hey, I've never done it before, but I can learn." As they fly to Lima, he writes, "For a week, he will once again become what he had always wanted to be, a disembodied soul without time or place—is this what the Brahmin sought?"

As they approach the mountain site, police and medical trucks pass them on the road. Several thousand feet further up, the snows have melted, and a peak has been uncovered, revealing an airplane and passengers that crashed and disappeared thirty years ago. Now they watch the ski patrols carrying down canvas bags with the preserved corpses removed from the precariously perched plane. He writes, "Will the bodies awake, and begin again their interrupted lives, or have they already entered the timeless realm of the dead?"

"Why doesn't the universe dissolve into chaos?" Heinrich asks. "Why has it shown the order, however uneven, of the creation?" His face slowly dissolves into microdots. . . . Dwight is sleeping next to Sabrina on the floor of the schoolhouse in Nicaragua—she has moved her gently breathing body against his. He wakes up on the mountain top in Peru. Nearby Heinrich sits in his sleeping bag quietly smoking his pipe.

* * * * *

A few months later, Beautiful Barbara bursts into his office, a sheath of papers in her hand: "The indices are all up. Our clients are now clearly stabilizing their economies, and even showing some growth. I think, Herr Doktor, we have, as they say, turned a corner."

As Dwight is reviewing Barbara's prepared press release, the television flashes news that war has broken out in Kashmir! Yes, as he had discussed with Derrick, the Paks and Indians had been exchanging territorial claims, dire threats, rumblings of military movements, just as they had for decades, but now, without warning, a limited exchange suddenly turns to full-scale war, as nuclear rockets rain down on both sides.

Hour by hour, he follows the war's progress on his special line, until the UN Secretary General, with the support of the U.S., China, and the European Union, patches together a cease-fire, and then a truce. He flies to Islamabad to discuss how the Fund can help in the reconstruction. Two days later, he is in New Delhi holding the same conversations.

Then he is donning a radiation resistant suit and is being flown by helicopter to one of the blast areas. As he walks through the streets, there is simply nothing left—no mourning, no ruins; the buildings have simply vaporized, the bodies disappeared into radioactive particles—all forms have been obliterated—the world has returned to its primal state of chaos. The statesmen, the diplomats on both sides have lost their bellicose tone, and now seem almost embarrassed, as if they had carelessly run over an animal in the road. "Ten or fifteen million, more or less"—Father smirks, his very sound seems frozen in time. He writes in his journal, "Millions of years pass, as life slowly develops into the very species which once were destroyed. Will nothing change, if the conditions appear again to produce exactly the world he knew? If time is infinite, would not a moment come exactly like the one which has just passed, and the world resume exactly the forms it had? Is the infinite of the Brahmin any solace for the tragedy of finite life?"

"How'd you sleep last night?" Bill asks. "Boy, I slept like a stone!"

Dwight takes another sip of coffee, and for just a moment, before he is swept with revulsion, he looks longingly at Bill. "Yeah, I know what you're thinking—of India and, uh, Pakistan, of all those people hit by nukes. I just talked to Emily—we always thought when we died we'd have a lot of time to think about it, and get ready, but what if we didn't?"

Weeks pass, then still another outbreak of violence in the Middle East—a spate of bus bombings by terrorists, a retaliatory razing of a Palestinian village. What is happening? Why now, like a disease, is the world being swept by violence? He is on his way to Israel, and then to Cairo and Tehran. He sits in the hollowed space of a Boeing 792 as he goes through his papers with his aides—Bill sits across the aisle reading *Sports Illustrated*—and then Dwight is just staring into the opacity of the window.

The seat belt signs flash, the plane begins its descent. At the airport, a banner reads, "FATHER IS DEAD." His bloated form is laid out on a gurney, his face turned to yellow wax. A bank of reporters waits for Dwight's statement—will he be judicious, will he be fair? Will he praise Father's dedication, his tireless energy, his inventive use of language? Dwight is screaming, "He was a brute, he sucked all the air out of the room, he sacrificed millions for his own power!" Sabrina's hair is coiling like the ringlets of a Botticelli angel. . . . As he wakes up, the plane is just landing at the airport in Tel Aviv.

In Jerusalem, the officials at the Ministry of Finance are cordial, technical, yet with a sinking sense of despair. The Arab countries are gaining strength, and now, in the case of Iran and Egypt, are armed for the first time with nuclear weapons and intermediate range missiles—can the standoff be continued, or has time finally run out? Dwight e-mails Washington, temporarily suspending the Fund's loans to both sides until there is more clarification, but the issues are political, not economic. Is there any way he can reach Derrick, or Lee Ashworth? What can he possibly say that has not been said a hundred times before? Father tells his joke again: "'Will there ever be peace in the Middle East?' 'No,' the Lord says, 'not in my lifetime.'" Father is a penis, two feet high. Dwight sits on the ground so he can talk to him at eye level. "Excuse me for asking," he says to Father, "but do you have a spine?" Dwight's hand ventures out to touch it. He feels a ridge of bone, and then a surge of pollution in his hand.

UN mediation diffuses the immediate tension, and the two sides back away. After conferring with Cairo and Tehran, Dwight returns to Israel for a last meeting with the Finance Ministry. As the meeting ends, Dwight says, "We hope, as the situation stabilizes, that we will be able to provide the funds you are seeking." The minister pledges to make a preliminary proposal. Dwight gathers together his papers. "That's it, Bill. . . . Listen, we've got a few unexpected days—maybe, we could just take off and see a bit of the Holy Land."

"Do you mean it? Oh, my God—I never expected. I never thought I'd get to see where he really lived—wait till I tell Emily!"

They hire a car, and then their Israeli guide is driving them into the Galilee. The car pushes through patchy grey-brown hills with outcroppings of rocks, an occasional shepherd tending sheep or goats, then through layered towns of white-washed houses. The sun has broken through the clouds, illuminating still another range of hills. There in the distance is Nazareth.

As they walk around the sleepy village, he says to Sabrina, "I know, darling, you would have wanted to be here." She says nothing; she is hovering above him in a private space. "I'll write you a letter, just as I did in Russia—is that all right?"

Doggedly, he begins to write: "As I walked about Nazareth, I thought to myself, he would have been one of several brothers, doing odd jobs for his putative father, the carpenter, Joseph; but then, Sabrina, I could actually see him—his eyes were naïve and yet preternaturally intelligent, like the eyes of Mozart or of Durer's squirrels. I wanted to ask him, what was quickening inside him, what new sense which would lead him to think that the Kingdom of God was at hand—or that it was in him?" . . . Bill walks around mumbling, "My God, my God, this is where he really was!"

"Here, Sabrina, he appeared before Peter. Here is where he walked on the water, over the gleaming fish, the sun so bright, how could one tell the surface from the deep?" The car climbs into the arid hills. "Imagine, a man who would be God, or at least his messenger, and who actually knows he is going to die for it."

Sabrina is reading his letter as he travels through the Galilee, as he journeys south to see Masada. The vast fortress rises over the land like a sentinel, as the Romans move up their battering rams to the base of the walls, and the Jewish defenders prepare to die. Dwight and Bill walk through the gutted chambers, with their faint echoes of life, then descend the thousand feet to the plain beneath to begin their trip back to Jerusalem.

He sits in his hotel—"Outside the window is the Old City— white walls of fitted stone, the Mount of Solomon's Temple lit by floodlights. In the stone streets I heard the ancient call of longing, 'If I forget Thee, O Jerusalem.'"

As he falls asleep, the bed has become a long, narrow box which looks like a casket. From a point high above it, he tries to drive it through a crowd of masked youth protesting the International Monetary Fund. . . . "The next morning, our car took us to Yad Vashem, the Museum of the Holocaust. On the walls were black-and-white photographs, some sharply focused, others overblown and granular. Image built on image as if the camera were an unbelieving spectator. Sabrina, I saw photos of fear-stricken shopkeepers, rabbis, the blank eyes of children, legal decrees in bizarre Gothic script, reinvented ghettos, the boxcars, the crematoria, the gas chambers, naked women huddled with their hands over their breasts and geni-tals, piles of corpses—like a brakeless car plunging down a hill. I said to myself, I don't have to see this, I can leave.

"Then like the first, furtive mammals in the age of dinosaurs, I saw the Jewish resisters as they huddled and plotted around tables in dimly lit bunkers and basements. The S.S. was closing in. Were we there, Sabrina? Were we Jews of the Holocaust? Two women, wearing berets and the big-shouldered jackets of that day, young and unbowed, were photographed by their Gestapo cap-tors. Were you one of them, Sabrina? Wouldn't you have been one of the resisters?

"So few escaped. So many died against the walls, in the snow, in the gas chambers, or, yes, my darling, they were disappeared. In my imagination, I saw the sun rise over the winter-locked lands and abandoned camps—Treblinka, Belsen, Dachau, Auschwitz— over the sidings, the barbed-wire fences, as you wandered with your staring eyes through the gutted streets of an unknown city.

"The God of history, the judge, the so-called protector? That God had no role here. He was a character in a play who never appeared.

Then why is He even listed in the program? Why, Sabrina, must we pray to Him, why must we even think of Him?

"Even now, music stirred. I asked, if only you were here, like the soft receiving earth, to mourn and bless and hold the dead. If only in the night you were here by my side, as the one enduring opposition to emptiness, to affirm eternally what has been achieved of beauty or of moral worth. If only . . ." He stops in the middle of the street.

"We wandered about the city in widening circles until we found ourselves in East Jerusalem at a demonstration—Bill was nervously holding his pistol which was discreetly hidden in his jacket. Fifty, sixty Jewish women dressed in black were displaying signs in English, Hebrew, and Arabic: "STOP THE OCCUPATION!" "FIFTY YEARS IS ENOUGH!" "TWO STATES FOR TWO NATIONS!" On the edges, a group of men pushed the women and shouted insults.

"I found a demonstrator, with short bobbed hair and rimless glasses, who spoke English. 'What are those men saying?' I asked her.

"'They say, you Jewish women here make love with Arabs, that we are prostitutes, that we are traitors, that we are, how do you say, Palestinian *nikim*, Arab people.'

"'And the men?' I asked, 'who are they?'

"'They are Kach, they work for the rightists.' Then a Jewish woman was hit in the eye with a stone; she was screaming in pain as they carried her away. Now I saw the red Mogen Davids on the men's t-shirts.

"A tear gas canister exploded, then several more. The police hustled ten, fifteen, twenty women into trucks. I looked for the woman with the bobbed hair, but she had disappeared. In ten minutes the street was clear, as if the demonstration had never occurred. Sabrina, I saw us running from the police as the tear gas canisters exploded behind us, then ducking into a doorway, and holding each other, just as if we were together in Nicaragua, or Guatemala."

"The next morning, we began our last day. From the balcony overlooking Jerusalem, dark birds swooped and turned in the silver air, while you slept in our hotel room. A brief walk, and there before us like a blunt, opening statement, rose Jerusalem's ancient walls.

"We stood with a group of tourists on the Temple Mount. Two mosques gleamed: the silver-domed al-Aqsa and, facing it, the Dome of the Rock in brilliant gold. On the stone square, groups of tourists, under constraint by testy Israeli police armed with Uzis, left piles of shoes and cameras before entering.

"Inside, they stood by the side of the faithful, who prostrated themselves on rugs. The legend says this is the place where God told Abraham to sacrifice Isaac. In Rembrandt's drawing, I remember Abraham standing convulsed with grief, his knife suspended over his still believing son bound to the stone—he was about to tear out his son's heart at God's command."

"As the light was just beginning to fade, we entered the Christian Quarter. It was the last entry on our agenda—the Stations of the Cross, the Via Dolorosa. We stood in the courtyard where supposedly he was condemned. There with his unblinking eyes he faced his accusers; I could almost imagine them wearing the t-shirts with the red Mogen David. They were taunting him, they were calling for his death. Yes, the events he had anticipated were actually happening. Why was he so calm? 'Yes, I am He,' he said to them. 'I am the One.'

"They were waiting for him to beg, or try to make a deal. They shuffled their feet, they looked at each other. He said, 'Tomorrow you will be here, but I will not, and then you will gnash your teeth and rend your garments.' Angels swooped and passed overhead like helicopters, but he didn't call them.

"At the next station, he was flogged by brutish Roman soldiers. The pain was intense, but it must have come from somewhere else, from the body which refused to desert him. Nearby from a balcony, Pontius Pilate looked down and scoffed.

"He fell to his knees, surprised, as if he had suffered an attack. The women helped him up. There was Mother; there you were, Sabrina—you were there helping him. A man he didn't know carried his cross. Mother wiped his face with a cloth. He was losing track of time. Again he was on the ground; the pain from the beating seemed even more distant. Why were these people so concerned? Again, he had fallen.

"We entered the Church of the Holy Sepulcher, which wavered in the gloom of incense and grease-laden dust, as if we were swimming into a sunken ship. Priests and acolytes lurked in the shadows. Every cranny harbored crypts and shrines, lurid crucifixes, inept paintings, silver hearts. A guide told us about the Church's present division between Franciscans, Greeks, Armenians, Orthodox, Coptics, Ethiopians—all were fighting for space and rights.

"At the entrance to the Franciscan Chapel, he was stripped of his clothes. At the far end, he was nailed to the cross. His palms bled. . . . But then the church disappeared, and I saw the cross, his slight body on the hill of Golgotha—had he been murdered by his Father? It was clear that nothing of the sort had happened. He was there because of events he had put in motion himself. *He* had decided to enter Jerusalem, *he* had determined to be in this place, to risk his life for what he believed, and he was paying the consequences for his own decision. Father had left, with all his anger and prerogatives, putting himself forever out of reach—now, at last, he was truly alone. And then he fell through the hole."

"I've got to go!" he yells to Bill. He runs from the church. He's dead! He's dead! "The sun had already set, the sky was just turning from purple to black. The first few stars were out."

At the airport, he calls Mother in Sudan, and receives permission to speak to her. The phone crackles with static. ". . . just for a moment, to hear your voice. . . . No, no, I am fine. . . . All the places Jesus had been—how wonderful! . . . My work, so many sick . . . starving, terrible wounds we treat. . . . The tribes, sometimes the armies from the north. . . . I'm all right, Dwight. The Lord is with me. . . . So good to hear your voice."

"Be careful. Don't stay if the situation becomes too dangerous."

"I must do, I . . . what the Lord tells me, Dwight. . . . Goodbye, my son, goodbye." He puts down the phone. Bill signals to him: their flight is being called. On the plane, he reads stories in the *Jerusalem Post* of a new outbreak of hostilities in the Occupied Territories, menacing statements from the governments in Tehran and Cairo. Bill taps him on the shoulder. "Would you like a sleeping pill?"

"No, thanks, Bill." The night stares with the great eye of a predatory bird.

In Washington, Dwight makes his first phone call to the Fund office, and asks the chauffeur to pick him up in half an hour. . . . He continues to walk through the streets of Jerusalem filled with Hasids, housewives, American tourists, Arabs, soldiers—on the ramparts, clouds move over the city like dark angels. He writes, "When it was his time, did he want to go? When he entered Jerusalem with his prescient knowledge, was he ready? Was it only to create community with humankind that he pretended at the end to care, or was there truly something here which drew him? Surely, there were moments when it must have seemed like pure ritual, his riding in on a colt, his discussions with Pontius Pilate, even his assumption of the cross. And yet, he went through with it.

"What else could he have done in this life, than what he did? What else could he have done, except perhaps to write the very books which others wrote about him, and imagine in the quiet of his study a preacher born to simple parents, yes, to a carpenter in a provincial town, who, infused with divine energy, heals the sick, turns water to wine, raises the dead, and asks what is here for us to do but make straight the path, to prepare the Kingdom?"

* * * * *

The results come in as confident statements by administration officials, as rises in the Dow, as diminishing unemployment figures, then as articles in the *Post* and *Times,* and discussions on the talk shows. As he walks into a meeting of his Board of Directors, his "clients" sit before him in their impeccable suits like children beneath a Christmas tree.

At his parties, the guests stay longer—the word has been passed: he has won the tentative approval of the financial community. Editorials, even in the *Wall Street Journal* or *Washington Weekly,* now find Fund policies "closely followed by those of the Braendel Administration, the needed, if temporary measures which the current crisis has imposed." . . . In St. John's Hospital, Chandler Ellis lies dying of cancer.

When Dwight shakes Braendel's hand, it still feels like metal. "Treasury tells me your policies are working, and, of course, I read your praises in the press every day. Bravo, Dwight!"

"Bravo, Derrick, for all you have done for the country!" For a moment Derrick glows in the light not of his success, but of his determination. . . . Chandler's cancer is metastasizing with terrible speed.

Then Derrick asks him, "What do you think of these new attacks in the Middle East—are we into still another war?" The mandatory "light moment" has passed. Derrick also brings up the new missile deployment by the Chinese in the Taiwan Straits, the European Union's military missions around the Caspian Sea, and the move of the E.U. and China to compete with the United States in weaponizing outer space. Why in each meeting does he bring up such topics, and not just the economic issues? Is Derrick just seeking another opinion, or has he really some other motive?

As he walks through the halls of St. John's Hospital, Dwight passes a series of listless bodies in a field of white, as if life were losing its color. Chandler's body lies emaciated between the sheets, his skin pale, his eyes alternating between vague and unfocused, and hard and glittering—his bed has already been transformed into a casket.

"Chandler, it's Dwight. . . . I'm just back from the Middle East."

Chandler jokes about the distressing accommodations—"I'm afraid there's no brandy I can offer you."

"Your company will more than suffice," Dwight says, but then he sees that Chandler has forgotten he is there.

He visits him every day, as the cancer closes in, until a week later, Chandler lies grey, almost lifeless. "No, I do not want this to happen," he mutters. His body begins to contract, his words to speed up. "I wanted to write forever, I wanted to write a continuous accompaniment for humankind, now, and in the future, in times I can't even imagine . . . with cities glittering in the glow of information"—Dwight takes his hand—"with human beings and nanorobots . . . the soft glow of intelligence, like the first . . . like the first sunshine, the first sunshine on the waters. . . . I wanted to write . . ." A few minutes later, as Dwight continues to hold his hand, Chandler dies, as his intelligence fades from his mind, as it dissolves into molecules, then into atoms, particles. Dwight stands again over the dying soldier in Nicaragua: "So that is how it happens, as simply, as quietly as this."

He scans his e-mail, dictates notes into his voice-computer, reads the *Times*, the *Post,* the *Wall Street Journal*, studies a report on the economic effects of the new interest rates, another criticizing "the destructive policies of the Fund." He takes notes, prepares for the forthcoming meeting with his staff.

Barbara appears—"Yes, yes, I am again the bearer of bad news— I have to tell you, Herr Doktor, we have a problem in Africa. I am afraid that some of our clients are not as sweet as they appear. You know that default on our loans? I think it's a fabrication—I think we are dealing with the connivance of a New York bank, or, may I say, even the CIA?"

Dwight looks through the papers, and yes, again it seems that Beautiful Barbara is right. He will fly directly to Nairobi, and ask some tough questions. Again he dreams of predatory birds—he wakes up—hasn't he had enough of such fantasies? . . . He is sitting with Mother at Bergdorf Goodman waiting for her to emerge from the dressing room in a new creation. Birds are flying in and out of the racks of dresses and furs—she stands in a slip, her feet naked. He is holding up to her his weekly bouquet of flowers. As he wakes up again, he asks himself, why hadn't he seen her all these years? Had he just placed her in his past, and let her dissolve?

He asks an assistant to call her clinic and make the arrangements: a small plane will take them after the meetings in Nairobi to

Bentu on the bank of the Bahr el-Ghazal River where she has been all these years.

Again, he and Bill, and always Sabrina, are flying over a bank of clouds. The first night in Nairobi, he attends a reception at the home of one of the IMF delegates: a sumptuous house, a badminton court, a swimming pool overhung with bougainvillea. Monkeys swing in the trees on the edge of the compound as the moon and stars fill the clear night sky. In a stilted British accent, his host tells him of his still colonial style of life, of big game hunting, parachute gliding, of taking his private plane to a mountain plateau to watch herds of elephants—"I should say, it's not all bad here, as primitive as it might seem." The reception goes on for hours, as Dwight tunes his ear for telling financial gossip, picking up still more hints of collusion between some governments and the banks.

The next day, the Economics Minister tells him, "Ah, you should know the words of such people are like birds, Dr. Lockwood. They fly into the blue sky, and you cannot catch them." In another meeting, a bank president lowers his voice, and accuses the Economics Minister of engineering the suspicious default for his own profit—Dwight writes his report to the Board, pulls back several loans, while indicating that he has uncovered only the most superficial levels of still deeper deceits, which may, in the end, elude analysis.

Then he and Bill and Sabrina are flying over the swamps of Southern Sudan. They land at a crude airport thirty kilometers from Mother's clinic. As Dwight steps off the plane in the stifling heat—it is 120 degrees—adolescents, dressed in t-shirts and blue jeans and carrying AKs and Kalashnikovs, are eying him curiously—they must be part of the Sudan People's Liberation Army.

John Deng, the aged rebel leader, steps up to greet him. Once he had been a large, robust man with a round head and twinkling eyes; now after four decades of fighting the Islamic government in the north, his limbs have shriveled, his eyes recede into his skull. Yes, he understands, Dwight is not here on official business—he will not discuss any of his issues with Khartoum. "No," Deng says, "I fully understand your purpose in seeing your mother without distraction," and then he modestly retires.

As Dwight waits for their jeep and their bilingual driver, he sees small tents on the edge of the field made of stretched skin or fabric. Under their folds, or listlessly playing in the dirt, are children with pencil-thin arms and legs, whose skin hangs from their bodies, their eyes and noses swarming with mosquitoes. Bare-chested women follow him holding out their hands for alms.

As they drive by a food station, still more women with bowls and plastic sacks wait for the supply plane which may or may not arrive that day from Nairobi. An incredibly tall man walks across the road with high cheekbones and a t-shirt which says "Joe's Restaurant, Omaha, Nebraska." Emaciated cattle with lyre-shaped horns glide through the gutted streets of the town. A prophet in cotton robes wanders past with scarred ridges across his forehead, pink flowers behind his ears, as he sings and gestures—their driver says that God is the "spirit of the air" who takes possession of such men and makes them prophets.

The people they pass—the driver reels off a long string of tribal names—are all fleeing from the marauding bands, and the recent famine. The road parallels the grey-green Bahr el-Ghazal; Dwight sees the bloated corpses, dead cows, pelicans, crested cranes, a speckled vulture on a prow of a wrecked boat—yes, just as he had dreamed.

They arrive just before sunset at the clinic of St. Francis of the Meek. For a moment, Dwight looks up at the trees which seem to rise from the floor of the forest and then angle up into the sky to form an irregular white knot—again, the vision he'd first had in prison, and then in the hotel in Cambridge when he was with Stand Up and Be Counted. Mother waits on the wooden porch of the main building with a tall, bearded monk, who must be Father Antonius.

Although she is close to seventy, Mother is still exquisitely beautiful. The air is a symphony of bird cries, as the violet ball of the sun slips through the tall trees. Waiting patiently in line before the clinic—they must have been waiting there all day—are thirty or forty people, some clearly sick or starving, others with missing limbs, ugly wounds.

A thin smile is on Mother's lips, and her eyes are opened wide, as if she were gazing over the face of the waters—shouldn't he have known this is the life she would choose? They embrace; then with lowered eyes, she says to Brother Antonius, "This is my son."

"You may speak, Sister Lockwood has received permission for your visit." Thunder rumbles as Dwight sees the first flashes of lightning.

When they are finally alone, Mother's face tenses; she stands for a few minutes in silence. "I . . . I am so glad you've come. . . . For years, I . . . I wanted to be alone just with God, and . . . with the necessary indifference I suppose which this must have meant for you, for which now I am so sorry. . . . I am not speaking well, I have little practice here, and I have only a short dispensation. . . . I wanted to see you, and, and if I saw you, I needed to speak." Suddenly, she takes his hand, and draws him to her. He is unable to say anything at all—she stands in the stasis of time.

Brother Antonius reappears to show them a metal-sided building where he and Bill will sleep, the switch for the battery-driven lights, the outhouse, the well, while Mother stands silently by his side. An hour later, before they will retire, Mother says as if for the first time, or is it the last? "I love you, Dwight." Then he stops, and turns her head, and from the bottom of his being wells up pure grief— "Mother, Mother!"

In the cool night air, as he lies under the mosquito net, the birds still chirp and sing. . . . He and Bill are flying in a small plane through the clouds which hover just over the trees, as sometimes the faces of Mother, or Sabrina, congeal into images, then dissolve.

He awakes to the cry of roosters, the croaking of frogs. At the clinic, he watches Mother assist at an operation of a boy who has had both his hands chopped off with a machete in a raid by a paramilitary group. Mother stands as if for communion, holding the scalpel and the stitching as a German doctor sews up the wounds. Outside the line of sick and wounded shuffles forward—Sabrina is operating at San Miguel Acatán, her image almost obliterated in the lights over the operating table.

"Now," Mother says after the operation, "we have only a few minutes, and then, I . . . cannot speak." Tears are in her eyes. "It is time now." He waits for her to say goodbye; he looks down to see her gnarled hands.

The air is damp; it will rain soon again. Mother's shape lifts away from the portrait on the living room wall. For a moment he holds her, or she him, until he can feel no shape nor mass, until she dissolves into the blue sky. . . . The sun suddenly breaks out over the forest as they ride to the airfield, and then he sits with Bill and Sabrina in the private plane which will take them back to Nairobi.

The images of Mother and Nairobi slowly fade as he renews his Washington life, and his duties at the Fund. As the election moves closer, the bitterness against President Braendel intensifies—despite the economic recovery, or perhaps because of it. In op-eds, on talk shows, the conservative ideologues appear to Dwight as angry, dismissive, arrogant, more like thugs than discussants, as their candidates and representatives in Congress raise increasingly dangerous amounts of money.

"By our deeds you shall know us"—there is Derrick on the television screen shouting to a working class crowd in Cleveland. "Think where we were four years ago, and think where we are now. Do we want to go back to those days? Do we want to put into office the people who will take us back? Or do we want to keep in office the people who have delivered the goods, and who will go on delivering the goods for another four years? *By our deeds you shall know us!*" The crowd roars.

Afterwards, a group of analysts sit around a table on a television talk show accusing President Braendel of "demagoguery," of "Leftism," of "shameless appeals to the street." In sync with the Federal Reserve, Dwight calls in Beautiful Barbara, and lowers still further the interest rates on IMF loans.

Now the opposition accuses Derrick of accepting bribes from the steel workers union when he was a congressman; repeats the charge that he is bringing the country to the brink of socialism; claims he is gay, and speculates on his putative lovers, which, of course, include Dwight Lockwood. "Does it hurt?" he asks himself. Sabrina smiles at him, and shakes her head—"How could it, my darling?"

The economy continues to improve, despite the opposition's dire predictions. "What is the long-term possibility of success of the

policies of the Braendel Administration?" the *Wall Street Journal*
asks. "It is useful to consult history. After eight years of the New
Deal, ten million people were still unemployed. If it had not been
for the war, a war Franklin Roosevelt was perhaps only too eager to
fight, the economy would not have turned around, and we would
still be in the Great Depression. . . ."

"They're desperate," Sig Harris snickers.

Derrick calls him in for still another White House interview—
he lowers his voice to tell him that the FBI has just uncovered an
assassination plot, involving the maintenance crew of the White
House, and behind them, of course, more important figures. "As we
speak, we are learning the names." While he and Sabrina watch, spiders crawl over Derrick's body, and then begin to penetrate into his
kidneys, his liver, as Dwight begins to wake up. . . .

A few days later, the story breaks! Arrests follow, as an investi-
gation reveals the involvement of former CIA agents and possibly
several members of Congress. For weeks the incident dominates
the headlines, the talk shows, and the visible Net, lifting Braendel's
ratings still higher. . . . On a back page in the *Times*, a brief story
depicts still more violence in Southern Sudan.

With threats of further fraud—"Now the federal machinery is
in our hands, Dwight"—Derrick dispatches government officials
to make pre-election checks of the voting machines. As the election finally takes place on a clear November day, federal troops and
the FBI stand guard by the controversial polling places. As Dwight
presses the "Vote" button, he watches his vote disappear like a stone
into a dark well.

By seven-thirty, the statistics are overwhelming—Derrick
is declared the winner! Dwight sends in his congratulations—
"HURRAH FOR YOUR SECOND TERM!"

What was it Derrick was thinking during their last visits? He
had something on his mind. In a week, the answer comes: Derrick
is nominating him—it will be the first time for an American—as
Secretary General of the United Nations!

If the plan works, in three months, he will be elected. In four,
he will fly to New York to the glass skyscraper, and confer with the

outgoing Secretary General, Peter Constantinescu. In six, he will assume office, Braendel's assistant simply informs him, as if the decision were already made. Who can he ask if this is his task—if this is what he is intended to do? Father smirks, "My God, do you really want to waste your talent on the UN?" Will it be Todd Jacobs, now grizzled and even pudgier, who will smile like a whimsical rabbi? "If that's what you want to do, Boss." Will it be Heinrich, who will see in the decision a peculiar combination of molecules, or Mildred, who will suggest still another dinner at Le Corbusier? . . . In their bedroom, Sabrina, as vibrant as in their last months together, says "Yes!" He can barely breathe as she fuses her dark shape into his. Later he sees her looking into the darkness, as if she could see beyond it into an unknown light.

IF I FORGET THEE

As Dwight waits for the vote at the UN, Derrick proposes a still stronger set of measures to pull the country out of the lingering remains of depression. The opposition filibusters to block his appointments and sidetrack his legislation, but, piece by piece, Derrick pushes his program through as the dreary Washington winter moves into spring.

"Yes, Lockwood would be excellent," the E.U. spokesperson says. "His appointment will realign the United States behind the UN, not just for another five years, but perhaps for future administrations." He receives similar endorsements from India, Japan, Nigeria, Brazil; and then an agreement to abstain by Russia and China.

Two months before the final vote, his election has been all but confirmed—as Derrick congratulates him, Dwight sees that his eyes have taken on a peculiar glitter.

"I cannot tell you, Dwight," Lee Ashworth assures him, "how delighted we are that we will have our representative at the helm of the United Nations. If we are going to work together, we might as well begin now, although, of course, one could say we began the first day of your appointment at the Fund"—had he accepted the nomination on these terms? Has his position already been compromised?

When the election finally occurs—even China and Russia vote for him—the ambassadors of all 196 members present their congratulations, each attempting in their allotted time to achieve the significance of a memorable encounter with the new Secretary

General. Dwight packs up his papers at the International Monetary Fund, says goodbye to his staff; to the Beautiful Barbara, whose touch lingers on his hand; to his Georgetown house—all the furniture will be stored temporarily in a warehouse, as he moves to New York to begin his new job.

He stays up night after night—when will he have time even to unpack?—storing up information on each country—the foreign ministry, its issues, its UN history—achieving his now famous "total comprehension," "immediate recall." His eyes are a screen making report after report to his brain until it cannot hold another name, another set of problems.

Now his every word must be even more carefully scripted. The last traces of his flamboyance or trusting intuition will be crushed beneath the infinite weight of responsibility. His hand is already warm with handshakes, as if it were a stone almost melted into clay, as he mounts the podium for his first address to the General Assembly, with a bank of press agents pressed up against the raised platform. Behind them, the delegates are waiting in a broad arc. Again as he approaches the podium, the Zeno game, a half, a quarter, an eighth . . . "Pillow'd upon my fair love's ripening breast . . . To feel for ever its soft fall and swell. . . . And so live ever . . ." Sabrina sits in the front row smiling up to him.

"In 1945, your predecessors assembled in San Francisco with a vision of a world organization which would 'save succeeding generations from the scourge of war.' Each secretary general who has mounted this podium has had as his primary responsibility the fulfillment of this promise. That responsibility is now mine. But I hasten to say, it is not a responsibility I bear alone. . . ." At the end, the delegates appropriately applaud; the clock begins to tick.

He goes from office to office greeting members of the Secretariat, shaking the hands of clerks, office heads, elevator operators, computer technicians; he sees their genuine excitement in actually shaking the hand of the new Secretary General—now they can tell their friends, their wives and children. . . . In meeting after meeting with the senior staff, he receives briefings on pending substantive issues, budgetary limitations, and on the thin line the UN must tread on conflicts between the great powers.

As new federal programs open around the country, President Braendel officiates at dozens of venues, cutting ribbons, exhorting local administrators, explaining his "Just Deal" to the local constituency. Like Dwight, the wiry little man must rise every morning at five, shower, shave, dress, rehearse each day, as his staff assembles to make concrete his intentions. . . . Even now, he is on his way to Atlanta, although he will not arrive for still another three weeks.

Bill follows Dwight at the customary distance as he walks through the streets, through the halls of the UN, glancing nervously at the crowd, once throwing himself in front of him when a bearded man in a shabby suit makes an ambiguous reach into his breast pocket—it was nothing, just a pack of cigarettes—"Yeah, but you never know." . . . Dwight reads a report on Southern Sudan, as still another war with the North breaks out, renewing the threat to the aid stations and clinics—what is Mother doing? Isn't it time for her to "retire"? Do people "retire" from such service? Isn't there a moment when she can rest, or must she demonstrate her devotion without limit to her imperious God?

In Haifa, another restaurant is gutted, two more buses are blown up in Jerusalem, and in retaliation, a Palestinian village is leveled. Menacing statements by the Arab League, and belligerent rebuttals by the Israelis, mobilization of both sides—it's starting all over again! . . . "The Lord says, 'Not in my lifetime.'" Dwight confers with his staff, particularly his number two, a crafty young Canadian named Peter Larkin—tall, blond, athletic, whose face—blue eyes, red lips, white skin—yes, resembles his. "Isn't it time, Mr. Secretary General," Peter suggests, "particularly now, as the incidents multiply, and with nuclear weapons on both sides, for the UN to move in with a peace force?"

"Perhaps," Dwight responds. "Of course, as you well know, this is not a novel idea, but perhaps now . . . Yes, I think you're right—it is time!"

Peter smiles. "It's going to be lovely working with you."

They spend the next few days putting together the plan for the UN peace force. Peter is so brilliant—Dwight will take him on his first trip as Secretary General to the Middle East. In his briefcase, he carries the plan they have crafted for a peace force—will he be able to sell it to both sides?

As he and Peter walk off the plane in Tel Aviv, and the reporters press around him, as he repeats the anticipated phrases, "the need for calm and statesmanship at this moment of crisis," "to speak with the principal parties to attempt to secure an immediate cessation of violence," "to seek the basis for a lasting peace," his image superimposes itself on a half dozen other secretaries general of the UN who had made similar statements at this airport.

"No," Chaim Ginzburg, the Israeli Prime Minister, says, when he broaches the idea of the peace force, "the Israeli Knesset would be quite wary of anything of that sort."

"Wouldn't such a force," Dwight asks him, "be preferable to a nuclear exchange? We cannot rule that out, now that Egypt and Iran have acquired . . ."

"Yes, yes, but you must understand our reticence here." Bushy eyebrows, a furrowed brow, a prominent nose, he is staring directly into Dwight's eyes. "After so many years of humiliation, of becoming the butt of condemning resolutions, of being excluded from key bodies like the Security Council, why, tell me, should Israel put its trust in the United Nations?"

"I can certainly understand your position, Mr. Ginzburg, but in these times, and, may I say, with new management at the UN itself, perhaps it might be worth a try. I offer this for your government's consideration, with the clear condition that I personally guarantee the objectivity and fundamental fairness of any force which might be deployed."

Ginzburg smiles, places his hand on Dwight's arm. "Ah, you are new to this position, Dr. Lockwood, and although your reputation at the Fund precedes you, I think you will find this a far more intractable organization."

"I am sure that in the years to come, I will indeed learn the wisdom of this remark"—Peter shoots him a look, with just a faint suggestion of a smile, "but I cannot see how, without some imposition of external force, the two sides will avoid even more hazardous clashes."

"Yes, yes, of course, you can try, but I doubt you will have any luck." . . . Dwight meets with the heads of state in Cairo, Tehran, Baghdad—the reactions are tentative, evasive—after all, it is just the first stage. Dwight and Peter return to New York—Peter says, "I think we did better than I expected."

Air Force One leaves for Atlanta, and in less than an hour, President Braendel is shaking hands at the airport and talking to reporters before entering the limousine on his way to Byrd Auditorium. . . . Dwight asks Peter to call in the ambassadors from other key UN members, as Derrick's car threads its way into the abstract, high-rise cityscape. Hawks and eagles circle the air—or are they just helicopters?—with a high-pitched electronic whine.

The delegates sit in Dwight's office carefully listening, asking questions about the composition of a UN peace force, and its possible terms of deployment. . . . Derrick's car crosses a major intersection, and enters the last stretch of boulevard lined with his shouting supporters.

"No, I think we can safely say . . ." As the limousine passes the last street light, a man in a leather jacket emerges from behind a trash bin—he's holding a hand-held rocket . . . "that the mandate would necessarily include guarantees for both sides." It fires—the shell arches over the crowd, the presidential car bursts into flames.

Bill runs into his office—"The President's car has just been attacked!" He switches on the television: the car is crossing the intersection, it is entering the last stretch before coming to the spot where a man emerges from behind a trash bin with the rocket. The shell arches over the crowd—Derrick's car bursts into flames.

His charred body and two of his aides are pulled from the wreckage. . . . Again and again, the car moves down the street, the missile is fired, the car bursts into flames. . . . On the mantel, the clock stops. . . . The car moves down the street, as it will ten, twenty, a hundred times—Dwight turns off the set, his face wet with tears.

Bill doubles the security around him, as Dwight and the staff make the necessary arrangements for the memorial—he must deal with a million details—why couldn't he just be alone with his grief? Before the assembled delegates at the General Assembly, he delivers his tribute to President Derrick Braendel, to his humanity, to his broad, compassionate vision, to his endorsement of the World Organization, while underneath his own words, he hears, "Did not our hearts burn within us . . . when he spoke with us by the way?"

The official funeral will be in Washington—at St. Paul's Cathedral and Arlington National Cemetery, with banks of soldiers firing their salvos into the air. . . . No, it will be in a simple church in Gary, Indiana, with Derrick's family, his mother who bore nine children, his alcoholic father, and his workers who for years went door-to-door getting out the vote.

The trees bend over the river in a fierce wind, as he and Sabrina slide by in their canoe, as the corpses pass, the vultures perch on boats, and rapacious birds turn and wheel in the air. . . . Vice President Barton assures the country that he will continue the "brave program begun by our late President," but unstated is the assumption, by Left and Right, that the "experiment" has been stopped. Each day the newspapers will be written, the televised interviews take place, and the current, augmented by a dark wind, will push the boat down the river. . . . He writes in his journal, "After Derrick had died, they were on the same earth just as they had been before he arrived, facing the same problems, but now they searched their faces to seek, in the glint of sunset on the cedar trees, in the import of sacred texts, if something had not changed."

A major rocket attack on Israeli towns—over thirty dead. "NEVER AGAIN," the Israeli banners read, as thousands troop through the streets of Jerusalem, Tel Aviv, and Haifa. The government sends the Israeli army into Lebanon. The delegates from

Egypt and Iran allude darkly to the "disastrous consequences," if Israel does not immediately withdraw.

"Will they really risk a nuclear confrontation, or is this just posturing for local consumption?" Dwight asks his staff.

"I think we need to act fast," Peter says, "to separate the sides."

"Yes," Dwight says, "now is the time to put forward our peace force."

"How will we sell the plan to the Israelis? If we can't get their approval, the whole business goes down the drain."

"What if they didn't altogether withdraw?" Dwight asks. "What if they were restricted to compounds *within* Lebanon—as a face-saving measure?"

Peter blinks his eyes: "Yes, that's it." In a double mirror, he sees Peter's multiple reflection—brilliant, tireless, like himself, with his blond hair, his fair skin, his athletic body—is he his son? . . . Or, God, is he repeating, even in his mind, his father's lust? Sabrina is shaking her head. "Let me contact my Canadian friends," Peter says. "It'll go down better with the Arabs than having an American propose it."

Ashworth calls to say that State's contacts indicate, despite the bellicose language, a willingness now on both sides to back off—if a face-saving formula can be devised. Dwight initiates a series of meetings on the UN peace force which goes on day after day, and then deep into the evenings. Sabrina stands hovering in the air—exhausted, he cries to her, "Are you there, are you there with me now?"

"What do you think?" she asks, bewildered, hurt, then dissolves right in front of him—he reaches out into the void, and touches nothing.

Peter stands in front of him, quizzical, confused before his "mentor."

"We will need to draft a statement for the Security Council," Dwight tells him—"Can you do that?"

With the "Lockwood Plan" on the table, Dwight speaks to the Security Council of the need for military restraint, for seizing the opportunity to "forge a new policy in the heat and danger of the present moment." The delegate from Lebanon suggests that his country could accept some kind of international police force "provided that the Council censures Israel for its iniquitous conduct in clear opposition to the principles of the World Organization. . . ."

After another week of Council sessions, more meetings in his office with members of the Arab League, with Israel, with the E.U., with China, and, of course, with the United States, after the continual all-nighters with Peter and the staff, the Council drafts a totally anodyne resolution which calls upon the Secretary General to submit a "plan for the resolution of the conflict."

"Leave it to Dwight" becomes the catchword of the Council. Within a few hours, he submits the resolution empowering the UN Secretary General to devise a force capable of insinuating itself between the two sides. It passes after only token objections. Dwight, surrounded by banks of press, expresses "gratification for the confidence of the member states in allowing the Secretary General to act in the interests of all the parties to effect a temporary and then possibly a more permanent solution to the conflict."

Enough, enough! He heads for his apartment to sleep, if, after staying awake for thirteen straight nights, such a thing still exists, if there will ever again be a moment in which he can lie untroubled, as darkness invades his body, as . . . Sabrina slowly turns to him: she is naked, her breasts rise and fall; she takes his head and pulls him toward her, as his senses drown in her tenderly taken breaths, and "so live ever . . . or else swoon to death," and he sleeps.

Another ugly skirmish as the UN force is being assembled; both sides announce that their missile forces are on full alert—any provocation will be met by instant and devastating retaliation. Frantic meetings at UN Headquarters, as Dwight secures emergency funding, arranges the logistics, assembles the force, and Swiss Air flies the first units to the Middle East.

A few days later, Dwight leaves with Peter and a small staff for still another round of talks. In Jerusalem, Chaim Ginzburg, now chatty and perhaps overly familiar, invites him for a "home-cooked meal." Ginzburg introduces him to his dumpy, unattractive wife, who squints at him through thick rimless glasses—she cooks the meal herself, as she shuffles back and forth between the kitchen and the living room; and to his son, Aaron, a rabbinic student at the *heder*, pale, thoughtful, with starring eyes, already immersed in the intricacies of the law—is he Todd Jacobs' son? . . . As Dwight flies from Tel Aviv to Cairo, he glances over to the next aisle—Father is gazing out the window. "Does it matter, my boy, if you are right or wrong? The point is that you are in control of the action, though, God knows, not all of it."

He meets with Anwar Said, the Egyptian foreign minister. With a meaningful glance, Dwight quips, "Could we possibly seek a final solution of the Jewish problem?—I hesitate to use that term with your Israeli counterparts, as you might imagine." The "light moment" passes; Said sits puffing on a cigarette, and for the next few minutes, Dwight barely controls his disgust at the insensitivity of his own remark, as he attempts to lay out the arrangement to prevent an accidental engagement with Israeli forces.

"Yes," he tells Peter, "it just might be possible that Said could be recruited into being a supporter for a permanent settlement, but how much he will be willing to trade—time will tell."

Peter smiles to him, "I wouldn't count on it."

When, the next day, Dwight suggests Said broach diplomatic recognition of Israel to his Arab League colleagues as one of the terms of settlement, he just scoffs. "No, not that helpful," Dwight laughs. He goes on with Peter to meet with a host of new names added to the list of statesmen who are "conferring with the Secretary General."

In Baghdad, after a meeting with the Iraqi foreign minister, with the situation at least temporarily stabilized, Dwight, Peter, and Bill fly off in a helicopter—he can afford a few hours—to view the ruins of Uruk, the ancient city-state once ruled by the Sumerian king Gilgamesh. He reads again the epic he had first read at Harvard: about the frivolous prince starting wars, enjoying his first night rights with the women of his kingdom; how the gods kill Enkidu his friend who fights with him in his wars, sometimes against the gods; how, shaken by his death, and now, for the first time, realizing his own mortality, Gilgamesh wanders for years over the face of the earth seeking the secret to eternal life. In the end, his quest fails—all that is left for him is to return to his city and dutifully serve his people. As he stands before the great walls of Uruk, he says, "No, it does not matter that I will die. My city will survive me, and my people will live into the future which I cannot have."

Dwight sees some mounds of gray-brown earth, a few tombs; he and Peter and Bill stand before the crumbled walls, then board a helicopter, which rises over Uruk, which just a few years before had been looted of most of its relics. He writes in his journal, "I am the keeper of the museum, with all the clay tablets and ancient statues as the looters come. I stand powerless, cringing against a wall until they leave with their sacks bulging with all the artifacts of my culture. Almost nothing is left, as I walk ceaselessly through the savaged rooms and despoiled vaults. No, time, which once seemed my ally, can no longer be considered even neutral."

A few hours later, he is back in Palestine to review the UN force. As he "troops the line" past the young men of fifteen countries, they are saluting him—the Secretary General of the United Nations! Of course, it is the "UN presence" that matters, not him. Will they ever fight? The British ambassador tells him, "These lads are quite willing to do just that, to establish their authority."

The next day, a strike by Hezbollah provokes an exchange in which the UN force kills eight terrorists and inflicts a score of casualties. Dwight reads that two of the injured were permanently demented in the attack—"How did that happen?" he demands.

"Some UN troops were armed with a new U.S. laser rifle," Peter tells him, "which both kills and strips information from computers, and from the brain." The dementia is already creeping into his mind, draining it of information; as a clock ticks, each bit of information flares, and is then permanently extinguished—is this Chandler's "Alzheimer War"?

Dwight moves on for talks in Cairo, then to six other cities. The truce is working, at least at this point, while under the table, the

Arab bloc is frantically developing its missile systems, although, in the CIA reports, which Ashworth forwards to him, the Israelis still hold a substantial advantage.

Even while the crisis in the Middle East seems headed toward a possible settlement, Dwight proposes a special session of the Council on the increasing friction between the E.U., China, and the United States around the Caspian and South China seas, with their still largely untapped reserves of oil. Representatives from all three parties reject the offer, but then reluctantly accept a mediating role for the Secretary General, as he flies from capital to capital, attempting to work out a *modus vivendi* for the disputed oil rights.

"No," he says on a second visit to Lee Ashworth, "I must keep himself clear of any identification with the U.S. position—I simply cannot be seen as a mouthpiece for U.S. policy if I am to be effective . . ."

"Why do you think we supported you, Dwight? Why otherwise would we have used up our credit?"

"Of course, I understand your position, but wouldn't I better serve U.S. interests if I maintained at least the appearance of neutrality? Otherwise, none of my actions will be credible, and the Organization itself . . ."

"Yes, yes, if that's what it's got to be!" They shake hands, they smile—the special relationship is over. As if now Ashworth were a few steps behind him, watching his every move, Dwight pursues the settlement, dividing the oil rights according to an "equitable" formula. President Barton seems to accept the arrangement, but then issues a statement, "The UN Secretary General, in his rush for agreement, has clearly forgotten any sense of equity or fairness, or, I may say, any sense of loyalty to his own country." Ugly editorials burst out in the *Wall Street Journal*, the *Washington Monthly*, even in the *Post* and *Times*. On Fox News, one commentator remarks, "Has the Secretary General forgotten who he is? Does working for the UN mean ceasing to be an American? Or are we just seeing the true colors of the Left? No longer will Americans work for America. They will work for the world, and America be damned!"

He sits with Mildred at Le Corbusier having a magnificent dinner and an even more glorious wine. "What did they expect? Don't they see that we had to reach an agreement before the situation got out of hand? Is their hatred simply the price I must pay to do my job?"

Mother has finally been assigned to the nunnery in Portland. She is dangerously ill, the order writes him, with a number of still undiagnosed diseases. He flies to Portland, and for two days he sits by her bedside. He sees her gaunt face, the purple patches on her arms and legs, the skin hanging from her bones, as she stares vacantly into space. Nurses pass in and out with bedpans, attempt to feed her, draw blood to make even more tests—she can wrinkle her face, she can talk, though not move her body.

"I still . . . I still cannot believe I was there all those years . . . though, that is where the Lord sent me. . . . I have nothing further to give. . . . I am ready to die. . . . I thought of you all that time, but, of course, in silence." She smiles, "Did you hear my thoughts?"

He sits by the bed as time moves toward his last glimpse of her—no, not this sunken skull and withered bones. He writes, "Does it matter that she served humankind, or that I walked through the world always without her?," and then he crosses it out.

He takes one more look at her accepting face, signals to Bill, and leaves. As they walk in the street, the cars pass up and down; Bill signals for a cab. Mother looks down on him from a place in the sky. The Interchange clicks on: the new Taiwanese President, Ah Shaogong, is proclaiming once again his country's independence of Mainland China.

"Can't the world stop even for a few weeks!"

"Just when you thought it was safe to go down to the water," Sig Harris quips as they sit in the lounge of the Cosmos Club. Sig smiles, sips his Martini. "I don't envy you this one."

He writes, "The wheel in the sky turns still again, and I must go on." . . . La Shih-fa, the Chinese premier, declares, "If Taiwan continues to maintain its independence, the Chinese will consider their declaration an act of war," and then evokes a doomsday scenario of missiles and massed landings.

Dwight receives Shih-fa's assurance that China will be open to negotiation, but Ah Shaogong refuses to back down: "It is not our role in history to be a laughingstock. We are not simply an illusion of a country, but a land, a people, a culture"—he stands two inches high on his little rock looking up at the sky.

The next day, the Chinese launch a missile attack, which is followed by a Taiwanese attack on the Mainland—whole blocks of cities burst into flames, killing an estimated seventy to eighty thousand people.

"Why now?" he asks Peter. "Why after decades of threats and narrowly averted crises are real attacks occurring? Has a virus infected the world? Why now? Why did La Shih-fa give me no inkling, no inkling of what would happen?"

Again, an immediate cease-fire, all-night sessions of the Security Council—Dwight, empowered by the Council—"Leave it to Dwight"—flies to Washington to block a retaliatory U.S. strike; then meetings in Beijing, Taipei, Moscow, Brussels—crushing fatigue until he cannot even imagine himself in the world; a renewal of the cease-fire for another week, still another, until the crisis is diffused, and Taiwan reverts to its original anomalous status.

He writes in his journal, "A year, two, three, now the fourth year, as the crises continue. Are they real, are human beings suffering, or is it all some vast illusion, like the shadows on the wall of Plato's cave?" With the funding for the UN peace force in the Middle East draining away, his trips increase from capital to capital as he pleads with each government to keep up its contribution, to be met with blank, indifferent eyes. If he does not get at least half the funds he needs, the force will simply dissolve—don't they understand that?

Sabrina is staring at him—he writes, "Is there a peace which can only be sought but not known? Or is eternity just the absence of time and place and events? Is that the 'peace of God, which passeth all understanding'—is that all it is?"

To Enter Jerusalem

Sometime during an ebb of crises, Dwight had bought an elaborate mid-town apartment in New York, and had furnished it with expensive postmodernist art. In the midst of relentless work, he can stop time and stand in front of one of the compositions: it will connect to no place or train of events, but seems waiting to be configured into any reality he might imagine. At parties, he sees his guests and social staff being transformed into a block of blue, a red line, a squiggle of green. . . . The apartment and paintings had drained the last remains from his estate—was the investment worth it? "'The poor are always with you,'" Sabrina gently chides him, "'but the son of God. . . ?'"

In Felicia Dewar, a Cuban novelist, whom in his "spare time" he is translating into English, he catches the faint glow of lost lust. She stands now beside him, dignified and discreet, still handsome with her dark eyes, flowing dark hair. She insists on diverting the conversation to world affairs, particularly to his handling of crises like the Middle East or the Taiwan Straits—"How do you manage to do it, and so well?"

"I should prefer," Dwight says, "to speak of *The Lost River*."

Felicia holds up her cocktail glass. "Which is more important? Yes, I write novels, but you change the world."

He shakes his head.

She purses her lips, and smiles. "Are you just being modest, Mr. Secretary General, or are you simply seeking more praise?"

"I wonder now if any intervention can ultimately be successful, if the world can be changed at all, or if it just changes according to its own inner dynamics." Sabrina stands nearby holding up a glass, eying him sharply—"*We* have had this pretentious conversation before!"

Felicia places her hand on his arm.

"*The Lost River* is a beautiful, tragic work," Dwight says in a voice now devoid of energy, "but you must excuse me for a moment," as he turns to greet a new guest, the ambassador from Algeria. Felicia recedes into the crowd. Then he greets Ami Hussein, the Jordanian ambassador, who launches immediately into the only topic he can discuss, the Middle East: "The situation, as you must understand, Dr. Lockwood, has totally degenerated. Soon, I fear the funding for the UN force will be reduced to a mere token."

"You must be aware," Dwight says, "of my continuous efforts to fend off that reduction—I have pleaded that case again and again."

"Of course, you are doing whatever you can, but if the United States and the E.U., not to speak of China, continue to withdraw their support, it goes without saying that the force will be disbanded and the security of the region will simply collapse."

"I suppose what Washington and Brussels and Beijing are telling me is that enough time has passed to test that proposition."

"The situation will simply explode with violence!"

"Yes, I know that—I have simply run out of options! . . . I have tried"—Ami Hussein is turning away—"nothing I do works!"

Guests drift in and out of earshot, the ambassador from Egypt, the foreign minister from Iran, France, who now are joined by deceased ambassadors from the United States, Henry Cabot Lodge, Adlai Stevenson, John Bolton; former secretaries general, Dag Hammarskjold, U Thant, Kofi Annan, who form a little convulsive knot discussing for the thousandth time the crisis in the Middle East, with still no resolution—Father smirks, "'Not in my lifetime.'"

The evening draws to a close. Felicia hovers over him, then asks him if he would like her to stay, and moves her body against his. "I think not," Dwight says—has he any time for this? Sabrina lets out a puff of air. . . . Through the open windows, a cold wind is blowing into the reception room, piling snow against the liquor tables, the musicians' stand. As he climbs into bed, and Sabrina presses against him, he's gripped by his old fear of impotence. After only an hour's sleep, he wakes up at four, and for an hour—Manuel will bring his coffee at five; Bill will arrive at six—he dutifully translates *The Lost River*.

As light slants through a window, Dwight sits as he does each day in the Contemplation Room in UN Headquarters. In the center is a huge block of iron illuminated by a single shaft of light. . . . What had given Derrick such energy, what had propelled him into the future—until Atlanta? Even now his car is leaving the airport—the iron block sits in the middle of the Contemplation Room—the car is passing the last intersection; the man with the hand-held rocket emerges from behind the garbage bin—can no one stop this?—the missile is slowly arching over the crowd!

Later, as he takes the elevator to his office, there, standing right by him with his beard and piecing eyes, a dagger projecting from his burnoose, is the chief of Hezbollah, Sheik Mohammed Yassin. "We will kill, if we need to—we will do what we must to redeem the lost land, and reclaim it for the glory of Allah!" Yassin reaches down for his dagger—Dwight closes his eyes, and Yassin disappears, eventually to be hunted down by Israeli rockets and cruise missiles.

He writes, "What did the passing events of the world matter, thought the lonely man walking through the streets of the city, if beneath the surface all was still? What did it matter if towers crashed and cities fell, if beneath resided untouched the generative power to create a thousand civilizations?"

Of course, Ami Hussein was right—with the withdrawal of funding, the last full units of the UN police force must now leave the demilitarized zone. Dwight appears on the TeleScope, thanking the troops for "their courage, their perseverance, their dedication to world peace," as digital cameras record the final scenes for CNN, Fox News, the BBC.

"The UN withdrawal," Sheik Yassin proclaims, "can only be interpreted as a sign that the world community will now no longer go through the sham of protecting Israeli interests, and that Hezbollah must now resume the *jihad*." The next day, rockets explode inside an Israeli compound killing thirty-seven troops. Then more Arab attacks, a truck bombing at a check point, killing seventeen; a school bus, killing twentty-two children; the body of a college professor found mutilated in a Jerusalem side street with an inscription, "Death to the Jews."

The Israeli army moves into Lebanon and Palestine, occupying one village after another, demolishing buildings, killing suspected terrorists as well as innocent civilians. Behind the army are corps of engineers who begin to lay out new roads, electrical wiring, water and gasoline piping, to create the infrastructure for an extended occupation. The Israeli move is followed by dire threats from the Arab League, which now include nuclear annihilation.

As the crisis deepens, politicians in Washington, Brussels, and Beijing speak of the failure of the UN to create a lasting peace, blaming the Secretary General for lacking the necessary vision and follow-through. "Don't they know what has really happened?" he asks Sabrina. "Haven't I spent months warning them—that the withdrawal of UN forces would result in precisely what they are witnessing now?"

"I know that, my darling."

"Did they think that the problem would just go away? Is the real use of the UN just to be a scapegoat for their own failures?"

A frantic round of calls, an emergency session of the Security Council, as he skates over the ice, does incredible turns and twists, while a huge bear stands watching his foolish maneuvers. "There is no resolution," Lee Ashworth tells him—does he need this increasingly pompous man to lecture him?—"because the Arabs think Israel has no right to exist."

"Of course," Dwight responds, ". . . and your point?"

Ashworth begins breathing heavily—his head is alive with maggots! "My point, goddamn it, is that we cannot always be coming to their aid. Does a Jewish state like Israel, which now has become little more than a military machine, even deserve to exist?"

"And the alternative? . . . You should be glad these discussions are confidential."

"You see, I already know what you're going to say—you've already said it. Reinstate the peace force—but *I've* taken another look at the situation, and *I* no longer see the demographics in Israel's favor—did you know that today they are out-voted three to one by the Arabs in the United States, and that someday they will even be out-voted by the Arabs in their own country? So why, except to stop your constant begging, should we put ourselves out to save them?"

"If two thousand years ago, they'd only rallied around some Galilean preacher, would you have felt differently?"

"I'm not getting into this discussion!"

"Then consider this—as you know, both sides have nuclear weapons. In a matter of hours . . ."

Ashworth sighs, "Yes, yes, it's probably true, and it's probably unfair to ask you to indulge me in my little fits of ill humor. You want to know something—I like to see you mad, makes you human, instead of this saintly, uh, cloying, virtuous—whatever, I don't know, Nobel Peace Prize tone you assume. Yes, set up the goddamn peace force again, and, I can't guarantee it, but maybe, just maybe Uncle Sam will pick up some of the bill!" A phone rings. Ashworth answers it. "Good to see you, Dwight," and signals him out.

With Peter's prompting, the Canadians and Australians take the initiative, but now the Norwegians can only provide two hundred troops, Belgium cuts its contribution to a third, the Indians come up with nothing. . . . In the final vote, the Egyptians vote no—a reversal of their agreement made personally to him just two days ago.

At the Tel Aviv airport, Chaim Ginzburg greets him and Peter warmly, but as Dwight presses Chaim to move the army units back into the compounds, he stiffens. "We will not go through still another charade. We tried that, and look what happened. Our army will freely operate on Lebanese and Palestinian territory until we have a full guarantee!"

"Isn't cooperation here preferable. . . ?"

"The cooperation you have suggested has already been breached, and will be breached again."

"Not if the Security Council makes clear that such attacks will be met by international sanctions."

"But they won't, not at the cost of its members' precious oil—it was *our* side, *our* army, which had to respond to the attacks, not the UN! I know you have come here with the best of intentions, but until we have firm guarantees"—he is almost shouting—"we will continue to deploy our troops—do you understand!"

"A cease-fire?" The Egyptian Foreign Minister scoffs: "And freeze a situation in which Jewish troops are permanently on our territory, and sanction their theft of our land still another time? For almost seventy years we have had to watch this imposter squat on our land—land that was given to us by God, by *God!*" Maggots are streaming over his desk, climbing on his shoes, up his legs. "Now we are armed with the same weapons with which they have threatened us. Make no mistake, we are willing to die to win the final victory! We hope it will not come to this, but if it does, we are willing, let me assure you, we are willing to pay the price!" . . . A house bursts into flames as men with torches scurry away.

Beirut, Baghdad, Tehran, Damascus, then back to Jerusalem—the response is the same. The Arab states have already decided on war, or is it, as Peter suggests, only a collective maneuver of intimidation? "The cobra coils and uncoils, then hisses its poison, before it will strike."

The emergency beeper of his computer begins to flash—a major clash between the Israeli army and "volunteers" from Syria. A few hours later, units from Egypt spill over the Israeli border and engage the army in a major fire fight. "It is too late, the moment for your peaceful maneuvers has passed." Ginzburg shakes his head.

His trip with Ginzburg to the Tel Aviv airport is accompanied by half a dozen armored cars—Bill sits by his side clutching his pistol. His "son" Peter is with him, and Sabrina—forever by his side. As his limousine moves through the streets, they pass again the walls of the Old City, and for just a moment, they are stopped by a group of pilgrims as they make their way toward the Via Dolorosa. An hour later, they reach the airport, and hastily board the plane.

As they reach the first bank of clouds, Dwight sees a huge flash in the direction of Jerusalem, and then a shock wave hits the plane, taking his breath away. The plane falters as if it would fall from the sky, dips, and then rights itself, and continues its flight. From the direction of Jerusalem rises a mushroom cloud.

The pilot's voice comes on: "Jerusalem has just been hit by a nuclear missile. Another, aimed for Tel Aviv, has been destroyed by the Israeli missile defense system." Peter switches on the U.S. Defense channel—"The Arab rockets are in the low megaton range. The Israelis have intercepted several others, although another has just hit Jerusalem, and one more an outlying section of Haifa." Twenty minutes later, the centers of Cairo and Tehran, as well as their launch facilities, are hit by more powerful Israeli nuclear rockets.

Dwight instructs his undersecretary in New York to secure an immediate cease-fire through the Council—Peter says Canada will put through the motion. Then he calls Ashworth: "Lee, only you can stop this!"

"What's the plan?"

"Threaten an immediate nuclear strike against any party which breaks the cease-fire."

"What cease-fire?"

"We'll have a cease-fire in half an hour—Canada will propose it—but do it *now!*"

"Okay, okay, I've just got to clear it with the President. . . . I want to say . . . you were right. I was just being a . . ."

"It's all right, Lee. I've got to switch off now—I'm counting on you!"

In a week, the UN force is back in operation, and the cease-fire is in force, supported by the U.S. and the other permanent members of the Security Council. Major sections of cities have been leveled to the ground as if the blasts had wiped out parts of the world's memory: the Via Dolorosa is a seething ruin, the walls of the Old City, even the Dome of the Rock, a heap of radioactive rubble. In Cairo and Tehran, even more destruction—how could they have done this? Is there no end to human hatred? "Now you know," Father says.

As Dwight descends from the plane in Tel Aviv, Chaim is standing on the field, his face pale, his eyes unfocused—he had escaped by accompanying Dwight to the airport, but his wife and his son, Aaron, were consumed in the blast. He barely greets Dwight, then suddenly he is pressing his body against him. "Forty thousand Jews have been killed," he cries, "a hundred thousand injured, many more exposed to lethal doses of radiation. I . . ." He breaks down.

". . . I am so sorry for your personal tragedy, for . . ."

"It is not your fault—I know you tried, and you cannot, even if you would wish, prevent all the evils of the world."

"Chaim, if there is anything we can do to honor the dead, it is to make arrangements, permanent arrangements, that this will never happen again."

"Yes—like after Hiroshima and Nagasaki?"

"Help me!" Dwight says. "We cannot look back now. We can only look forward, and do what must be done. . . . Will you help me?"

Ginzburg stands quietly for a moment, as tears course down his cheeks. "My grandfather, Hanoch, survived two years through the hell of Belsen, while millions died. And now, because of his spirit, I am here, and in front of me, yes, you are right, is another Holocaust, so, of course, I will work with you. I will bury everything inside my soul, everything, and I will work with you, so this will never happen again!"

All night Dwight paces up and down in his hotel suite, as Peter sleeps in the next room, knocking every hour or so to see if Dwight is all right. Chaim debates with his cabinet, and at five in the morning, he calls: Israel will withdraw its forces from Lebanon and Palestine, and make a full commitment to work for the establishment of a Palestinian state, if the Arab states will sign non-aggression pacts, guaranteed by the great powers.

In Cairo, half the city has been leveled, and many in the government killed. A high pitched keening fills the air; women with covered heads, half-naked men, wander the streets—the Cairo

museum, historic mosques have been leveled. Men in radiation protected suits dig out the rubble. Dwight's limousine stops at a hotel
further up the Nile which has become the new foreign office. Anwar
Said had died in the attack. Dwight puts forward the Israeli offer to
his deputy—"Can I count on your government to accept it?"

"We believe, Mr. Secretary General, that the sanctions imposed
by the major powers are enough."

"But without an agreement, Lebanon and parts of Palestine stay
in Israeli hands, and in time, this will precipitate still another crisis.
Should there be no agreement to end the conflict?"

"If that is the will of Allah . . ."

"Israel made its offer in good faith! Now you must do your
part!"

"Was it in good faith to kill our people, destroy our cities, to . . ."

"Who started the attacks, who first used the missiles? . . . I
understand your grief, of course, but now is the time to rise above
sorrow and anger, and proclaim before the world the greatness of
your souls."

The deputy foreign minister blinks, then mumbles, "I am
without instructions."

Dwight leaves with nothing, but the next day, in Baghdad, he
learns that Egypt has accepted, though in the UN it castigates Israel
as a "criminal state," "a cesspool of infidelity," etc., etc. After still
more weeks, with the permanent members of the Security Council
holding firm with their threat of nuclear sanctions, Jordan, Syria,
Iran, then the other Islamic states accept the agreement and with
Israel sign the non-aggression pacts. . . . "Let us pray that through
suffering we can secure wisdom," Dwight says at the concluding
meeting of the Security Council. "Let us pray that through these
statesmanlike acts on both sides, we will see the permanent end of
hostilities. Let us hope that arrangements concluded here will over
time redeem the grief and pain of so many decades of conflict, and
usher in an era of hope and mutual cooperation." The faces of the
delegates stare without a trace of emotion as if he had caught them
with a flashlight in a darkened room.

As Dwight wanders down the Via Dolorosa, his arm slowly dissolves, then a leg. As he lies helplessly on the ground, Sabrina leans down and places her hand behind his head, as she had the first time when they were still in school.

He writes, "He wandered through the world as if it were a desert, but it was teeming with life—he could not see it, not only the small animals which darted in and out of their holes, but even the human beings, an endless number of strangers, who still walked the earth."

That morning, he cannot even go to work, until Peter—"You're worrying me"—hands him still another cup of coffee, holds him as if he were his father, while Dwight cries in his arms, and then says, "Yes, yes," and, with Sabrina watching over him, begins the new day.

* * * * *

Franklin Morgan—will he be the candidate? Dwight has his staff prepare a report—a senior senator from Ohio, a decorated veteran of the second Iraqi war, a virulent conservative. Even before the primaries, the Republicans had blasted the Barton Administration, and, of course, the UN Secretary General, for providing no leadership, for permitting a nuclear war, for allowing the Holy Land—"the land of our Lord"—to be destroyed. Once again, their spokesmen say, the United States must "affirm the moral basis of our society, assert its righteous power to reorder the world."

As Dwight walks through the streets with Bill and Peter, New York is a foreign country. How curious these three and four-story townhouses, these little shops on the corners, these massive skyscrapers rising from the center of the city. The inhabitants here— what language do they speak?

A placard reads, "The world is drifting toward the kind of nuclear exchanges which have just destroyed the Holy Land. Is America next? Vote for the party which can defend America!" The economy, as if in full cooperation, enters a recession. By November, the ratings favor a huge victory. On election night, as the victory is confirmed, he writes, "Is it true, as Lord Bryce once said, that a country gets the government it deserves? Am I still adrift in the sands, mindlessly contemplating, while history has taken yet another ugly turn?" He opens his journal to reread the passage—it's blank.

The new Secretary of State is a stocky African-American with a benign smile, named Ellesworth James—an internationalist, an ex-general, the former head of The Good Life Foundation, which serves disadvantaged children. Even before his first address to the General Assembly, James meets with Dwight in his office, and they begin the expected *tour d'horizon:* Palestine, Taiwan, Kashmir, the civil war in the Sudan, the continuing aggressive programs of the E.U. and China in outer space, and a host of other problems which take up over an hour.

"May I also add"—Dwight twists his face into a smile—"the forthcoming election in the General Assembly? Can I still count on U.S. support for a second term?"

"Yes, yes, I understand your concern here. . . . I'll do what I can to blunt any attacks on you, but your initial alliance with the previous administration is a known fact—I think you're in for some trouble. You've got to understand that the line here is 'Americans work for America.' "

He leans forward, his voice lowers, "If, in the next six or eight months, you play it quietly, or should I say, you put yourself in no straight-out confrontation, I think I can pull it off—if not support, at least abstention. . . . It's not going to be easy, either for you or for me."

Now U.S. security agents appear regularly in the UN building; Dwight's staff members find their communications intercepted and discover cameras and sophisticated surveillance equipment planted in meeting rooms and offices. Now the government is selectively denying visas to members of the UN Secretariat—several even receive subpoenas to appear before congressional committees. Hawks and eagles circle in the sky, perch on the ledges of the building, even swoop down into the rooms and halls.

Dwight avoids any confrontation. "Yes, I have been informed of the concerns of Washington. The Secretariat will continue, as it has in the past, to fulfill its international obligations with the impartiality demanded by the Charter." But he also agrees—it is difficult to look Peter in the face—to transfer quietly a few particularly objectionable Secretariat employees to less strategic posts, and to supply Ellesworth James with reports on certain hitherto confidential operations—has he given away too much? Who is he doing this for, the Organization or himself?

In the General Assembly, he listens to the new U.S. ambassador: "We in this country deplore the United Nations' willful blindness. We cannot say if we are simply seeing the usual signs of its ineptitude or, perhaps, even more disturbing, genuine malice. In either case, the World Organization should contemplate what would occur if my country should simply withdraw."

"I told you it wouldn't be pleasant," James says. The months pass, as Dwight must play the waiting game, but some weeks before the election, James is able to tell him that, yes, the U.S. will abstain, and Dwight is eventually reelected with virtually no opposition to what the *Times* calls "the world's most thankless job." The next day, Dwight hires additional security experts, systematically removes cameras and surveillance equipment, and forbids any Secretariat member, on pain of immediate discharge, from speaking to U.S. security agents. "Out, out," he runs through the halls as the hawks and eagles depart in a noisy burst of wings.

The war in the Sudan intensifies. The Sudan People's Liberation Army (SPLA), with its motley force of tribal groups, still led by the aging John Deng, resists the Khartoum forces and its paramilitary groups with some success. Then Dwight reads that Deng has entered into negotiations with the Sudanese president, General Ali Muhammad Abboud, and in a surprising move, they agree to a cease- fire, with Deng designated as the first vice president of a united country.

Dwight sends letters of congratulations to Deng and General Abboud—can the peace last after forty years of civil war, and now almost three million deaths? A week later, Deng's helicopter mysteriously crashes over the forest not far from the Bahr el-Ghazal, killing Deng and all the crew. The news is followed by angry accusations that this is the work of Khartoum—the war resumes, now led by Deng's son, Thomas. Will the world ever know who shot down the plane, could it possibly have been an accident? He opens his journal with barely enough energy to write: "It doesn't stop, this perverse belligerency of the world. Why must it go on year after year—is this savagery what it is to be human?"

In the middle of the night, as his breath comes in pants, he and Peter and Sabrina are leaving the earth to begin a journey into the outer reaches of the galaxy. . . . Mother stares at him with a preternatural look. That morning, he receives an e-mail from the nunnery in Portland that Mother has finally had a stroke and died after three years of suffering.

"Did my dying surprise you?" Mother asks—her body is lying in an open casket in full habit with a simple wooden cross between her praying hands. "No, Dwight, I could not live forever." Even in death, she is breathtakingly beautiful, as if for this last time, or for her appearance before God. Father is standing over the casket: "It happens to everyone, though it took her longer than I thought. She was beautiful, wasn't she?" He wipes his forehead. "Surprised I care? I cared—though, of course, how could you have known?"

He hears nothing in the funeral, except the music—Palestrina, Buxtehude—with its projection of eternity, its denial of ephemeral life. Father says, "What are you waiting for? Are you still waiting for me to apologize? Is that why you're staring at me?" Then he is screaming, "Your lips were so red, your eyes so blue, your skin so fair and dazzling—I'd do it again, and again, and again! Take that! Take that!" The lid of the coffin cracks. As Dwight sits in his pew, he is running down the aisle, out the door, and into the street.

Ellesworth James resigns as Secretary of State—he had served less than a year—to resume his work with The Good Life Foundation.

His replacement, announced even before James has left, is Jack Templeton. Peter shows him Templeton's recent book containing a quoted passage that had become part of the presidential campaign—yes, he had read it—"If the glass house cracked and fell to the ground, the world would suffer no loss." "Jack, Jack," Dwight repeats to himself—a wolf, no, a jackal, stalks through the halls of the UN building.

"Does it make any difference at all what I do?" he cries aloud. Every morning he gets up and prepares for the next day, and then the day after that. Where is he? What's happening to him?

Father stands over him, Sabrina hovers like mist, Mother gazes down, Peter waits prepared for the first briefing, while every day Dwight rises before five, has his coffee, reads his papers, takes a second cup of coffee, stuffs more than he can possibly do in a week into his briefcase, and walks with Bill to Headquarters, which, when he arrives, will have crashed to the ground—blown away, his body drifts off into the thin New York air.

It flashes on the computer screen—a huge deposit of oil has just been discovered in Southern Sudan! In the next few weeks, with the world-wide shortage, the great powers, the U.S., the E.U., and China, begin to weigh in on one side or the other of the ongoing civil war, supplying military equipment, then directly putting in their own troops. Is this still another crisis? Will he be able to deal with this? Can he still focus, can he distinguish any more the real from. . . ?

He flips on CNN: in the South, teenaged soldiers of the Sudan People's Liberation Army are posturing with their AKs and Kalashnikovs. Then Thomas Deng is making a brief statement—"Once more," he is saying, "the Khartoum government, driven by its greed for oil, and backed by the United States, is moving its armies into the South to effect a full occupation."

He turns off the set, sits in his office making notes, which then dissolve until he is staring at a blank sheet of paper; he calls in Peter and members of the African bureau. Peter is saying, "With U.S. support, the Islamic government in Khartoum, the NIF, is proclaiming that *sharia*, the traditional Islamic law, will finally prevail throughout the country. No more talk now of regional autonomy, which is, of course, a Christian plot, they say, augmented by the intrigues of the Zionists. No more holding back the inevitable Islamic revolution which will sweep the world."

Is Peter actually saying this? Or has Dwight read it somewhere? When was it that time had begun to slip?—he stands again on the edge of the Bahr el-Ghazal as corpses, cows, even houses pass. . . . He still remembers; he has a memory—even if it is no longer relevant.

"Behind the intervention of the U.S. government," Peter continues, "stands the oil conglomerate, C.O.I., which has poured millions into its coffers, and after years of covert support, the Morgan Administration is finally . . ." Peter sits before him, talking, outlining the world, which he will manage after Dwight is gone—Peter, his son.

"What are you going to do?" Father snaps. Sabrina hovers in space, ethereal, compassionate. Slowly, Peter begins to remove his clothes, showing his bare chest, his hips. "What are you going to do?" Father insists. "You sit pissing around here all day—I asked you a question, for Christ sake!"

"If the great powers were not involved," Dwight begins, as he gropes for words as if he had dropped coins in the dark and was desperately now trying to pick them up, "the issue would continue . . . to be a mere civil war. But now . . . the great powers are involved, and the killing will increase. . . . The UN must intervene precisely at a time when the involvement of the great powers is making it so difficult . . . ."

A legal team arrives in three-piece suits, with spats and academic keys, carrying piles of thick tomes. "Mr. Secretary General, we can assure you that the majority of precedents would favor the position that the United Nations could be considered to have a legitimate basis of involvement . . ."

The piles of books begin to teeter, then fall. Father shouts, "I didn't ask you for some goddamn legal opinion; I asked you, Dwight, what *you* are going to do!"

"There is, of course, the danger," he says, "that the United States, the E.U., or China will veto any action which might be taken." A huge truck backs into the building. In the sudden explosion, the building sags, then collapses into a pile of broken glass.

"Clearly," Dwight declares, "under the circumstances, our initial actions must be quite circumspect."

"Clearly," Peter says, nodding his head.

"We should probably get started. . . . We'll need appointments in all the major capitals, and, of course, in Washington." Can Peter see the change, that behind his image, he is no longer even in the room?

"Is the trip safe?" Peter asks. "A lot of people will be gunning for you—the NIF, the CIA, who knows, even the Chinese or the E.U.— I've got to say, this might be a time to conduct our diplomacy from home base."

Dwight waves his hand, as if he were cleaning mist from a window.

"No, I mean it—don't go, it's not safe!"

"I'm going."

"Dwight. . . ?" Peter is shaking his head.

Jack Templeton turns down his request for a meeting in Washington, and follows with a press release: "Dwight Lockwood's intended trip to Sudan can only be considered as a gross interference in the internal affairs of a sovereign state by the UN's ambitious Secretary General. It is time that the United Nations becomes what it was intended to be, the servant of its members, not an international government which breaches their sovereignty!"

The press swarms around him like hungry flies. "I can, of course, fully appreciate Mr. Templeton's concern, and that of his government, that the UN Charter be faithfully fulfilled; and I can admire his support for the sovereignty of all its members. No one, however, is more conscious of this principle than the Secretary General of the United Nations. It is my hope that in the weeks to come Mr. Templeton will see this trip not as a usurpation of powers but as an attempt to carry out my responsibilities as prescribed by the Charter."

The computer reports an attack on the E.U.'s satellites—U.S. ASATS are stripping them of their information with laser beams. Sabrina extends her hand, as energy flows from her fingers into outer space, lighting up the moon and the stars, which then burst into flames.

Jacques Lefèvre, now the E.U. foreign minister, sits in Dwight's office. "We must have a meeting of the Security Council immediately to deal with this flagrant act of aggression."

"At this juncture, what would be the purpose?" Dwight asks.

"Do I mistake your position—are you questioning the relevance of your own organization?"

"I would not argue with you in the slightest on the merits of your motion, but can any good come of it? Might there not be grounds for more quiet diplomacy with perhaps a better chance of success?" . . . He is falling through space—his disappeared body, splayed limbs, spiral down as the air rushes past.

"Are we to live with this kind of arrogance? Clearly, the United States has distanced itself from any constraint under international law, and is making a full-scale attempt at world hegemony."

"Yes."

"There is always a danger with a nation that believes it is morally superior to everyone else, particularly if it is as powerful as this one."

"Of course, of course," he mumbles. . . . A huge lizard crawls out from under a log, lurches down the hall, its voice a high electronic scream.

He sits immobile before his computer screen, as the U.S. continues its attacks on the E.U.'s and China's satellite systems, stripping their satellites of information and computer capacity. As he and Sabrina and Peter orbit the earth, ASATS approach and spurt their energy at them—they continue circling the earth, but now are devoid of memories.

Peter appears, and takes him over to the Council meeting. As Dwight continues to occupy the chair of the Secretary General, the E.U., then the Chinese delegate accuse the United States of direct acts of aggression. The U.S. has already made its point. No power can challenge it. As he is returning to his office, a security officer rushes up to him. "Don't go in! We've just discovered a bomb. We've got to clear the area!" The limousine makes its way down the boulevard in Atlanta, as a man steps out with a hand-held rocket; the missile arches over the crowd. Bill stands by him, his hand on his pistol. Will he still make the trip to Sudan? Isn't Peter right, isn't he now at risk? . . . The car bursts into flames.

He writes, "What would happen if he left his soul unattended? Will there be a time when he can no longer find himself?" Yes, he will go to Khartoum, he will do his job. That is what he has chosen to do: he will fly to Khartoum; he will meet with General Abboud, and then with Thomas Deng.

. . . Peter stands before him: "Why can't I go with you? Why do you have to do this alone?"

"Because you need to be here. I need you here, Peter!"

As he sits in the plane, his computer picks up that an E.U. satellite has directed a hit against a forward land base of the NIF, killing several hundred more government troops. Waiting for him at the airport—they will finally meet—is the turbaned and bearded Sudanese Chief of State, General Ali Muhammad Abboud. "Yes, we will have much to talk about," Abboud declares, then, for the rest of the trip, sits in stiff silence as the limousine drives them into Khartoum.

They enter the statehouse, a monstrosity of reinforced concrete that looks like a modern Russian hotel. "Now there is no possibility of compromise with the infidels of the south," Abboud states. "My government must break out of the humiliating trap of subservience which has constrained Islam for over a thousand years. We cannot hope to keep Allah on our side if we do not act as His agent."

"But the involvement of the United States in securing its supply of oil . . . Aren't you really fighting *their* war?"

"Would you, Mr. Secretary General, sell out your God for peace, could any benefits here outweigh the price we would pay in eternity?"

"But surely, the revolution which you believe must come with the sword can only come through the word. And just as you would rightly resist any effort on the part of the SPLA to impose their views on you, so you should expect them to resist any such effort on your part."

Had he said this? Abboud stares, without reply.

"It is not a war you are directing, but one in which you are carrying out the wishes of an external power." Several minutes pass. "It is important, at this juncture," Dwight ventures again, "that Sudan not become a tool for a larger power, that you not fall into the trap of believing that you are being supported rather than exploited. It might be useful to think who on both sides is being used. In my view, it makes no sense for you to succumb to a new form of colonialism."

Abboud waves his hand in dismissal.

"I shall only urge you, perhaps in a more reflective moment, to consider what I have said." A clock turns slowly inside its disc; he notes from time to time how it has advanced, five minutes, ten, then half an hour, an hour, until, with the requisite courtesies, he departs.

Still another plane trip. Bill sits by his side reading an automotive magazine. The plane swoops down for its landing on the small airfield. Thomas Deng stands before him with a motley group of adolescent soldiers—like old pictures of John, he is larger than life with the same round head and twinkling eyes.

"I remember well my most pleasant encounter with your father when I was visiting my mother, then at a clinic near the Bahr el-Ghazal River." Thomas had been educated, Peter had briefed him, at a British public school, and then at Oxford; he had worked for several years for a British corporation. The pleasantries pass. "Tell me, how would you state the objectives of the SPLA in this present conflict?"

"Let me assure you, Mr. Secretary General, all we wish is the arrangement we thought we had concluded with the Khartoum government when my father was still alive. What we wish is a state which accepts the full diversity of the country, where different regions can receive the benefits of their local resources, and where we can walk through the streets of our towns and cities and farms, and not see the appalling poverty and disease which have been the products of this endless war."

"Yes, of course, I can understand these objectives. Let me pose a possibility: if I were successful in persuading the NIF, would you agree to meet with them under UN auspices, say, in New York, or perhaps in Nairobi?"

"'Any place, any time in the cause of freedom.'" Deng chuckles.

Dwight blinks his eyes—wasn't he quoting John Foster Dulles? Had he said that? . . . "Yes, quite so. And if we were to secure a cease-fire, would you abide by it and essentially stop military operations pending a larger settlement? And would you use your good offices to persuade your allies to do the same?"

"The E.U. and China? I am not sure how much influence we would have here, Dr. Lockwood. At this juncture, they are perhaps even more militant than we are." . . . They walk along the river, accompanied by the SPLA's ragged band of armed young men. They pass little makeshift villages of tents and flat-roofed mud houses—off the side of the road, three children hover over a woman who has been disemboweled.

The sun is just setting with flickers of orange as he shakes hands with Deng, and he and Bill board the small plane—will it be now? . . . The rocket lifts off from the ground and zeroes in as they fly over the trees. He turns—he needs Sabrina—there she is sitting by him on the plane, looking right into his eyes—he reaches out into the air to touch her cheek as Bill watches him and shakes his head.

After a change of planes in Nairobi, as they fly to Brussels, the computer picks up the news of several satellite-directed attacks on SPLA training bases. "Of course, it is oil," Lefèvre exclaims, as they sit in his elegant office. "What did you expect? But what the E.U. and our ally China wish is simply a fair division. If we do not fight for oil here, when will we be able to make a stand—when we have no oil for our forces?"

"I understand," Dwight says, "but when I attempted to discuss these issues with Mr. Templeton, he would not meet with me."

"Welcome to the club, as you say. Only you must persevere in attempting to mediate this crisis, as it could, and is already, we fear, spiraling out of control. We shall, of course, back any cease-fire you may reach. Consider us, Mr. Secretary General, your allies, although I needn't tell you that our allegiance will be as discreet as our position requires." Dwight smiles as he shakes hands with the wily M. Lefèvre.

Again—he is back at the Security Council—the U.S. vetoes the motion for a cease-fire, which had been supported by China and the E.U. The U.S. ambassador declares, "In taking the position of one side of this dispute, Secretary General Lockwood has abandoned any pretense of neutrality. He has clearly rejected all necessary restraints which must be observed by an international civil servant. We have been clear about what our next action will be." Dwight rises to give an immediate reply—Peter strongly signals him to wait.

The delegates leave their chairs, and file out of the room. Then, slowly, the chairs are refilled by Mother, Sabrina, Todd Jacobs, Roberta Sánchez, Father Dietrich, Heinrich, Chandler, John Deng. . . . Will they vote, will they support him, even if with a few abstentions?

That afternoon, in the General Assembly, Dwight offers "the defense of a Secretary General whose record is transparent, and who leaves his fate in the hands of the membership. I have not worked for the benefit of any one nation, as the delegate from the United States suggests, but for all. Can a nation truly object to a cease-fire as an infringement of sovereignty unless it is using its objection as an excuse to mask its own ambitious activities? This is the time to take stock, and before more damage is done, to re-engage in the dialogue of nations envisaged under the Charter."

His speech is met by cheers from the usually sedate delegates—if only Templeton cared what he had said. Country after country boldly defends the Secretary General against "any slurs which might have been made on his impeccable record," although in a few cases, of countries tied closely to the United States, the delegates are silent. Most of the membership gives him a standing ovation, and endorses his suggestion that he negotiate a cease-fire.

Yes, as delegates buzz about him, he has been vindicated, but what does it matter? Outside the hall, energy beams light up the reaches of outer space, as E.U. and Chinese satellites battle the U.S.—aren't they as culpable or as greedy as the U.S., only less powerful? . . . Dwight sits behind his desk as cats slowly enter the room, still wet from the ocean, leaving puddles of water on the floor; and then he is caught up in the swirling air. It begins to churn, then roar, as he turns and twists—he cannot breathe, he will die. . . .

"Are you alright?" Peter asks. "Should I get a doctor?"

"No, no, I'm alright!"

Templeton directs still another virulent personal attack, and as a "preliminary step," officially withholds the country's UN dues. "The United Nations could actually dissolve," Dwight tells Peter. "It would not require my best to save it, but ironically my absence. But if I left, the precedent would be set, and that, too, would inevitably weaken the Organization, as it would imply that a major power could make me leave." Peter listens politely—do words, especially his words, matter at all any more?

"In a steady voice, he says to his staff, "Now I must fly again to Khartoum, then to Nasir, and arrange for a summit between the North and South." Sabrina looks at Dwight: "What are you trying to do—are you still deliberately trying to. . . ?"

Peter asks, "Can we trust Abboud to provide for your safety?"

"Do I have any alternative?"

"The situation has so deteriorated—can you trust Khartoum, the CIA?" Dwight says nothing. Peter goes on, "The only way I'll let you go this time is if you let me go with you. Otherwise, if anything happened to you, I could never forgive myself—I want to be with you!"

He looks into Peter's eyes, so like his own, but he cannot let him go! If he should die, Peter must be there after him. . . . "No, I will not let you go!"

As Dwight prepares for the trip, he makes the call to Abboud to confirm the meeting, and receives a reluctant response—yes, he will meet, as he promised, but there will be no agreement, not even on an agenda.

"I am flying to Khartoum," Dwight says at the press conference, "to meet with General Abboud, as Chief of State, and then to Nasir in the South to meet with Thomas Deng, the head of the opposition group, the Sudan People's Liberation Army. I should add that I am pointedly not taking any side in the civil war in Sudan, nor in the larger conflict which has the Sudan as its focus."

"A criminal attempt to interfere in the domestic affairs of a member state," the U.S. responds. Peter holds him at the airport before he boards the plane to Naples. Then he will change planes, still on a regular commercial line, for the trip to Khartoum. On the way, he sits devising alternative scenarios for a tentative cease-fire, and possibly the beginnings of a settlement. . . . Beyond the clouds gather the hawks and the eagles.

"It is the time now," Dwight tells General Abboud, "when all parties to this conflict must act in reverence for life. If your country is destroyed in the conflict, what will remain, even if at the end you and your powerful ally prevail? . . . I understand what is at issue here for you and for your people. But it is no longer your fight if you continue, and there will be no victory, but the most abject subservience to a foreign power."

Abboud stares off into space. "You are just mouthing words which others have put into your mouth—do you think I am such a fool?"

"It is yours today to show the world that Sudan's Chief of State is a man who acts for all its citizens, not just for those in the north but for all the Sudanese, north and south, who together, under your leadership, will achieve the greatness of a united country."

"By just giving up, by . . ." Abboud stops and looks at his hands.

"Years from now when you think of this moment, you will understand you had this chance to act with compassion for all your people, to see even in the eyes of those who think and feel differently from you the common humanity which unites them, which . . ."

"By giving up?" Slowly now his head turns back and forth.

"No, by . . ."

"Enough! Enough! I do not need to listen to your words which you manufacture so easily!"

Dwight waits, and then very slowly Sabrina, who had been sitting in the empty chair, stands up and walks to Abboud's side, and takes his hands into her own and looks into his eyes. "All right, I will sign a cease-fire, if that is what you want. We cannot go on like this. I cannot sit while the West kills our people by the thousands."

Dwight waits.

"I will make the announcement here. I will then meet with the SPLA to reach an agreement by ourselves—with neither the Americans, the E.U., nor with China—it will be *our* decision, the decision of the Sudan!"

He flies next to Nasir, where Dwight tells Thomas Deng the outcome of his talk. Like Abboud, Deng agrees to the cease-fire without conditions, and to meetings in Nairobi without participation by the great powers. Then Dwight and Bill leave the metal-sheeted building, and walk out with Deng into the early evening. The sky has already turned lavender and purple; on the river white pelicans, crested cranes, and vultures fly from bank to bank. "I did not think this would happen," Deng says, "and yet it has. You have done this. If we can agree to a decent partition of resources . . . who knows if our 'bosses' will accept it? Maybe it is too late for this, but it is worth a try."

A puff adder curled around the head of a dead antelope hisses as they pass. Deng looks up into the sky.

Bill radios Nairobi, and receives flight clearance. Dwight and Bill board the single-engine plane that will take them to Nairobi, where they will await the two parties for further talks. Dwight writes into his journal, "I never knew, Sabrina, if what I was doing was right, only that at some point we had said we would do our best. I never had the assurance of a blessing, but only this inner assent—how could it be otherwise, as long as you were with me?"

The plane coasts down the runway, and turns. The pilot guns the engine, the plane shoots into the air, and then is flying over the treeline toward Nairobi. The sun is just setting, a huge violet ball with wisps of colored clouds, as for twenty minutes the plane heads south. Suddenly, there is a huge explosion inside the cockpit. The plane swoops down, crashes into the trees, and plummets to the earth.

Dwight is flooded with pain, his back, one leg is broken, his ribs are sticking through his shirt. He has been thrown clear of the wreckage which he sees burning—he had not fastened his safety belt. "No, no," he tells Sabrina, "I was not trying . . ." A fire from the plane engulfs the fuselage—Bill will die. Dwight cannot move, he cannot save him! The fuel explodes in a huge flash. Waves of pain sweep over him, then recede. . . . He is sitting in front of General Abboud waiting for his reply. . . . He is in the Security Council listening to Jack Templeton—he will speak next, he will defend what he has done. . . . A meeting over Palestine—Chaim Ginzburg agrees with his proposal. . . . A meeting with Ambassador Henderson, with Todd Jacobs, with Luis Fuentes. . . . He is in Nicaragua telling *Comandante* Raven, "I am the son of Bradford Lockwood, who, you will remember, was a great friend of the *Contras* . . ."

Mother looks in, "Didn't you know, didn't you always know, Dwight?" . . . The light flashes through the tall trees that hover over the wreckage, and at the very top is that strange white knot—is it a sign, has he now really seen God?

Father laughs, "What did you expect, my boy? A brass band? They'll be lucky to find even your dead body. No, no, don't look for anything from this quarter. I warned you, or I tried to—you have to give me credit for that."

Sabrina stands at the operating table in San Miguel Atalán— "We talked about it then. It was no surprise. Only when, only when. . . ."

Peter says through his tears, "I think you did the right thing—you did what you had to."

Is he dead? He tries to move his arms—nothing happens. His leg, even his eyelashes, seem inert. . . . How long has he been here? A few minutes, a few days? Distantly, he hears the slash of machetes, the stomping of feet, the sound of human voices. . . . He is being lifted by several men, and is being placed into the back of a truck. Sabrina and Peter are sitting with him as the truck rumbles down a road to an airfield—he asks, "Is it Nasir?" Sabrina smiles. "Does it matter now?"

The plane takes off. "So you know," Sabrina says, "now and then you will appear in the mind of this person or that who knew you, Father Dietrich, Thomas Deng . . ." The plane would be flying now over the Atlantic over a bank of clouds; then it would be putting down—would it be met by a brass band and an honor guard of UN troops? . . . No, it does not matter now. He had done what he needed to do, he had made the trip, he had agreed to accept what might happen—yes, he had decided to enter Jerusalem!

* * * * *

Before the vastness of the stars, he looks out into the face of the world. He had inhabited only the smallest part, a tiny planet circling a minor star. Had it mattered what he had done here? "Yes, yes!" Sabrina shouts. She is with him as he stares into her eyes, only now they are his own, this his shape, as he merges his being with hers—"Still, still to hear her tender-taken breath, And so live ever," as the light of the world fades away.